When Rainbows Walk

Bob Adamov

Other *Emerson Moore* Adventures by Bob Adamov

Rainbow's End   Released October 2002
Pierce the Veil   Released May 2004

Next *Emerson Moore* Adventure

Promised Land   To be released Summer 2006

The following publication provided reference material:

THE SEARCH FOR THE ATOCHA by Eugene Lyon, Copyright 1989 Florida Classics Library

ISBN: 0-929774-35-4
Library of Control Number: 2005925370

Cover art by John Joyce, red inc.

Layout by Greenleaf Book Group

Submit all requests for reprinting to:
Greenleaf Book Group LP
4425 Mopac South
Austin, Texas 78735

Published in the United States by:
Greenleaf Book Group LP, Austin, Texas
and
Packard Island Publishing, Cuyahoga Falls, Ohio

www.greenleafbookgroup.com
www.packardislandpublishing.com

First Edition—June 2005

Printed in the United States

Acknowledgments

I'd like to acknowledge the support and wealth of guidance that I received from the following: Kim Fisher at Mel Fisher's Treasure Sales in Key West, Rod Althaus at the New Wave Scuba Center in Port Clinton, Roger Roth, Captain Steve Luoma and the crew of the *Fish Check* in Key West, the Key West Police Department, the Key West Fire Department, and a special friend with the Organized Crime Task Force who shall remain nameless. I'd also like to extend my appreciation for the continued support from my Put-in-Bay friends, including Jeff and Kendra Koehler, Bob and Judy Bransome, Dale and Kathy McKee, Patrick and Jill Myers, Tim Niese, Tom Ohlemacher, and the last of the barnstormers—that roguish Dairy Air Bob.

A special thank you to my team of editors and advisors: Hank Inman from Goldfinch Communications, John Joyce at Red Incorporated, Jay Hodges from Greenleaf Book Group LP, Joe Weinstein, Krystie Stone, Ron Fields, and Greg Hite.

The National Multiple Sclerosis Society will receive a portion of the proceeds from the sale of this book.

They that wait upon the Lord shall renew their strength; they shall mount up with wings as eagles; they shall run, and not be weary; and they shall walk, and not faint.
—Isaiah 40:31

Western Lake Erie

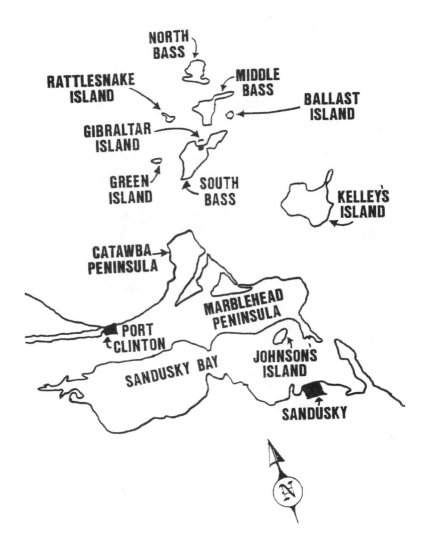

Put-in-Bay
South Bass Island

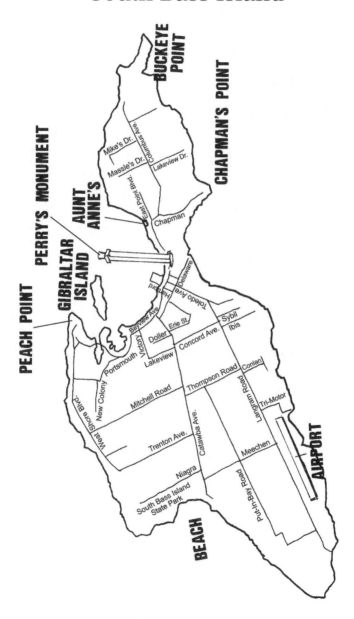

Key West

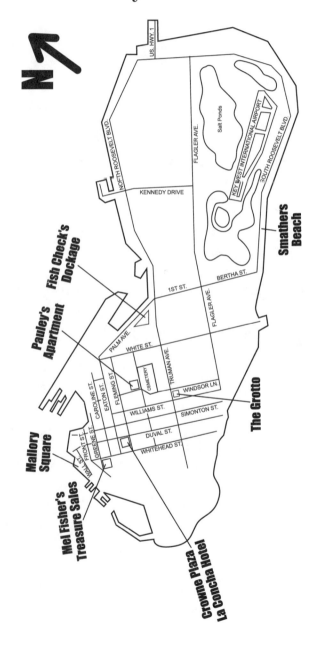

Prologue

A Note to Readers

While completing my on-site research in Key West in April 2004, I picked up a copy of *USA Today*, dated April 2, 2004. There was a story written by Patrick O'Driscoll with the following headline: "Expert: Major Hurricane Likely to Hit USA This Year." The story referenced predictions by William Gray who headed the Tropical Meteorology Project at Colorado State University. He predicted an above average hurricane season for 2004.

How uncanny his prediction was for one of the worst hurricane seasons on record for the people of Florida, who were pummeled by Hurricanes Charley, Frances, Ivan, and Jeanne. Billions of dollars in damages were caused during Florida's record-setting storm season as the state and its residents were pounded relentlessly by the wrath of the four hurricanes. Countless homes were damaged and lives disrupted.

This book, in part, is dedicated to those hardy Floridians.

Havana, Cuba
September 5, 1622

~6~

After a brief overnight stay, the fleet of twenty-eight Spanish ships sailed out of Havana's harbor on Sunday morning. Since loading the fleet's rich cargo at the Portobello, Panama port, the fleet's commander was anxious to be under way with his heavily loaded treasure vessels, especially since their departure had been delayed six weeks, and would cause them to traverse the Bahama Passage during the hurricane season.

One ship was significantly overloaded. Its main hold was filled with wine, bales of indigo and tobacco, ceramic jars of olive oil, slabs of copper, and the usual ship stores. This galleon, with its twenty bronze cannons and cases and barrels of muskets, pikes, powder, and shot had been assigned to guard the fleet's rear and carried an entire infantry company. Forty-eight passengers and their voluminous luggage were crammed into her small cabins.

More importantly, the ship's hold carried a vast treasure of 901 silver ingots, 255,000 silver coins, 161 pieces of registered gold, crated silverware, gold rings and chains, emeralds and other fine jewelry from the artisans of Lima. In addition, the ship was laden with hidden, unregistered contraband bullion. One important merchant had secreted sixty silver bars—averaging sixty-five pounds each—on the ship. The galleon's name was *Nuestra Senora de Atocha*— "Our Lady of Atocha." Built in Havana in 1619, the 110-foot-long vessel was named in honor of the Virgin Mary in a Madrid shrine, and had a depiction of the Virgin painted high on her sterncastle to bring the ship good luck.

The fleet of ships tacked to the east of Havana and sailed easily northward with the wind toward the lower Florida

Keys where they would enter the Gulf Stream for their sail to Spain. After a night of steadily increasing wind, the fleet sailed into the Gulf Stream and encountered a strong northeast wind. The wind raked the Gulf Stream's current in the opposite direction, causing vicious cross-seas.

The ships reduced sail as the weather worsened and the day darkened. The wind rose to a whole gale, and the height of the seas around the convoy rose to more than ten feet.

The *Atocha's* waist was almost continuously awash as it lumbered through the heavy seas. The ship began to plunge wildly, causing some of its cargo to break loose in her lower decks.

After another night of fighting waves that crested at fifteen feet, the *Atocha* found itself along with the *Santa Margarita*, separated from the rest of the fleet, and about forty miles to the east of the Tortugas. The *Atocha's* foremast had been carried away, and the ship was suddenly lifted high on the crest of a towering wave. As it fell into the trough, it crashed with sickening impact on a reef, causing the ship's mainmast to snap off. The impact on the reef ripped open her lower bow, and the sea began to pour in.

The ship wallowed under the weight of the incoming seas, her ballast, the cannons, and her heavy treasure. Losing her buoyancy, she sunk just west of a circle of mangrove islands, carrying 260 shrieking passengers and crew to an agonizing, watery death.

The next morning's dawn brought clear blue skies and calm waters. The only evidence of the previous day's ferocious storm was floating debris.

Fifty-five feet below the glimmering surface lay the *Atocha* with over $400 million in gold and silver bars, emeralds, and coins. She would rest untouched by human hands at the bottom of the sea for three hundred fifty-one years until discovered in modern times by a persistent treasure hunter with a contagious enthusiasm—Mel Fisher.

In 2004, the name, *Atocha*, would again be linked with death—the death of some 200 Spaniards in Madrid caused by Al-Qaeda.

Sidewalk Café
Jerusalem
April
◈

The two fourteen-year-old Palestinian boys were enjoying the early morning sun as they sat at a table next to the sidewalk. Curly-haired Hani, and Bishr with his dancing, black eyes, were deep in conversation as they enjoyed some of the fine goat cheese from the hills of Shavuot, which the café had delivered daily.

Their breakfast meal consisted of salad, tea, and a platter of goat cheese, which included Omer, a semi-hard French-style goat cheese; Chevre, a soft goat cheese; Ofira, a goat camembert; Tom, a hard goat cheese; and Shachar, a soft French-style black rind cheese. Hani had ordered Banyas, his favorite goat cheese flavored with locally grown fresh herbs and mixed with pine nuts.

Engulfed in their lively, fun-filled chatter, they were oblivious to the passers-by and didn't notice an anxious-looking, gray-haired Israeli who was walking on the sidewalk. The Israeli's eyes were darting from side to side and then ahead of him as he neared a Palestinian who was walking toward him. The Israeli had a covert task to complete and he knew the risks of being caught. He would have to be very careful to execute the task that he had trained for over the last few weeks. He thought he had been successful in class, but worried that he would not be able to complete it when the time came. He glanced again at the approaching Palestinian. Their intelligence had been correct in indicating that he would be attending a nearby meeting, and this was the most probable path that he would take to arrive there on time.

Strolling with the controlled ease of a powerful animal, Asad Malmud allowed his trained, dark brown eyes to cautiously sweep the area for potential danger to himself. He was crafty in his sinister ways, and in the last few years, had avoided any direct involvement in carrying out terrorist activities. In his early days he had fought fiercely in attacking the Israeli forces. But now, in his late thirties, the lean, bearded Asad with his dark-skinned features and black hair was more focused on the planning side. He had built a reputation for planning and directing the successful execution of a number of meaningful attacks on the Israelis.

He knew that there was nothing more that the Mossad, the Israeli intelligence service, would like to do than capture or assassinate the Lion of Terrorists, as he was known in many circles. Asad had found it relatively easy to avoid capture by the Mossad. In his youth, he had made sure to cover his face on his raids, and as he grew older, he would not allow any photos of himself to be taken, to avoid the possibility of them getting into the hands of the Mossad. He felt comfortable with his ability to disappear in a crowd and avoid capture.

In recent weeks, he had heard the rumors that the Mossad had changed its tactics and was not planning on capturing him. They were going to seek retribution for the deaths he had caused, and assassinate him in order to send a message to the other key leaders in the terrorist organizations. But first they would have to identify him. He smiled to himself as he thought about the precautions he had taken to avoid his identification. He continued walking as he thought about his upcoming meeting with an arms dealer.

What Asad was not aware of, was that two weeks ago an informant contacted a Mossad agent. The informant, who was in need of cash for his son's medical care and who was a competitor of Asad's, told the agent that he would be willing to snap a photo of Asad for the right price. Negotiations for the price were finalized quickly and the informant snapped the photo of Asad leaving a meeting. The camera was turned over to the Mossad so that the film could be developed. The film produced several clear shots of Asad, which the Mossad would put to good use. One of the agents drew a red circle around Asad's face. "This is our target," he had said with a satisfied smile on his face. "It won't be long. It won't be long!"

Asad's eyes continued to scan his surroundings. As had been his past practice, he would often stop and stare into a storefront window to see if he was being followed. He was wary, very wary of the Mossad and its vast network of agents.

The gray-haired Israeli was now next to Asad, and bumped into his right shoulder. He paused momentarily to apologize. The two men's eyes locked onto each other's for a brief second, and then the Israeli continued walking, but at a faster pace. He stopped in a doorway and radioed to his partner who had been observing what had transpired from a vantage point in a second floor window across the street.

"It is done," the first Israeli, who was a Mossad agent named Peled, radioed.

"Good. And now, I will finish it!" the second Israeli, Sharret, stated firmly as he picked up his cell phone and dialed a number.

Asad was approaching the sidewalk café and saw the two teenaged Palestinian boys standing to leave. He recognized Hani who was the son of the leader of the dangerous Al Majid terrorist cell. He smiled at them as he saw them leaving.

The phone in Asad's right coat pocket rang. A look of concern crossed his face as he reached into the pocket to pick up the phone.

From the security of the doorway, Peled watched Asad as he picked up the cell phone and began to raise it to his ear. For a moment, Peled's view was blocked by passers-by. When he saw Asad again, he saw him walking on the far side of the sidewalk café with his right hand to his ear.

From across the street Sharret smiled confidently as he held his cell phone to his ear and heard Asad's phone ringing. Answer this quickly, he commanded silently as he watched Asad.

Asad stopped suddenly and looked directly past the café until he spotted Peled standing in the doorway staring at him. He grinned sinisterly as he began to lower his right hand from his ear, showing his empty hand to Peled.

Peled stared in shock because he could hear the cell phone ringing. He looked around quickly and saw that it was lying on an empty table next to the sidewalk at the café. It was next to the table that the two teenagers had just vacated.

Asad smiled as he started to turn to escape. He paused as a motion caught the corner of his eye, and he looked back to the cafe table where the phone was ringing. Hani had heard the phone that someone had apparently forgotten and thought he would take possession of it.

He quickly reached for it and picked it up to his ear.

Asad and Peled shouted a warning to the energetic teenager, but they were too late.

Hani pressed the answer key as he held the phone to his ear. Pressing the answer key closed the circuit in the explosive-filled phone, which detonated, killing Hani instantly. The sound of the explosion filled what had otherwise been a quiet morning, and was quickly followed by shrieks from the café's occupants.

Hani's body crumpled to the ground as Bishr rushed to the side of his now-dead friend. Tears streamed down Bishr's face as he held his friend close, not caring about the blood flowing from the devastating head wound.

Peled rushed to Bishr's side, and began to comfort him as the sirens of the police vehicles began to fill the air. Peled looked down the sidewalk to where Asad stood.

Asad pointed an accusatory finger at Peled and shook his head before turning to disappear in the crowd. Asad quickly went around the corner, thinking as he walked away. The Mossad must have been able to get a photo of him, or someone had identified him to the Mossad. He was suspicious when the man had bumped into him, and having been a pickpocket in his youth, realized that it might have been a ruse to pick his pocket. Their agent had been extremely adept in picking his pocket for his cell phone, and replacing it with the deadly one. He had noticed several subtleties in the phone when he first retrieved it from his pocket. Although the phone brands were the same, he hadn't felt the deep scratch on the cover that he usually felt every time he had picked up his cell phone. That had been his early warning that something was amiss, and prompted him to discard the phone on the table.

It was a mistake on his part that he hadn't thought quickly enough about the possibility that someone would have picked up the phone. He certainly didn't anticipate that Hani would return to answer it.

Asad was concerned about Hani's death. It didn't matter that, in the end, the Mossad was responsible. He knew how revengeful Ra'id, Hani's father, could be, especially if it was triggered by the loss of his only son. Asad continued walking deep in thought about possible repercussions from Ra'id.

Gaza
Two Days Later

❧

The dingy room on the second floor of the old apartment building overlooked a small courtyard at the rear. The window shades had been drawn. The room was lighted by a single overhead bulb, and was bare, except for a well-used table with two chairs. One chair was empty.

The other chair was occupied by a man with a black hood tied over his head to obstruct his view. His arms were tied securely behind his back with plastic ties that cut into his blood flow. He was closely watched by a guard who stood next to the door.

The figure in the chair tried to stretch to loosen the tight plastic and bring relief to his aching arms. He had been sitting in this position for hours.

Asad swore under his breath at his negligence. He had crossed easily through the Erez checkpoint between Israel and Gaza just as 15,000 Palestinian families made the same crossing daily into the Erez industrial area.

Asad had been careful to watch the Israelis because he suspected they had a photo of him, but he hadn't been watching his fellow Palestinians closely. After he had walked through the checkpoint, he had turned onto a long narrow street. When the old man had stumbled and fallen in front of him, he stopped to help him to his feet. Focused on the old man, he didn't sense that he was in a trap until it was too late. His arms were grabbed and pulled behind him as four men overpowered him. The hood had been quickly placed over his head and he was shoved into the backseat of a car that appeared suddenly next to him.

He found himself wedged between two of his captors as the car sped down the crowded street, narrowly missing several street vendors who were slow in getting out of the way. None of the captors spoke to Asad during the twenty-minute swerving ride to their final destination.

His captors dragged and pushed Asad up the flight of stairs and secured him in the chair. They all left the room except for one who had been assigned to guard him. Asad could hear him as he paced about the small room.

Asad waited.

As he waited, he recalled several of the attacks and assassinations that he had been involved in during his early years. His first was as simple as riding by a café where senior members of Jerusalem's police force were meeting. He had casually pulled the pin from the grenade he was carrying, and lobbed it into the middle of them, killing them all.

His memory carried him to his first assassination by handgun. Four of them had been given the assignment. Two would drive the two cars, and Asad and the other terrorist would act as the gunmen. The two cars had pulled up in front of a public café. The other gunman, armed with a Kalashnikov, had fired a barrage of bullets over the heads of the patrons. Asad, carrying a handgun and ignoring any thoughts about anyone in the café being armed, had walked directly and boldly up to an informant, and pumped five bullets into the informant's chest. Asad dashed into his car while his partner continued firing overhead to cover Asad's escape. The other gunman then fled with his driver.

It had been a daring attack and Asad's stature in his terrorist cell had risen dramatically.

The sound of approaching footsteps in the hallway interrupted Asad's recollections. The door burst open and five people entered the room.

Asad heard the other chair being moved as it was pulled back from the table and someone sat on it. He sensed that there were others around him.

Someone began to untie the bottom of the hood, and then they roughly pulled it off of Asad's head. He winced in the light as his eyes adjusted and he saw Hani's father, Ra'id, sitting across from him. Looking towards the shaded window, Asad sensed that it was nearing dawn.

Asad knew Ra'id's reputation for violence and recalled that Ra'id had ordered an author of a series of articles criticizing the terrorists, and in particular Ra'id, to stop the series. The author ignored Ra'id's warning, and was found dead by his son and daughter after he went to his rooftop to use a satellite phone. The author had a bullet hole in the back of his head and another in his right hand—a symbolic attack on his writing.

Ra'id didn't waste any time.

"Asad, you're responsible for my son's death!" he stormed.

"It's not me, but the Mossad that bears the responsibility," Asad explained stoically.

"They were after you. Bishr said that he saw you place the cell phone on the table where my son, my only son, picked it up and was killed. You are responsible!" Ra'id shouted angrily.

"Ra'id, anything that I say to you will only fall on your deaf ears. Your grief will block out any explanation that I might try to provide you. Do with me what you wish. I know you well enough," Asad said as he resigned himself to his fate.

An evil smile crossed Ra'id's face. "I will do with you as I wish. I do not need your permission." Staring directly into Asad's eyes, Ra'id commanded, "Unfasten his hands and place his right hand on the table here in front of me."

The plastic tie binding Asad's arms was cut by a sharp knife and his arms were gripped by two of the terrorists as a third one held him firmly in his chair. One terrorist extended Asad's right hand and splayed his fingers on the table.

Asad's arms tingled as blood surged and circulated in his freed arms. He flexed his fingers and then recoiled them when he saw Ra'id pull out a large knife.

"Your death will not be as fast as my son's. You will die slowly. A bit each day until you are nothing more than a quivering mass, begging for me to end your life."

He stared intently into Asad's eyes as he looked for fear. He didn't see any as Asad stared back defiantly.

"I am not a beggar."

"That's easy for you to say today. Let's see what you say in a few days. Hold him! We'll start with the trigger finger on your right hand. The one with which you have ended the lives of so many."

Asad surprised them. He calmly and fearlessly extended his trigger finger.

"You don't need to hold my hand. Here's my trigger finger."

Ra'id's sharp knife quickly cut through Asad's finger. Ra'id was disappointed when Asad didn't scream, although he did flinch as the bone was cut.

Ra'id put the knife away and looked sinisterly at Asad as blood pumped from the finger. "No reaction this time. Let's see what happens tomorrow. Tie his arms behind him and put the hood back on."

"Should we bandage the finger?" one of the terrorists asked.

"No, let him bleed!"

The captors replaced the hood on Asad, and abruptly pulled his hands behind his back to retie them. No one did anything to stop the flow of blood from his finger stub. The captors, except the original guard, left the room.

Asad twisted in pain as he felt the blood continue its flow, with drops covering the floor beneath his hand. He heard the guard's approaching footsteps.

"Asad," the guard said quietly.

"Yes?" Asad replied.

"You saved my cousin's life ten years ago. You remember him? His name was Qasim."

"Yes, I remember him. The police were chasing him and I hid him." Asad paused as the throbbing in his finger stub increased in waves. "How is he?"

"Dead."

After a moment, the guard continued hesitantly. "For what you did for my cousin, I might return the favor, but in a very small way."

"How so," Asad asked slowly. He sensed that this guard could be helpful if he didn't appear to be too aggressive with him.

"The blood still flows from your finger. I could free your hands and give you a cloth to hold over it to stop the blood. You must leave your hood on. Agreed?"

Asad saw an opportunity developing. "Agreed."

"You must not do anything that would require me to kill you. I will be covering you with a pistol while you tend to your finger. I won't hesitate to use it."

"Agreed. I just want to stop this blood," Asad responded quietly.

The guard moved in closer and swiftly cut the plastic ties holding Asad's arms. Again his arms ached as the blood flow increased not only to his arms, but also to his finger stub. The throbbing increased with the release of blood. Asad felt a cloth shoved into his hands. He quickly took it and wrapped it around his finger stub as he held his right hand up to ease the amount of blood flowing to his finger stub.

He sat quietly as he listened to the guard nervously pacing the floor. He was taking a risk. If the others returned and saw that he had helped Asad, it would mean severe punishment or even death.

After five minutes, the guard began to move closer to Asad. "Let me see your finger."

Asad pulled the cloth away from his stub and displayed it to the guard. "I believe it has stopped bleeding."

"Yes, it has. I must retie your hands. Put them behind your back like they were before."

Asad placed his hands behind his back. As he did, he heard the guard set his pistol on the floor. Not wasting a second as the guard pulled Asad's arms together, Asad pushed back on his chair and sent it and him flying into the guard and onto the floor. Asad ripped off the hood and grappled with the guard on the floor. When the guard reached to retrieve his pistol, Asad kicked out his foot and connected with the pistol, sending it ricocheting to a corner of the room.

The guard grunted in surprise at Asad's strength and roughly reached for Asad's neck. Asad slipped through his grasp, and wiggled free, rolling to the corner where the gun lay. He reached for the gun and picked it up in his right hand. He looked down as he realized he didn't have his trigger finger and quickly switched hands.

The guard stood. "This is the way you treat my kindness?"

"Turn around and face the wall," Asad commanded. The guard turned around and waited for the inevitable bullet to end his life. He began to pray and was in the middle of his prayer when all went black and he slumped to the floor.

Asad looked at the prone figure and hefted the gun in his left hand. He had used the gun butt like a hammer and knocked the guard unconscious.

"Be grateful that I did not kill you," he whispered to the unconscious guard. "That was in return for your kindness in untying me, which, unfortunately for you, was a stupid thing to do. I hope your friends are as kind when they return and find me gone."

Asad turned to the shaded window and peeked around the edge. He saw the courtyard one story below, and the early morning light. He carefully raised the shade and as quietly as possible opened the window. He stepped back from the window and listened. He didn't hear anything unusual. It was still early.

Asad carefully edged his way out of the window. Holding onto the window's ledge and ignoring the pain in his hand, he took one more look below before letting go and dropping one story to the ground. He landed and rolled. Standing quickly, he brushed the dust from his hands and looked around the courtyard. It was still quiet.

Asad made his way to the courtyard's gate and opened it. Stepping through, he pulled the wooden gate shut and began to walk rapidly in the early morning gray light through the deserted street.

As he walked with long strides to his home, he thought and planned. He would have to move quickly with the Mossad and Ra'id after him; it would be time for him to leave the country. But he needed to end their pursuit of him.

One hour had passed. Asad had entered his apartment, called his driver and taken from his hidden compartment the cash that he had been saving for more operations. He had $25,000, enough for his quickly concocted escape plan. He heard a beep from a car below, and looked out his window. His driver, Ghalib, was waiting for him in his old, dusty Mercedes.

Asad, carrying a suitcase, ran down the steps and entered the car.

Noticing the heavily bandaged finger, Ghalib asked, "You had an accident?"

"In a manner of speaking, I did. I will tell you more later. Did you arrange for us to meet with Nazim?" he asked hurriedly.

"Yes, I did. We pick him up in about five minutes."

"Good. We must move quickly if this is to work for all of us."

Ghalib waited a moment and then asked, "Is this anything that you can tell me about?"

"No. But I will tell you that it is a very important plan that I've put together."

"I see," Ghalib commented. It was frustrating for him not to be fully involved with the plans that Asad put together. But he understood that, at times, it was better for him not to be aware.

"Did you place the bicycle in the trunk as I asked?"

"Yes, I did."

Five minutes later, the Mercedes pulled over near the opening of a narrow alley where a figure stepped out and jumped into the back of the car.

From a distance the man looked like Asad. Nazim had been very useful in providing alibis for Asad when Asad needed to slip away to secret meetings and didn't want people to know that he was gone. Nazim's job was not difficult: just be sure to be seen so that people think that Asad is where he is not.

Asad produced bandages from his kit and had Nazim wrap them around his right index finger, which he bent, so that he would look more like Asad.

The car entered a side road and bumped along into the countryside where it picked up speed. Thirty minutes later, the car stopped along the roadside and Asad opened the door.

"Make sure you follow the plan as I outlined it. Don't stray from the plan at all," Asad warned the two.

"I understand my part," Nazim smiled as he ran his hands over the currency that Asad had paid him.

"I will see you soon," Ghalib responded confidently.

Asad walked away with a small backpack that he had pulled out of the duffel bag, and began to climb to the top of the hill that overlooked the small airport. The car sped off to the airport, leaving a trail of dust in the morning light.

A few minutes later, the car pulled to a halt in front of a small charter service. Nazim, carrying the duffel bag, stepped out of the dusty Mercedes and walked to the office. He saw a girl inside peering out the window at him and Ghalib. She would later recognize him from photos as Asad's driver.

The Mercedes turned around and drove away.

Nazim smiled as he started this new mission for Asad.

"Yes, may I help you," the girl yawned and looked up at Nazim as he entered the cluttered room.

"Yes. I am Asad Malmud. I called earlier to arrange a charter flight to Tel Aviv."

The girl looked down at his bandaged finger. She would comment about it later to the police and to two rough-looking Palestinians who would come around later and ask questions about Asad.

"Yes. This last minute, emergency flight is going to cost you dearly. It will be $5,000," she said nonchalantly.

Nazim grinned at his good fortune. Asad had told him it would cost $10,000 so he could keep the difference plus the $10,000 that he had been paid to do this rush job. He counted out the cash from his duffel bag and then sat down to wait.

Within minutes, the pilot strode into the room and completed some paperwork for the flight. He then turned to Nazim and asked him to follow him out to the aircraft where the engine had been warming up.

"Won't take us long to get to Tel Aviv," the pilot responded as he took the duffel bag from Nazim and threw it in the plane.

On Top of the Hill
Near The Airport
⋘

The Mercedes came to a dusty halt at the top of the hill. Ghalib was able to find Asad easily. He was standing where he could see the airport.

Ghalib slammed the car door behind him and joined Asad. They watched as the small plane taxied to the end of the runway and turned. The single-engine plane picked up speed as it flew down the runway and lifted off.

The plane was airborne for thirty seconds, and still climbing to a higher altitude when an explosion interrupted the morning's solitude. A fireball engulfed the plane as it broke up and its fiery remains plummeted to the ground.

Ghalib's eyes widened in horror, and he turned to look at Asad. He was surprised by what he saw. Asad was smiling.

"I want you to return to the airport and see if you can help. Make sure that they believe it was me in the plane," Asad instructed Ghalib.

"Of course. Of course," Ghalib stammered.

"Before you go, I want to take the bicycle from the trunk," Asad said slowly. "I'll ride on to a safe house that I have nearby and contact you later. It would be better from this point, that I'm not seen with you."

"Of course." Ghalid opened the trunk and started to help Asad lift the bicycle.

"I'll get it," Asad said firmly. "You can get in the car. This will only take me a moment."

Ghalib did as he was told and returned to the driver's seat.

Asad lifted the bicycle and set it on the ground. He extracted a small device from his backpack and set its timer. He casually set the device in the Mercedes' trunk and slammed the trunk lid.

"To the airport, Ghalib! Don't waste time!" Asad ordered.

The car roared down the hill and raced back to the airport.

Asad watched the car as he opened the backpack and pulled out a hat, which he placed on his head. He reached inside again and pulled out a pair of large work gloves, which he slipped over his hands in order to hide the bandaged finger.

He glanced anxiously at his watch as he saw the Mercedes nearing the airport. He wondered if he had set the timer incorrectly or misjudged the driving time back to the airport. Asad was mounting the bicycle when he saw the Mercedes explode as it pulled into the airport's small parking lot. Ghalib was killed instantly.

Asad smiled again to himself. He hoped his strategy would pay off and the hounds would be thrown off his scent permanently because they would think that he had been killed in the plane explosion. He didn't need the Mossad or Ra'id chasing him.

Asad mounted the bicycle and began to ride north to the Mediterranean for the next step in his plan—to disappear permanently from Israel and Gaza.

His finger throbbed as he rode in silence, planning the start of a new life for himself away from the reach of Ra'id and the Mossad—although the Mossad's reach was virtually worldwide.

A few hours later, Asad's bicycle had a flat tire. He pushed it several yards off the road, then he returned and began to walk along its side in the growing heat of the midday. He was pleased when a passing lorry pulled over, and the driver offered him a lift to the next town.

Within a matter of twenty minutes they arrived in a town where Asad thanked the driver and, pulling his hat low over his eyes, walked into a nearby store for water and food. He took his purchases, and found a bench in the shade where he pulled off the gloves, which he still wore to hide his wounded, throbbing finger. While he quenched his thirst and hunger, he looked around the small town and watched as a motor scooter parked next to the store. Its rider bounded off the scooter and walked inside.

Watching the store's door close, Asad decided to check out the motor scooter, and walked across the street to where it was parked. He was surprised, but pleased that the unsuspecting owner had left the keys in the ignition. Pushing the scooter off its stand, Asad pushed it around the block where he quickly started it, and rode it out of town.

Later that evening, he would abandon the motor scooter and steal a lorry, continuing his escape from Israel.

La Plaza de Toros
Madrid
May

ঔ

"This is something that I've always wanted to do," Peled said to Moshe Kagan as they settled onto the concrete bench at Madrid's main bullring, La Plaza de Toros de Las Ventas del Espíritu Santo. The red brick and ceramic tiled building had been in use since 1931, and more recently housed rock concerts and political meetings.

Peled had taken time off from his work in Israel to visit his good friend, Moshe, with whom he had worked on several Mossad assignments when Moshe was still stationed in Jerusalem. Moshe, who was a lean five feet seven, was in charge of the Mossad's Madrid office. Peled was still recovering from the psychological blow wrought by the death of the young Hani. He had planted the cell phone bomb, and even though Asad had placed it on the café's table, Peled felt responsible for the young boy's death.

"You picked the right time to visit me. The best time to see a bullfight in Madrid is during the months of May and June when they have their famous San Isidro bullfight festival. It brings together the best fighters and bulls every night at seven o'clock for thirty days," Moshe explained.

"Do they have bullfights during the rest of the year?" Peled wondered.

"Yes, they actually do. They are held every Sunday evening at seven o'clock from March to October. You'll see fights involving young bulls and less experienced bull fighters during that period," he responded as his eyes gazed over the quickly filling stadium.

One of the vendors approached them, and they rented cushions to place on the concrete bench-style seats. It would be a two-hour event and the hard concrete could become very uncomfortable as the late afternoon and early evening wore on. Another vendor who was selling shots of liquor appeared at their sides as they reseated themselves. They dismissed him, and also the vendor behind him, who was selling soft drinks.

"These vendors can be very aggressive," Moshe offered as an explanation to Peled. Peled nodded his head as he watched the vendors approach others seated across the aisle from them.

Peled's head whipped around at the sound of the horns announcing the start of the day's fight. The gates at one end of the stadium opened and a parade of people entered. Moshe quickly explained the role of each one.

A few minutes later, the first fight of the day started.

"There will be three matadors today, and each matador will fight two bulls, so we will watch six fights. Each fight will last about fifteen minutes," Moshe offered as the first bull entered the ring.

The large Brahmin bull rushed into the ring, and was full of fury and dangerous energy. Tossing his head up into the air, the bull rushed around the ring to the cries of the crowd, and came to a halt near the middle as one of the three matadors began to approach him.

"Each fight has three phases. In this first phase, the matador judges the bull's strength and courage. He will receive the bull with that large fuchsia cape," Moshe added.

Peled watched carefully as the first matador attired in purple spandex with gold braid teased the bull. The large bull charged the cape and the matador deftly stepped aside as he raised the cape, and the bull ran by harmlessly. On the next charge, the matador had to retreat behind a protective barrier as the bull bolted at him rather than the cape.

From the other side of the barrier, another matador entered the ring and captured the bull's attention. With dangerous bravado, the matador began to drop to one knee as the bull charged. The matador skillfully twirled the cape, and remained on one knee as the bull charged through the cape harmlessly, but much to the boisterous delight of the crowd.

A horn blew to announce the next phase of the fight.

"This next part of the fight is the unfair part for me," Moshe said with a touch of sadness.

"How is that?" Peled asked curiously.

"It involves the picadors and banderilleros. The picadors are the guys on horseback," he said as two rode in on their horses. "They use the long lances that they're carrying to stab at the bull and weaken its neck muscles."

"Why is the horse blindfolded?" Peled inquired seeing the large blindfolds over the eyes of both horses.

"So he doesn't spook when the bull charges into the horse. They don't see the bull coming. Watch. You'll see what I mean."

They watched as one of the heavily padded horses moved toward the bull. The stocky but powerfully built picador seated himself firmly on the horse and gripped his lance tightly as they approached the bull. Seeing the approaching horse and rider, the bull lowered its head and charged into the side of the horse as its rider brought it to a halt and braced himself for the bull's charge. The bull thrust its horns several times into the sides of the horse, trying to gore it.

Realizing that it couldn't gore the horse, the angry bull began to toss its massive head underneath and upward in an attempt to knock over the horse and its rider. The blindfolded horse struggled to keep its balance against the powerful surge of the bull, which was becoming more agitated by the pain being caused by the picador thrusting his lance several times into the bull's shoulder, drawing blood. The dark wine-colored blood flowed down the bull's shoulder.

"If you were that horse and saw the bull charging, don't you think that you'd panic?"

"Most definitely," Peled responded.

"The horses will fight to keep their balance—and they do a good job. A bull's courage is measured by his willingness to approach the horse and lance."

The picador stabbed the bull a few more times, and more blood flowed.

The horn blew again announcing the beginning of the next phase of the fight.

"Watch this part," Moshe advised as three brightly attired men began to approach the weakening bull. "They're called banderillas. See the barbed sticks they're carrying?"

The weakening, but angry bull swung around to confront its new threat as the picador retreated from the ring. The picador raised his tan, wide-brimmed hat to the crowd's applause as he left the ring through the main gates at the far side.

"Yes."

"The banderillas will charge at the bull and whirl at the last moment and attempt to stab the barbs into the bull's back around the shoulder area. The idea is to continue to weaken the bull so that the matador is not facing a strong bull."

"That seems unfair to the bull," Peled said.

"That's exactly how I feel. I was surprised when I attended my first fight."

They watched as the banderillas danced and whirled around the charging bull and tried to stab him with their colorful, two-foot-long barbs. The first banderilla carefully approached the angry bull and shouted at him to make him charge. As the bull charged and lowered its head, the banderilla reached over its head and stabbed two barbs into its shoulders while skillfully dodging the bull's rush. The barbs didn't stick and fell to the ground, much to the displeasure of the watching crowd who filled the air with their whistles of disgust.

Another banderilla stepped toward the bull that was pawing the ground and kicking up dust. The bull began to charge the banderilla who was running backwards, shouting at the bull and watching for the opportune moment to stick the agitated bull. As the bull lowered its head, the banderilla was able to reach over the top of the bull's lowered head and stab both barbs into the bull's back to the approving roar of the crowd.

The bull whirled around with its dangerous horns and tried to catch the banderilla off guard, but the banderilla deftly stepped aside, touching the top of the bull's head with his hand. Two more times the bull charged him, and two more times the banderilla showed his bravery by tapping the bull on its head as the crowd rose to their feet, applauding the banderilla's daring performance.

After two more banderillas successfully inserted their barbs and further weakened the bull, the ring's horns announced the final phase of the fight.

The matador received the bull alone in the final phase. Holding a small red cape, which hides a ceremonial sword, the matador walked toward the weakening bull. Teasing the bull, he watched as it charged the cape, but deftly danced aside when the bull, at the last second, avoided the cape and whirled into the matador. When the bull stopped, the brave matador turned his back on the bull and walked a few steps away as the crowd cheered his bravery.

Taking several deep breaths, the matador turned to confront the bull. He placed one hand on his hip and stretched his lean body at an angle, then he held out the cape and taunted the bull to attack. The bull started to charge, but stumbled to its knees. It slowly arose and charged.

In a display of bravery, the matador allowed the charging bull to pass dangerously close to his body. Narrowly missing the matador, the bull stopped to gather its strength.

Next, the matador stepped to the wall of the bullring and exchanged his ceremonial sword for the killing sword. Holding the sword behind the cape, he approached the bull again. Three more times, the matador entertained the crowd as he allowed the bull to pass close to him as he pulled aside the cape.

Dropping the cape, the matador began to approach the bull, but carefully watched him as he walked, and began to aim the killing sword at the bull. He stopped and yelled at the bull to again taunt him and display his bravery to the crowd.

The bull charged him and lowered its head, but the matador thrust the sword deep into the area behind the bull's head and between its shoulder blades. He skillfully stepped aside. The bull whirled around and stopped to face the unarmed matador. Weakening, the bull stood and stared silently at his killer. A few moments later, he dropped to the ground.

The crowd roared its approval as the matador bowed. The jingling of bells on their harness announced the entry of the three horses who were led to the fallen bull. The four attendants quickly harnessed the bull to the horses and dragged the bull from the stadium.

Peled observed, "Not much of a fight when you've got so many people weakening the bull."

"True, although I've seen a weakened bull gore matadors and banderillas before. If they can catch them on their horns, they can toss them a fair distance," Moshe replied.

"And the bull still ends up dead after fighting back?"

"Not necessarily. He does have one chance to live. If the crowd judged the bull to have been especially brave and the matador to have done poorly, the crowd can demand that the bull be spared. I've seen it happen a few times."

"I'm glad to hear that the bull wins once in awhile."

Between the third and fourth bullfight, Peled's attention was distracted by one of the whiskey-selling vendors, whom he had noticed near at the bottom row of the ring.

"I've got to check something," Peled said as he arose to descend the steps of the stadium.

"Is anything wrong," Moshe asked as he read the tone in Peled's voice.

"No, no. I thought I saw someone I know working here," Peled said nonchalantly. He didn't want to raise a stir until he could confirm whom it was that he had seen. "I'll be right back."

Peled arose from his seat and walked down the steps to the main level where he paused and looked around. He looked back towards his friend, Moshe, and waved. Moshe returned the wave and turned his attention to the next fight.

Peled began to scan the faces of the vendors from his closer vantage point.

Through a small group of people who were descending the ramp to the street level, Peled thought that he spied the bearded vendor in whom he was interested. Peled recognized the clothing and began to make his way through the group. A lady in front of him, who was carrying a baby, unknowingly dropped the baby's blanket.

"Señora, un momento," he called.

She stopped and turned to see him stooping to pick up the blue blanket. As Peled handed it to the lady, she spoke, "Muchas gracias, señor."

Peled grinned. "De nada," he replied with the limited amount of Spanish that he had learned over the years. The lady continued on her way and Peled anxiously looked from one side to the other as he tried to spot the vendor whom he had been following. During his attempt to be a gentleman, Peled had lost sight of him in the crowd.

Peled moved farther down the ramp as he searched for the elusive vendor. Just before he reached the street level, he heard a door open behind him and at the side of the ramp. Peled turned to see who it was and stared into the eyes of the vendor.

"Yes, it's me," the vendor said ominously as he thrust his knife into Peled's abdomen and then pushed in upward. "You should have stayed in Israel." He gave the knife a hard twist to the right, making Peled gasp in pain. "That was for killing Hani!" Asad scowled with a face filled with hatred.

Peled's eyes widened in terror as he felt the knife penetrating him and his life beginning to flow out of him. Still gasping, he dropped to the ground as the vendor looked around coolly for any witnesses. The group of people on the ramp had dissipated, and from inside the stadium he heard the roar of the crowd, approving the matador's skill as he plunged his sword deep into the charging bull.

Seeing no witnesses, he smiled wickedly to himself as he kneeled over Peled, and wiped his blade on Peled's shirtsleeve. The matadors were not the only ones doing the killing here today, he thought.

With his sight fading, Peled noticed that the vendor was missing the trigger finger on his right hand as the vendor raised the knife from Peled's shirt.

Asad rose to his feet and walked quickly toward the exit. As he passed a large trash container, he flipped the knife into the container, and went to the line of waiting cabs in front of the bullfight stadium. He entered the first cab, gave directions to the driver, and then looked cautiously over his shoulder. He wanted to be sure that he wasn't being followed.

After a few blocks, he ordered the driver to pull over, and he exited the cab. He entered the doorway of the nearest store and stopped to peer carefully into the street to again check that he hadn't been followed. He waited five minutes and took a deep breath as he relaxed. He left the store's doorway, and walked several blocks where he found a bus stop and caught a ride.

After ten blocks, he exited the bus and walked into a small café. He had to take time to think about what he needed to do. He had been reacting to the situation and now he needed to wisely plan his next steps. He still wasn't sure if the Mossad had tracked him to Madrid and was on his trail.

La Plaza de Toros
Madrid

∽

Moshe began to grow anxious as the bullfights continued and Peled had not returned. He wondered whom Peled thought he saw. Finally, Moshe decided to find Peled. He arose from his seat and followed the path, which he thought Peled took.

As he began to descend the ramp to the street level, he saw a small circle of people staring at something on the ground. He moved into the circle and saw that a seat cushion vendor was starting to turn over a body. As the face came into view, Moshe realized that it was Peled. He brushed aside the vendor and cradled Peled's head in his arms as he felt his emotions rising. It was obvious that Peled was dead, especially from the large amount of dark red blood that covered the ramp.

Then Moshe saw two letters scribbled in blood on the ramp near to where Peled's outstretched hand had been. The letters read *AS*. Moshe would pass this along to the Mossad when he completed his report on Peled's death.

The crowd parted as the police arrived and began their investigation. Moshe identified himself as working for the Israeli embassy and provided what he knew about the circumstances surrounding Peled's death.

As he watched them trundle away Peled's body, he swore an oath of vengeance. He would not rest until he tracked down Peled's murderer.

A Small Cafe
Madrid
∽

Tucked into a far corner, a furtive figure sipped a cappuccino. Taking refuge in this nondescript café off the Paseo de Recoletos to gather his thoughts was paramount to Asad as he assessed his situation and options. He was trying to determine what had brought Peled to Madrid. Had the Mossad, in some manner, traced him to Madrid, or was it a coincidence that Peled had run into Asad at the bullfight? Asad wasn't sure—and one of the reasons that he had survived as long as he had was that he didn't believe in coincidences.

Taking the more conservative approach, Asad decided that the Mossad had been able to track him, and that it was time for him to disappear one more time. He wanted to return to his small apartment to retrieve the stash of cash that he had there, but decided that it would be too risky.

Reaching into his pocket, Asad pulled out a handful of Euros. Not enough to get him anywhere. He thought for a moment, and then quickly put together a plan as he observed the café's employees huddling together at a table at the rear of the café. Only one employee was working at the front of the café and running its cash register. There were only two other customers in the café—and they were obviously a couple in love, and oblivious to their surroundings.

Asad approached the employee with his check, and asked for a hot cup of tea to go. The employee poured the hot water into a cup, and set the cup on the counter for Asad. He then presented a box of tea bags so that Asad could make his selection.

Asad smiled ominously as he picked up the cup of hot water, and abruptly threw it into the eyes of the café's unwary employee. The employee shrieked as the hot fluid burned his eyes.

Asad ignored his cries and ran behind the register. He opened the drawer and, to his satisfaction, found a small handgun, which he pointed in the direction of the other employees who had rushed from the rear of the cafe to aid the injured employee, still shrieking as his hands rubbed his eyes. Asad emptied the register of its cash and motioned threateningly with the gun for the employees to stay back from him as he stuffed the cash into his trouser pockets.

Motioning the employees and their injured co-worker to the rear of the café, Asad made one last threatening move with the handgun, and darted out the café's front door. He rushed down the street and turned left at the next intersection. He found an alley and darted through it where he emerged onto a busy street.

Spotting a pharmacy a few doors away, he entered it and walked down several aisles until he found what he would need to alter his appearance. Carrying them in his hands, he walked to the register where he set his items on the counter.

The clerk held up the bottle of hair colorant and looked at Asad, who glared at him. Smirking, the clerk rang up the hair colorant and the rest of the items, then placed them in a bag.

Paying for the items and taking the bag, Asad left the pharmacy and walked briskly away. He smiled as he heard sirens in the background, probably reacting to his robbery at the cafe.

Asad approached an apartment building and climbed its stairs. He casually leaned against the doorway and waited. His wait didn't take too long.

Walking slowly down the street and carrying a bag of groceries was an elderly lady with a slight limp. Her small frame was topped with a head of white hair.

Asad watched her from the top of the stairs, and hoped that she lived in the apartment building behind him. Asad hoped that she lived alone, and selected her as his target.

Her weary steps stopped in front of the apartment where Asad waited. He held his breath, hoping that she would begin to ascend the stairs since it would make matters easier for him. Slowly, she turned and began to climb the stairs on her fatigued legs. Halfway up the stairs, she realized that there was a man leaning near the doorway. She raised her head and looked at the man who spoke.

"Mother, I'm early for my visit with the Cisternos family," Asad began in English as he remembered one of the names on the apartment directory. "Can I help you with your bag? These steps are so steep for someone like you."

The lady didn't understand what he was saying but recognized the Cisternos name, and saw that the demeanor of this man seemed to be one of being helpful. When he gently reached out for the bag, she allowed him to take it.

"Follow me. The Cisternos live across the hall from me," she replied in Spanish.

Asad flashed a disarming smile, and watched as she unlocked the front door. She motioned for him to follow her inside. Motioning up the stairs inside of the building, she said "Cisternos."

Asad smiled in feigned thankfulness. "Sí," he said.

She smiled at the nice young man, and began to climb the stairs to the second floor, closely followed by Asad. When they reached the second floor, she said, "Cisternos." She then pointed to the door across the hall from hers.

"Gracias," Asad replied as he motioned that he would carry the bag for the woman into her apartment. She inserted her key into her door lock and swung open the door to reveal her quaint apartment. Asad swept by her and her open arms, which she had expected to be filled with her bag. Asad walked to the table in the small kitchen, set down the bag and looked around. From what he could see, she lived alone.

The lady stood in the doorway. "Cisternos, alli," she said as she pointed to the doorway across the hall.

"Gracias," Asad replied again as he started by her. At the last moment, he stepped to the side and slammed her door shut. A look of fear crossed her face as she saw Asad's friendly demeanor transform into a manifestation of evil. She opened her mouth to scream, but no sound emitted as Asad swiftly moved to her side and clamped his hand over her mouth as he backed her toward the kitchen counter.

She struggled with Asad, but she was no match for his strength and training in the art of killing. He broke her fragile neck and dropped her lifeless body to the floor onto a thin, red rug.

Stepping back to the door, he made sure that it was locked and then quickly searched through the apartment to confirm that they were alone. Satisfied, he walked into the apartment's bathroom and extracted the items he had purchased from his bag.

Turning on the water, he cast aside the shirt he had been wearing and wet his face and the black beard that he had grown years ago. Applying lather to his face, he very carefully shaved it off. The newly purchased razor pulled at his hairs, and it took longer than he expected. He looked at himself in the mirror and was surprised at how much younger he looked without the beard.

He opened another package and began to dye his hair a reddish tint. After an hour, no one would recognize him as the same individual who had entered the apartment building. Now he needed to replace his discarded shirt; he rummaged through the apartment, looking for a shirt and anything of value that the old lady may have hidden.

He found one hundred Euros, an old pair of dark sunglasses and a frayed tee shirt, which he decided he could use. He looked out the window and saw the lengthening shadows from the afternoon's sun, and realized that he needed to leave for the train station. He had decided to take the late afternoon train to Barcelona where he would secure a passport in the black market and try to get a job on a freighter.

If the Mossad and the Spanish police were looking for him, they wouldn't check departing freighters as closely as airlines and border checkpoints. He wanted to leave the Mediterranean and find asylum where no one would look for him.

Asad glanced down at his missing finger and swore again at Ra'id for dismembering him. He picked up his shirt and the bag from his purchases. He didn't want to leave any traces of his visit other than the dead body. The apartment looked ransacked as if a thief had entered and had been looking for money, killing the old lady when she discovered him.

Checking the hallway to make sure that no one was about, Asad slipped on the sunglasses as he stepped out of the apartment, and closed the door behind him. He walked down the steps and out to the sidewalk. He walked down the street and turned the corner where he found a waiting trashcan into which he threw his discarded shirt and bag of trash. He hailed a taxi and was transported to the train station for the ride to Barcelona.

"I don't know who he saw. It was someone working there. He just left and said he'd be right back," Moshe explained as he talked to his superior in Mossad's Jerusalem office. "One thing that was very interesting, though."

"What is that?" Yosi Megon asked.

"He left a message for us."

"How did he do that? What did it say?" Megon asked urgently and in disbelief.

"Peled scrawled two letters in his blood, apparently before he died. They were *AS*. Any idea what that stands for?

"No, we'll check to see what Peled was working on before his visit, and run a search for anything else that he might have been working on in the last few years to see if it reveals an answer to this."

"I'm not sure what it is. I've been playing with the letters. Maybe something like blank Spain or Arabs Spain. I'm not sure," Moshe said perplexed by the initials. "It could be the initials of someone that he knew."

"We'll run it down and get back to you," Megon replied.

They ended their call and Moshe sat at his desk. He was scribbling names on a sheet of paper as he tried to solve the mystery of what or who *AS* signified.

Two days later, Megon called him with the answer.

"We think he saw Asad Malmud. Peled might have been writing his name and couldn't write the entire name before he died."

"But I had heard that Asad was recently killed in an airline explosion," Moshe countered.

"Maybe. Or maybe it was a cover up to put us off his trail for good."

"But, his driver was killed too!" Moshe protested, as he was sure that Megon was headed in the wrong direction.

"Could have been a part of the cover up. We heard that he had a run-in with Ra'id over the death of Ra'id's son. Asad may have decided that life was getting a bit more complicated than he needed it to be with Ra'id and us after him."

"We're sending you a photo of Asad that we were able to obtain. Take it to the bullfight ring, and see if anyone recognizes him there. If they do, then we're on the right track."

"Okay. I'll watch for it and let you know what I learn."

Moshe hung up the phone and anxiously awaited the photo, which was going to be e-mailed to him. He didn't have to wait long. The e-mail arrived, and Moshe opened the file. Asad's evil face stared at him. Moshe printed the photo and locked his office door as he headed to the bullfight ring.

U.S. District Court
New York City

~§

Being sworn in at the witness stand was a sixty-two-year-old Mafia informant. He was a stocky, tough-looking man with graying hair, dark-brown eyes, and chalky-white skin covered by red blotches.

"Do you swear to tell the truth and nothing but the truth, so help you, God?" the bailiff asked

Nervously, the witness looked at the bailiff, and then at Joey "the Rock" Rankito, the crew chief for whom he had worked for so long. Rankito was seated with his defense attorney, and was shocked when the state called this surprise witness. Rankito glared at the witness stand's occupant.

"I do," he replied with a gravelly voice that sounded like it belonged to someone who smoked twenty-five packs of cigarettes a day.

"State your name for the court."

"Paul Pocatello," he responded as beads of sweat formed on his brow.

"Please state your made name to the Court."

"Made name?" the witness asked in feigned misunderstanding.

The balding judge leaned toward the witness and looked down on him over the rims of his glasses.

"Come, come Mr. Pocatello. Please reply to the question." The judge sat back in his chair and waited.

"Pauley Pockets," the witness replied as he looked at the icy stare from Rankito. There was no doubt in Pauley's mind what Joey would do to him if he could get his hands on him. No one, but no one testified against Joey. If Joey thought for a second that someone was going to rat on him, they disappeared from the face of the earth. Pauley was the only one who had made it alive to the witness stand.

Pauley had entered the Federal Witness Protection program in exchange for testifying against his former Mafioso boss. He had been caught red-handed during a heist of cargo at Newark Airport and would have been sent to prison for years. That's why he balked and made the tough decision to turn against Joey. He couldn't be away from his wife, Laurie, who needed daily care with her emphysema. The disease had advanced to the point where she had to pull a small oxygen container on wheels anywhere that she went. She was becoming weaker, and Pauley needed to care for her.

The government had been trying to convict Rankito for a number of years, but was unsuccessful. This promised to be their strongest case against him, thanks to Pauley's cooperation.

By entering the Witness Protection Program, he would avoid penitentiary time, and he would be able to care for her. Over 7,500 witnesses and 9,500 of their family members had been protected, relocated and given new identities since the program was authorized by the Organized Crime Control Act of 1970. By using witnesses in this program, the government was able to obtain an overall conviction rate of 89 percent. They were anticipating another increase in their percentage today.

The prosecutor approached Pauley and leaned on the witness stand. Looking first over his shoulder at Rankito and then back at Pauley, the prosecutor asked, "Mr. Pocatello, we understand that you were a member of the Mafia. Is that correct?"

"Yes, that is correct," Pauley responded as he produced a white handkerchief, which his wife had given him that morning, and wiped his brow.

"And you were involved in the interstate trafficking of stolen merchandise?"

"Correct."

"Was there a person for whom you worked trafficking in stolen merchandise?"

"Yes."

"Is that person in this courtroom, today?"

"Yes, he is," Pauley answered as he twisted the handkerchief in his lap.

"Could you identify him for us?"

Pauley pointed to Rankito.

"Let the record reflect that Mr. Pocatello pointed to the defendant, Mr. Rankito," the prosecutor clarified.

"Mr. Pocatello, could you tell us what happened on the evening of November 13th of last year?"

"Yes, I can." Pauley wiped his brow one more time. "Me and Joey and two other guys picked up Little Louie about nine o'clock."

The prosecutor interrupted, "Little Louie? Could you give us his proper name, please?"

"Oh, sure. Sorry. His real name was Louis Larcarno. He ran some numbers for the crew, and we thought he was skimming some of the profits. So we were going to have this talk with him, but it turned out to be more than a little talk when Joey got mad." Pauley stopped and looked uneasily at the prosecutor.

"Please proceed," the prosecutor instructed.

"Well, we picked him up, and took him for a drive into the country."

"Could you be more specific, please?"

"Sure. We took him out about sixty miles west of here for a little chitchat. I pulled the car into a field, and drove down a driveway to an old barn. There, I parked the car and we all got out. Then we walked into the old barn. One of Joey's in-laws owns that farm."

"Could you give us the names of the other men who accompanied you?"

"Sure. Donnie Salerno and Mikey Muscari."

"What, if anything, did you tell Mr. Larcarno about where you were taking him?"

"We told him that we needed to go somewhere where we could all talk openly without having to worry about you guys listening in."

"What happened next?"

"Joey doesn't waste any time. He tells Little Louie that we know that he's skimming."

"Do you have an understanding why he said that?"

"One of his guys squealed on him," Pauley explained nervously.

"And what is the name of the person who squealed on him?"

"Jimmy Fazzita."

The prosecutor thought about Mr. Fazzita, who seemed to have disappeared. No one, including his family, had heard from him in several weeks.

"What happened then?" the prosecutor asked Pauley.

"Joey gets a little hot. He's got one hell of a temper. He pushes Little Louie into a chair and we tie him up. He knows that he's in big trouble, and begins to scream that he won't do it anymore, and he'll make it up to Joey."

"What did Mr. Rankito do next?"

"He grabs a crescent wrench off the workbench. It's a big wrench, and swings at Little Louie's jaw. It crunches and Louie screams real loud! We think the jaw is broken. Louie begins to cry and begs for mercy. Then, he sees what Joey is lighting on the workbench."

"And what did he light?"

"It's a blow torch!"

"And what does Mr. Rankito do with the blow torch?"

"He burns out Louie's eyes and then half of his face. Louie was screaming and then he stopped, but Joey kept on burning him." Pauley paused for a moment as he recalled the odor from the burning flesh. He shuddered for a moment and then continued, "That burnt flesh stunk up that barn. It was a good thing that the chair he was sitting in was metal, otherwise, I'd bet that chair would have caught on fire."

"What happened to Mr. Larcarno?"

"He died. Joey had us wrap some barbed wire around his body, and then we threw it in the trunk and drove him back to town. It was about two in the morning when we pulled up in front of his home. We got out of the car real quick like, and dumped his body in the front yard so that his wife could find it in the morning."

Pauley had avoided looking at Rankito as he told his story. He glanced quickly at Rankito, and saw a hatred-filled Rankito staring at him.

"Mr. Pocatello, what did you do to the body before dumping it?"

"We mutilated it so that it was only identifiable from its fingerprints or dental records."

"Mr. Pocatello, why was it so important to mutilate the body so much?"

"Joey wanted to send a message to the others in the business. He said that you need to kill one to send a message to one hundred."

The prosecutor stepped down and Rankito's attorney tried to attack the credibility of Pauley's testimony, but it was a losing battle. The conviction on Joey the Rock Rankito was a fait accompli.

Pauley was dismissed and stepped down from the witness stand. As he passed the defense table, Rankito rushed at Pauley. The bailiff and several policemen ran over to separate Rankito and Pauley, but not before they both exchanged blows.

As they were separated, Rankito said in a low voice to Pauley, "We'll whack you. There's no place they can hide you that we won't find you. You're dead meat! You understand me? You're dead meat!"

Pauley had a grim look on his face as he was ushered out of the courtroom by the two U.S. Marshals who had been assigned to protect him. Pauley could hear the judge pounding his gavel as he sought to restore order in his courtroom.

In the building's basement garage awaited a vehicle. It was a white Chevrolet Suburban with another U.S. Marshal at the wheel. Seated anxiously in the backseat was Pauley's wife with her portable oxygen tank.

The marshals pushed Pauley into the back seat, and one followed him in while the other sat in the front passenger seat.

"Nice job up there, Pauley," the one in the passenger seat said. It was the first time that he had talked to Pauley since they had entered the courtroom that afternoon.

"You heard what Joey said when I was leaving?" Pauley asked.

"Yep. But he won't find you. We've got everything set up just as you requested," the marshal responded.

"Paul, what did Joey say to you?" Laurie asked with concern.

"Oh, just what you'd expect. He thinks he's going to whack me. He won't find us. We're going to where he won't expect to find us. And I'll be able to keep out of the sun. You know how I burn when I'm in the sun," he said to his wife as he thought about his skin's sensitivity to the sun. On especially sunny days, he would have to apply large amounts of sunscreen for protection.

Thinking about their plans, she responded, "It will be so nice to live a normal life."

"Yeah, that it will be," Pauley said as he sat back in the seat and thought about their new future and his upcoming business venture. It was something that he and his father had talked about starting, but never followed through on. He would honor his father with the new business.

The Suburban pulled into traffic and picked up speed as it headed out of New York City.

The trial of Joey the Rock Rankito ended a few days later. He was convicted of murder and sentenced to life imprisonment. Before he was taken away, he had an opportunity to talk with one of his crew and put out a contract on Pauley for $100,000. He would make Pauley pay dearly for turning on him.

The phone was ringing on Moshe's desk as he reentered his office. He had hoped it was Megon returning his call from earlier in the afternoon.

"Moshe here," Moshe answered.

"I'm returning your call," Megon said from his distant office in Jerusalem. "What did you find out?"

"It was Asad Malmud. I showed the picture to a number of the vendors at the bullfight stadium and to his manager. They all agreed that it was Asad. Several of them mentioned that he was missing the index finger on his right hand."

"That doesn't tie with what we know about him," Megon said as he contemplated this piece of new information.

"I had reviewed Asad's fact sheet that you had e-mailed with the photo, and there was no mention of him missing any fingers in the identifying features section. I probed them on that and they thought it was a fairly recent loss because the scar tissue wasn't aged."

"I wonder if Ra'id got his hands on Asad before he fled the country, and started to pay him back for the death of his son. We'll have to have someone try to run that down although I'm not sure how successful we'll be in penetrating Ra'id's cell," Megon mused.

"I heard that you guys had an informant, and that's how you finally got Asad's photo. Could you use him?"

"Not anymore. His body was found dumped on a street. It had been mutilated pretty bad."

"Did Asad do it?"

"We don't think so. We're not sure who did it."

"I'll see what we can discover here while his trail is still fresh. I've got a score to settle with him."

"How's that?"

"Peled was married to my sister."

"I knew that," Megon said as he sat back in his chair and smiled. How fortuitous it was that it was Peled, he thought. Moshe would be even more motivated to track down his killer. "Good hunting."

"Thank you. I've got to go. I've got a meeting set up with one of my contacts with the national police here. He's with their intelligence unit, and may be able to give me some information."

"Keep me advised of your progress," Megon said as he concluded the phone call.

Moshe sat back in his chair for a moment and thought about Asad. He leaned forward and dialed the number of his friend, José Maria Valasquez.

After two rings, the phone was answered. "Yes?"

"José, it's Moshe."

"Buenas Dias, mi amigo. Que tal?"

Moshe grinned for the first time in several days, but he couldn't mask the concern he had in the tone of his voice. "Asi, asi."

"Sounds like something is troubling you."

"Very perceptive."

"It is my job to be perceptive, right?"

"Yours and mine," Moshe concurred. "A friend of mine was killed at Sunday's bullfight." He quickly gave Valasquez the details of what had happened.

"I had heard that there was a murder there, but we're not involved," Valasquez mused.

"You may be involved after what I tell you. We think it's a terrorist on the run from us."

Valasquez sat straight up in his chair and began to take notes as Moshe provided him with background information and his suspicion that it was Asad. Spain had several levels of security forces with the National Police responsible for investigations countrywide, security in urban areas, and hostage rescues. If there was a terrorist link to this murder of a Mossad agent, Valasquez should be involved as it was within his scope of responsibility.

"Do you have a photo?"

"Yes, I can e-mail it to you."

"Anything else?"

"I've got some background data sheets. Let me sanitize it, and I'll send it over to you."

"Good." Valasquez held up his wrist and looked at his gold wristwatch. "Do you have plans for this evening?"

"No, why do you ask?" Moshe inquired.

"I was going to suggest that we meet for tapas around eight o'clock at a little tavern on Calle de la Victoria. I'll have some information for you by then, I'm sure, and I'd like you to meet a guest that I'm entertaining from the United States."

Moshe understood the Spanish approach to life. His host enjoyed a walk before the dinner hour and meeting at an outside café or tavern for aperitifs to whet his appetite for dinner. "I'd enjoy it."

Valasquez provided the tavern's name, and hung up to start his data gathering.

Early Evening
Moshe's Office
Israeli Embassy
◅

Driving out of the embassy grounds through the heavily guarded gate, Moshe nodded his head to one of the four guards on duty, and pulled his Toyota into the congested traffic of a city that had grown to a population of three million. Soon he was driving down a sunlit Atocha Street, and past the recently opened Tryp Atocha Hotel in the heart of Madrid's Arts Triangle, which included the Prado, Thyssen, and Reina Sofia museums.

The city's propensity for more clear, sunny days than any other city in Europe helped Moshe as he adjusted to his assignment in Madrid. The bright skies reminded him of the weather at home in Israel. He relaxed as he thought about his walks along the tree-lined El Rio Manzanares, the small river that carried water through Madrid. He enjoyed morning walks and sipping coffee at many of the outdoor cafes that bounded the small river. It was like an oasis with boulevard traffic on both sides.

Seeing the tavern ahead, he found a parking spot, and walked over to find his friend.

"Moshe! Over here!" Valasquez's voice called from the outdoor patio area. Moshe turned and waved as he saw his friend seated with a stranger. He approached them and sized up the stranger. Even had Valasquez not told him that the stranger was from the United States, Moshe would have guessed it. The stranger was wearing a brightly colored tropical shirt with a lightweight blue jacket and white slacks. On his feet were tennis shoes. American, Moshe confirmed. It was easy to spot an American in Europe; they were always the ones wearing tennis shoes and dressing down, compared to the more conservatively dressed Europeans who wore leather shoes.

The tanned, blonde-haired stranger with a medium build stood and extended his hand to Moshe as Valasquez introduced him. "Moshe, this is Detective Yanni Wilharm from the United States."

Moshe shook his hand, and then Valasquez's hand. "And what brings you to Madrid?"

"I'm here on an exchange program with our sister police department in Madrid."

Moshe looked at Valasquez for an explanation.

"Exactly. The Madrid police department has had a sister police department in the United States since 1997. It's the Miami, Florida police department. We're all a part of the International Police Association.

"Here, I brought along one of these for you," Wilharm produced from his pocket a Region 43 logo patch with a pink flamingo standing on one leg on a sandy beach with a bright, blue sky in the background. "That's our logo, and I'll tell you that our organization in South Florida probably gets more visits from other police departments worldwide than any other member police department," he grinned. "We're in the right location!"

Valasquez explained further. "He's on a ten-day visit with us, and I'll have to visit them for ten days after the first of the year." He smiled as he saw Moshe's look of understanding. Moshe wouldn't mind visiting Florida in January either.

"Welcome to Madrid," he said to Wilharm.

The waiter appeared and took their orders for tapas, light snacks that are customarily eaten at this hour. Their order included tidbits of fried fish, cheese, slices of sausage, and prawns fried in butter. To wash everything down, they ordered chato, a small glass of white wine.

As the waiter departed, Moshe looked at Valasquez. "I trust that you received my e-mail?"

"Yes, I did, and I forwarded it to the appropriate departments. There are a number of avenues that we need to investigate. Is this Asad truly on the run from your organization and in hiding? Or is he in Madrid planning an attack on us? From the information you provided, and our own sources today, we see that he is an expert in planning terrorist activities."

"And where are you leaning at this point?" Moshe asked.

"It's too early. We need to be careful. Ever since the bombings of the trains at the Atocha-AVE Station that killed over two hundred people, we've become more cautious." Valasquez's head turned toward Wilharm. "You may not be aware that there was a link between our bombings and your September 11 catastrophe in New York City."

"You mean with Al-Qaeda?"

"Yes, but there's more to it than that. We believe there was a message. If you look at our train bombings, they happened on March 11. There are exactly 911 days between your World Trade Center disaster and our train bombings. Furthermore, the October 12, 2002 bombing in Bali was one year, one month and one day after your September 11 attack."

Wilharm's eyes had widened at the comments. "I didn't know that."

"Just a bit of trivia for you," Valasquez smiled.

"I had thought that your bombings were originally Basque separatists," Wilharm said.

"The ETA, or separatists, were the first suspects, but there were several disconnects, to use one of the phrases that I picked up from you in the last few days. ETA always calls in a warning and they don't use that type of explosive, Goma-2. They typically use titadine, which is a compressed dynamite. The worst bombing incident that we've incurred was the Hipercor supermarket in Barcelona in 1987. It killed twenty-one and wounded forty. The ETA claimed responsibility for that one."

"What really happened with the bombings in March? How many trains were involved?" Wilharm asked.

"Four trains. Each of the four was bound for the Atocha station. They all stopped at Alcala de Henares station where the backpacks with bombs were planted in the front, middle, and rear of the trains. The Alcala de Henares suburb houses Latin American and Eastern European immigrants, and quite a few of the blue-collar workers and middle class people who cannot afford to live in Madrid.

"The bombs began exploding on the trains at about 7:39 a.m. The first three bombs exploded on a train just five hundred yards outside of the Atocha station. Not all of the bombs exploded in the stations, which must have been their original plan. If they had, the fatalities would have been in the thousands with all four trains in the stations exploding. Not all of the bombs exploded and, in one case, a train was delayed by a red signal, so it didn't make it into the station. In another case, the cell phone alarm used to trigger the bomb was set twelve hours late."

"How did you trace the bombs to Al-Qaeda?" Wilharm asked with intrigue.

"During the middle of the night, one police officer was sorting through belongings recovered from the trains, and opened a sports bag with an unexploded bomb. It was filled with twenty-two pounds of Goma-2, surrounded by nails and screws. Two wires ran from a cell phone to a detonator. We disconnected it and looked at the cell phone's call history. We were quickly able to trace the calls to local numbers and identify the callers, several of whom had already been under surveillance."

Moshe had been listening quietly. "So, you think Asad is planning something here?"

"Again, I'm not sure. It is something for us to investigate. We are running down our contacts to see where this takes us."

"I don't want his trail to go cold," Moshe said.

"Be careful about warning me. Based on what you told me this morning, your people were the ones who let his trail go cold in the first place," Valasquez said slowly, but deliberately.

"Here's our waiter," Wilharm said as the waiter appeared.

They changed the focus to their tapas and wine, and the topic turned to living the good life in Madrid.

Two Days Later
Moshe's Office
Madrid

౸

"Hello," Moshe answered as he picked up his phone after two rings.

"Did I wake you?" Valasquez teased.

"No, José. I've been going through our files," he responded as he looked from his desk, which was covered with file folders up to his computer monitor. "Did you find anything yet?"

"Yes, and no, and maybe. We're pretty confident that he's not planning anything here. Our informants don't seem to be aware of anything, and the chatter that we have been monitoring has been normal. Our best guess is that he's fled the country, although we haven't seen anything that would indicate that he left via plane or train. We're still checking to see if he might have left from the southern coast and crossed the Mediterranean, and we're running down ships that disembarked from Barcelona since the murder. We're able to e-mail his picture to them at sea."

Moshe was silent.

"I don't hear you saying anything."

"Just thinking about what I would do if I were him."

"And what would you do?"

"Change my appearance so that you would be looking for the wrong person."

"You mean, like shave his beard?"

"Yes."

"We've thought of that. One of our people prepared a photo of him without his beard to see what he might look like. The eyes, they cannot change though."

"The eyes can be hidden by sunglasses. No, this one is a smart one. He may have dyed his hair."

"Probably."

They talked a few more minutes and then hung up.

A few hours later, Moshe's phone rang again. It was Valasquez calling back.

"Did you find something?"

"Maybe. One of my men with who I was discussing your hair colorant idea found something of interest."

"Yes?" Moshe asked urgently.

"There was an elderly woman found murdered in her apartment. Her neck had been broken and the apartment had been ransacked as if someone had been looking for something of value."

"And why do you think this might be Asad?"

"It was what we found in the bathroom sink."

"Yes?"

"It appeared that someone had dyed their hair in her sink. There were reddish hair colorant stains in the sink that were not completely rinsed away. We're checking the taxi companies to see if they may have picked up a man who had a dark complexion and red hair in that neighborhood at about the time we've estimated the murder to have taken place. We'll let you know."

The early morning sun cast a warm glow on the front of the small hardware store located on Main Street in the older downtown section. The quaint storefronts reminded residents and visitors of a time before the mega stores and shopping malls pulled customers out to the town's fringes where most of the new business development was taking place.

Customers walking into the hardware store found a variety of fragrances greeting them. The earthy aroma could be traced to the wide selection of grass and vegetable seeds in open bins, and a number of bags of fertilizer that could be found near the front door. Some of the shovels and rakes for sale were covered with a light layer of dust, signifying how slow business had been for the little store.

Six weeks earlier, the store's owner had sold out to a couple in their sixties, who had decided to move away from the crowds of New York City. The couple resided in the house attached to the store's side, which made it easy for them to manage the business. They kept open the connecting door to the store so that they could hear the bell ring above the door whenever a customer entered. And, if they were in the residence, they would quickly walk over to the business side to serve the customer.

The owners' names on the sales contract read Paul and Laurie Smith. The first names were their true first names. The surname was fictitious. Their last name was actually Pocatello. Pauley Pockets was realizing one of his life's dreams under the Federal Witness Protection Program. He owned a hardware store.

As she walked from the refrigerator to the sink counter, Laurie pulled her portable oxygen tank. She hummed happily despite her battle with emphysema. She was happy that she and Pauley had a chance for a fresh start.

She noticed that he had been more content too, although at times she noticed that he was edgy. He still became agitated when the door opened and customers entered, but not to the degree that he was during the first two weeks. The first two weeks were especially trying as Pauley would nervously stare into the faces of the customers trying to see if they might be one of "the boys." She didn't know that a number of the boys were trying to find them so that they could fulfill the contract that Joey put out on Pauley.

"Laurie, I'm going over to see Marvin, and help him hang a picture in his shop. I'll be back in a few," Pauley called as he stepped out the store's back door.

"I'll have breakfast ready when you get back," Laurie yelled as she worked away in the newly remodeled kitchen. She reached into the vase of fresh daisies that she picked the previous evening, and with a smile stuck one of the daisies in her graying hair. She'd surprise Pauley when he returned for breakfast.

Pauley paused as he stepped onto the small porch behind his store. He breathed deeply and enjoyed the early morning air. The sun had been out for about three hours, but the dew was still glistening on the grass.

As the rays of the sun beat down on Pauley, he reached into his pocket and opened a small bottle of suntan lotion with SPF 30 and began to vigorously rub it onto his arms and face. While he liked the sun, his skin had developed a sensitivity to it, and he had to use large quantities of lotion to protect himself from burns.

Finished with his ministrations, Pauley walked over to the back door of the little antique shop next door and saw his new friend, Marvin.

The sixty-five-year-old, stout and white-haired Marvin had hit it off quickly with Pauley when he purchased the hardware store. Graciously, Marvin had introduced Pauley to some of the folks at city hall and helped him through a maze of initial paperwork.

"Here, I was just having a cup of coffee. Sit and join me for a few minutes, then we'll put up the picture," Marvin said cheerfully.

Pauley glanced at his watch and said, "Okay, but I've got to get back as soon as we're done hanging the picture. Laurie's fixing breakfast for us."

Marvin poured the coffee. "I won't hold you up."

Pauley grimaced to himself. One thing that he had learned since buying the business next door to Marvin, was that Marvin was quite a talker. There was no such thing as a short conversation with Marvin, Pauley thought as he sat.

On the street outside, a white van slowly and ominously cruised by the hardware store. The two people in the van noted the empty parking lot spaces in front of the store and the open sign in the store's window. They saw a car parked in the driveway next to the house, which was connected to the store. The van circled the block and then pulled into the house's driveway, blocking the car from leaving.

Two menacing figures exited the van, walked to the front of the store and entered. The ringing bell above the door startled both of them. One of them reached up and stopped its ringing while the other locked the front door and changed the sign in the window to show that the store was closed.

"I'll be right there," Laurie called out cheerfully from the residence. She didn't want to wait on customers with breakfast having been started, but she didn't have a choice. She turned the stove's burner on low and looked anxiously at her watch. She wished that Pauley hadn't left to go next door. She also knew what a talker Marvin was.

Pulling her oxygen tank, she entered the hardware store to greet her customers. When she saw them, her outward disposition changed from cheery to one of concern. She couldn't mask what she felt as a shudder went through her body. She knew their kind. The two men in front of her reminded her of the kind of guys that Pauley had hung around with when he had gotten into trouble with the police.

She asked nervously, "How can I help you?"

The taller of the two, and the most dangerous looking, Marioda, spoke first. "Where's your husband?"

"He's not here right now," Laurie stammered.

"His car is in the driveway," the other man, Ricci, said.

"He's out of town," Laurie lied, hoping that they would leave.

"You wouldn't mind if we took a look around then, would you?" Marioda asked as he retrieved a pistol from his pocket. Ricci now had a gun in his hand, too.

"I told you he isn't here. Now leave," Laurie said valiantly.

"We'd like to take a look around, if you don't mind," Marioda said sternly as Ricci quickly walked through the store and checked closed doors to see if anyone was on the other side. He opened the back door and peered outside, but saw no one. Closing the back door, he locked it.

"I most certainly would mind. Now you get out of here or I'm calling the police!" she said courageously as she worked her way to the massive sales counter where the phone rested.

Seeing where she was headed, Marioda bolted past her to the phone and ripped it off the counter, throwing it across the room. "You won't be needing this."

"Nothing in here," Ricci said as he joined Marioda.

"Come with us, we're looking in the house." Marioda waved the gun menacely at Laurie as he directed her into the residence. When she still didn't move, he shoved her and she fell to the store's worn wooden floor. "I said to get moving!" Marioda roared.

Laurie picked herself up and glanced at the back door as she hoped that the long-winded Marvin would detain Pauley. It might save his life today, she thought. She began to walk back to the residence side of the building—dragging her oxygen tank as she walked.

Entering the house, they smelled the aroma of breakfast cooking. Marioda noted that the table was set for two people. "Where is he?"

"I said he was out of town," she replied.

"Then, why are you setting the table for two?"

Laurie hesitated and then unconvincingly said, "One of my girlfriends is going to join me for breakfast. She should be here any minute."

"That would be bad luck on her part," Marioda said sinisterly as he turned to Ricci. "Search the house." Turning back to Laurie, Marioda ordered Laurie, "You! Sit down!"

Laurie sat in her chair and waited uncomfortably.

Within a few minutes, Ricci returned. "Nothing. No one is here."

"You're sure?"

"Check it out for yourself. There's no one here."

Marioda looked from Ricci to Laurie with a touch of remorse as he began to walk toward her. "I really need to know where Pauley is."

Marioda produced a length of rope that he had picked up as they walked through the hardware store. He slowly began to unravel it as Laurie watched nervously and began to squirm in the chair.

"Sit still!" Marioda demanded. "I just need to make sure that you don't do anything stupid while I take a look around," Marioda lied as he began to loop the rope around Laurie and tie a tight knot in the center of her back.

Satisfied that he had secured her, Marioda walked in front of Laurie and moved in close to her. His face was only inches from hers as he stared fatefully into her eyes. "Pauley didn't think we'd find him here. But Pauley was stupid. He used to say that he always wanted to open a hardware store, and that he never wanted to leave New

York. That made it pretty easy for us to track him down." Marioda stepped away from Laurie and approached the kitchen counter.

Laurie's eyes bulged as she listened and saw Marioda pick up a large knife from the kitchen counter. He carefully ran his finger over the edge of the blade as he gauged its sharpness.

Marioda began to brandish the knife in front of Laurie's eyes. "Now, I need you to quit feeding me the lies that you've been giving me since we walked in the door. Where's Pauley?"

"I told you. He's out of town."

"Oh, oh. We got company," Ricci said as he stepped back from the front window in the living room where he had been watching the parking lot.

"Who?" Marioda asked hurriedly as he looked toward the living room.

"It's a policeman on a motorcycle. He just parked it in the parking lot."

Marioda clamped his hand over Laurie's mouth. "What's he doing?"

"He's trying the front door. It's locked. Now, he's looking in the windows. Oh, oh."

"What?"

"He just saw our van in the drive. He's started to walk this way," he said with building tension as he gripped his pistol tightly. After a pause, Ricci continued, "It's okay.

He stopped and turned around. He's walking toward that antique store next door. He just went in. We'd better go."

Marioda looked sadly at Laurie and said, "I am truly sorry. We were really after Pauley, not you."

Laurie's eye's widened in fear. She didn't scream as she realized what was coming. She accepted her fate in order to protect her Pauley.

A minute later, the two thugs exited the house and got into the van. They quickly backed out of the drive and drove up the street.

Meanwhile, next door at the antique shop, police officer Rod Farmer walked in and called, "Marvin, are you here?"

Marvin's voice replied from the rear office, "Back here, Rod."

Farmer walked to the office and entered, "Hi Marvin." And seeing Pauley, he added, "I was just looking for you, Paul. I need some grass seed. When I tried your front door, it was locked and the sign in the window said that you were still closed."

Looking perplexed, Pauley responded, "That's strange. I unlocked the front door when we opened this morning, and I'm positive that I turned the sign to show that we were open." Pauley felt bile rise in his throat as a cold chill ran from the bottom of his neck to the base of his spine. "Come on, we'll go in the back door."

Pauley moved quickly with relief at being able to escape from the talkative Marvin, but with a sense of urgency as to what might be going on in the store. His mind raced with a number of scenarios, none of which bode well for Pauley or Laurie. The picture hanging could wait until another day. It was imperative that he understand what was going on next door.

Pauley and Farmer walked out the back door of Marvin's and the short distance to the hardware store's back door. Pauley reached for it and found it was locked, too.

"That's strange. I'm sure that I left this door unlocked when I left this morning," Pauley said with concern.

"I think it's one of those senior moments, Paul. You're just getting forgetful. It happens to everyone after age fifty," the policeman joked.

Pauley smiled nervously. "No problem. I've got a key here," he said as he reached for his key chain and unlocked the door. "I'm positive that I left this unlocked. I don't know why Laurie locked the doors."

They entered the little hardware store and Pauley called out, "Hey, Laurie, why did you lock the doors?"

There was no response. He called again. "Laurie? Where are you?"

Pauley walked over to the sales counter and saw the phone on the floor with its wire ripped from the wall. He reached underneath the cash register and his hand emerged with a pistol in his grip.

"Paul, you have a license for that?" Farmer asked.

Pauley ignored the comment and pointed to the phone on the floor, which Farmer had not seen. "You better unholster your Glock and come with me," he said ominously.

Pauley's change in demeanor startled Farmer. He had not seen this side of Pauley. He unholstered his Glock and he and Pauley began to walk to the attached house as Pauley repeatedly called out Laurie's name.

"This isn't like her. Maybe she's in the crapper," Pauley said hopefully. However, he sensed that his life would be taking another twist in what would be a life-changing day for Pauley.

Farmer touched Pauley's arm. "Better let me go first," he said as he stepped in front of Pauley and entered the house.

They saw that the living room was empty and started down the narrow hallway to the kitchen at the rear of the house. They could hear Laurie's favorite teapot whistling from the steam as it boiled on the small stove.

Pauley's eyes began to light up when he first saw Laurie staring at him as she sat in a chair that faced the hallway. There was a daisy in her hair. Then, Pauley realized that it was a lifeless stare. His heart sank.

He then saw the towel that had been stuffed in her mouth as a gag and she had been tied in the chair with a rope. They rushed to her side.

"I'm sorry, Paul. She's gone," Farmer said after checking her for any signs of life. "Here's what did it." He held the severed line to her oxygen tank. She had died of asphyxiation.

"Laurie!" Paul cried in despair and crumpled to his knees on the floor next to her. He began sobbing. "They were after me, and she paid the price," he moaned.

Farmer didn't understand, but then again he didn't know that Pauley was in the Federal Witness Protection Program. He raised his radio to his mouth and called for back up, the coroner, and an ambulance. "I'll check the house," he said as he drew his gun and began to search the house.

When he returned, Pauley confronted him, "Get them U.S. Marshals over here. You can tell them for me that their witness protection program sucks. I'll get my own protection program," he said as he mourned.

Farmer's eyes widened at the mention of the witness protection program. He quickly began to put two-and-two together.

Pauley curled up on the floor and began sobbing harder at the loss of his one true love.

Three days later they buried Laurie in a small cemetery on a rolling hill outside of town. Since they were new in town, there was only a handful of mourners who opted to attend the early morning graveside burial service.

Two of the mourners watched the proceedings from the top of a nearby hill in the cemetery. One was sitting on a tombstone while the other scanned the mourners with binoculars. Their black rental car was parked nearby.

"There's Pauley," Marioda said as he watched the burial service, and a figure vigorously applying suntan lotion to his face. Marioda knew about Pauley's skin sensitivity.

"I wish we could take him out right now," Ricci said anxiously as he thought about the $100,000 on Pauley's head.

"Our time will come," Marioda said with deadly seriousness.

Following the burial, Pauley, who was accompanied by three armed U.S. Marshals, was placed in a white Chevy Suburban. His two suitcases were in the rear of the vehicle. As he settled into the rear seat, Pauley whined, "Can't you guys drive something besides these? You might as well as put signs on the side of the doors advertising U.S. Marshal's vehicle."

"Bear with us. We know what we're doing. If you had listened to our advice, you would have relocated outside of New York state and gone into some other kind of business."

"If, if, if! I don't want to hear anymore ifs. It's because of you guys that my wife's dead."

The vehicle pulled out of the cemetery, and eased onto the road leading to town.

"We're being followed," the driver said as he watched the vehicle pull in behind them.

Pauley's head whipped around, and he stared at the black car behind them.

"Recognize them?"

"Yeah. Two killers—Marioda and Ricci. Pull over and give me a gun. I'll finish this," he said angrily as he tried to grab one of the guns from a marshal.

"I don't think so. You've got no proof." The marshal picked up the radio and called, "Jerome, you back there?"

"Yep. We're about three cars behind you. Need us?" the agent asked as he peered ahead at the white Suburban.

"There's a black car right behind us. Why don't you put on your lights and pull them over. See what you find out. You may want to take them in for questioning although we don't have any concrete evidence to use against them yet. Names are Marioda and Ricci."

Pauley watched as the trailing vehicle turned on its lights and pulled over the black car. He wished that he could do the questioning. He'd make them talk. He spun around in his seat and pulled his wallet out of his back pocket. From his wallet he extracted a small plastic bag. In the bag was a lock of Laurie's hair and the pressed flower head of the white Shasta daisy that had been in Laurie's hair the day she was murdered. He gazed at it for a long time, oblivious to the outside world passing them by as the Suburban drove on. Pauley was angry. He was angry at himself, the mob, the U.S. marshals and the entire system. His dreams for retirement were headed on a different track, a track he had not anticipated.

The white Suburban headed toward the Albany airport and a second new life for Pauley Pockets.

B Dock
Put-in-Bay
South Bass Island, Lake Erie

∽

As the early evening's sunlight cast a golden glow across the western edge of Lake Erie, the thirty-foot Sea Ray slowed as it entered the picturesque harbor of Put-in-Bay on the northern side of South Bass Island. The crowded harbor was filled with moored sailboats and docked powerboats.

The boat's 285-horsepower inboard-outboard engine fell silent as one of the two figures on board cut the engines, and the other figure bounded from the boat to the dock to secure the craft.

It had been a relatively short ride in the borrowed boat from Cleveland to the island as the two men took a detour from their trip to Detroit. They had been able to conclude their business a day ahead of time, and decided to make a stop at this island resort town.

"Carmine, you sure that Vinny isn't going to find out about this?" the figure on the dock called down nervously to his partner.

"So, who's going to tell him that we stopped here? You going to tell him, Carlo? I don't think so," Carmine mocked. "We're just going to stop here for a few hours, have some drinks, and check out the chicks. They had great scenery here the last time I was here."

"This is my first time here," Carlo said as he looked around at the park, the quaint downtown area and Gibraltar Island, which guarded the entrance to Put-in-Bay's harbor. "You know, the scenery isn't too bad. I like that little island over there," he said as he pointed toward Gibraltar Island.

Carmine looked to where Carlo was pointing and reacted quickly, "Listen stupid, that's not the scenery that I'm talking about. That's the scenery that I'm talking about!" Carmine nodded in the direction of the dock.

Carlo looked where Carmine was indicating, and realized too late that he was referring to the two bikinied girls strolling down the dock. "I knew what you meant!" he said weakly.

"Oh, sure you did!" Carmine said in a belittling tone as he jumped out of the boat onto the dock and started to follow the two girls. "Now, that's what I call scenery!"

"You think it's safe to leave the stuff onboard here?"

"So, who's going to bother it?" he said, disappointed as the two girls boarded a boat named *Monkey Business*, and began to dance to loud music blaring from the boat's sound system—much to the delight of the boat's male occupants. "Everything's locked up in the bow. No one's going to touch it here."

"I'm just nervous that something will happen, and Vinny is going to find out when we get back to Detroit. I don't want to piss him off. He's already running out of places to hide the bodies!"

"Nothing is going to happen unless you plan on getting in a fight at one of the bars here, and then getting thrown in jail. Now, just cool it!" Carmine said firmly as they started to cross Bayview.

"Hey, where do you think you two are going?"

Carmine and Carlo froze in their tracks, and turned to identify the source of the voice. Standing at the edge of the dock was one of the dockmasters. This one was better known as Michael the Dock Nazi.

"You need to report in and pay your docking fee," he called.
Relaxing, Carmine reached into his pocket and withdrew a wad of cash. "And what do I owe you?"

The Dock Nazi calculated the payment amount based on the length of their boat. Carmine paid him quickly, as the

Dock Nazi saw another boat crew that he needed to catch for docking fees. Leaving the dock, Carmine and Carlo walked through DeRivera Park toward the Crescent Bar.

"From what I recall from my last time here, there's a lot of wild life at the Crescent Bar," Carmine stated as he pointed toward the gray-and-white building with the large plate glass windows.

As they crossed Delaware, they could easily hear the band, the island's famous Maxx Band, playing with their backs to the windows. Carmine's face broke into a big smile as he saw the body-filled dance floor on the other side. Carmine and Carlo entered the bar's side door, and made their way through the crowded onlookers and drinkers to the bar with its large center mirror and smaller side mirrors framed by spiraled pillars.

The bar's four ceiling fans turned slowly below the ornate tin ceiling. The fan speed would be ratcheted up later that night as the heat and cigarette smoke intensified. The walls were covered with dark blue floral wallpaper set above a white tin wainscoting.

Ordering their drinks from the blonde barmaid who had her long hair pulled back, Carmine and Carlo turned to watch the crowded dance floor, where couples were dancing wildly to the oldies but goodies.

"Yeah, I like the wild life here," Carlo said appreciatively as he watched one dark-haired female shimmying in front of Dwight, one of the band's guitarists.

Wearing a black top hat, blue tee shirt with an American flag, and stars and stripes slacks, Dwight peered over the rim of his glasses, and a large smile emerged from his bearded face as he watched the lady shaking and dancing in front of him.

It's still early, Carmine thought to himself as he watched the same dancer. Get a few more drinks in her, he silently urged her partner—as if he could communicate telepathically.

"Shot, boys?"

Carmine and Carlo turned to face the source of the sweet voice. It was a tall redhead in a pink tank top and white short shorts. She was wearing a cowboy hat and holding a tray of shots.

"How much are they?" Carlo asked quickly.

Carmine looked with disgust at his companion. Why did they have to give him this idiot for this run, he wondered to himself.

"They're free," the redhead smiled.

"Sure, we'll both take one," Carlo smiled back as he answered for himself and Carmine.

"Don't be such a frigging idiot," Carmine loathed. "Try to blend in a bit."

Carlo threw back his shot and wiped his lips with the back of his hand. "When that girl comes around again, I'll take two more of those," he laughed.

Their attention was drawn to Dwight again as he turned to face the people gathered outside, looking in from the other side of the plate glass window, and he began to sing to them as they watched from the sidewalk.

"That guy is awesome! He's a pro," Carlo offered.

"At least there's one pro in the building," Carmine said condescendingly to Carlo, but it went right over Carlo's head. "Hey, look at what that guy's doing now!"

Dwight left the stage area and exited through the door on his left, to stand with the onlookers on the sidewalk where he continued to play and dance.

Carmine and Carlo continued to drink and watch the dancers. Before they knew it, they had stayed longer than they had intended and had more drinks than they intended.

Looking at his watch and seeing that it was near midnight, Carmine said to Carlo over the loud music, "We need to blow this joint. Come on."

They started to work their way through the crowd and exited the building onto the sidewalk.

"Man, I had too much to drink," Carlo said as he breathed in the fresh air and tried to remember at which dock they had left the boat.

"I'm fine," Carmine lied as they began to wobble through the park to "B" dock. He was caught in his lie two steps later when he stumbled over a section of raised sidewalk concrete.

Carlo saw him stumble but withheld commenting.

They crossed Bayview and walked down "B" dock to their boat. Carmine stepped into the Sea Ray and unlocked the cabin door. He slowly stepped down into the cabin, and checked to make sure that the two orange duffel bags were still in the bow berth. He may have had too much to drink, but he wouldn't forget about the valuable cargo charged to his care.

Meanwhile, Carlo was still struggling with untying the bow line. He couldn't untie the knot. Hearing footsteps behind him, Carlo looked around and saw an impatient Carmine approaching.

"What's taking so friggin' long?" Carmine demanded.

Sheepishly, Carlo responded, "Stupid knot won't come undone. I think someone retied it."

"Right. Someone came along and retied the knot to make it more difficult for you!" Carmine mocked. "Here stand aside, I'll handle it."

Carlo had barely moved out of the way when Carmine's knife blade swiftly cut through the line. "Now, that's taken care of. I'll get the aft line." Carmine didn't even try to untie the aft line. He just neatly sliced the line and stepped into the boat to join a waiting Carlo. "Nothing to it!"

"Yeah, nothing to it," Carlo echoed as he watched Carmine close the blade and place the knife in his trouser pocket.

Carmine started the engines and pushed the throttle forward to slowly ease the boat away from the dock. As carefully as he could in his alcohol-induced state, he maneuvered the sleek craft through the maze of boats in the harbor.

As they left the harbor, he pushed forward on the throttle, and the boat leapt out of the water.

"Look at that big boat!" Carlo exclaimed as a huge boat with dimmed interior lights passed on their right.

"That must be that Jet Express. It's a ferry boat," Carmine answered. The two watched the lighted catamaran as it approached its dock to pick up the evening's revelers and return them to the mainland. They were so intent on watching the Jet Express that they didn't notice that they were passing the red can on the wrong side by forty feet.

All boats passed the can on their left as they exited the harbor before heading west past Gibraltar Island. The floating can marked the dangerous Peach Point reef.

Carmine gave the boat full throttle and the boat picked up speed. A few seconds later the boat shuddered as it came into contact with the rocks below the water's surface. The sudden halt in its forward motion threw Carmine and Carlo forward and onto the deck.

The jagged rocks beneath the surface had ripped a gash in the boat's fiberglass hull as the boat's engines continued pushing the boat forward across the rocky reef and lengthening the hull's gash. The boat eased to a halt on the other side of Peach Point Reef where the water depth was thirty feet. The breached hull quickly filled with water and began to sink rapidly.

"Shit!" exclaimed Carmine as he saw how fast the boat was sinking.

"We're sinking!" screamed Carlo in a panic as he saw water emerging from the cabin and the boat sank deeper in the water. The next thing that Carlo knew, he was being propelled by Carmine out of the boat and into the murky water. When his head broke water as he surfaced, something splashed into the water next to him.

"There's a life jacket for you. You might want to use it," Carmine yelled as the water reached the gunwales of the

Sea Ray. Carmine jumped into the lake with his own life jacket.

They watched as the Sea Ray sunk below the water's surface, and followed its glowing aft light as long as they could see it.

Gripping his life jacket tightly as he struggled to put it on, Carlo asked worriedly, "What are we going to do about the cocaine? Vinny is going to kill us!"

A now-sobered Carmine thought for a moment and then answered, "We're not going to tell him."

"Not going to tell him? What do you mean not going to tell him? Like he's not going to wonder where the coke went?"

"Listen, stupid. He won't know anything about this. And the reason that he won't know anything about this is that we are going to recover the coke."

"Recover the coke? Who's the 'we' you're talking about? I'm not going down there!"

"You will if I fill your shoes with concrete! And you'll stay down there!" Carmine threatened.

Even in the darkness as they floated in the water, Carmine could see Carlo's eyes narrow at the threat. "We'll hire a diver to retrieve the coke for us. There's got to be divers around here," he said as he gazed at the islands on the dark horizon.

The growing noise of a boat's motor caused them to turn around. A voice yelled out to them, "You boys look like you've got yourself in a bit of a pinch. You know that reef can be real nasty to boats. That's Peach Point Reef!"

The wooden boat slowed and glided to a halt next to the two floating men. "Come on. I'll give you a hand," he said as he tried to help them on the boat. "I'll help you climb in as best as I can. Can't do too much to help you. I've got a bad back," the older man said as he ran his tongue over his lips. "The name's Cassidy," he offered as he did the best he could in helping them into his boat. He turned his head as he smelled the alcohol on their breath. "Been drinking a bit too, I'd gather," the seventy-year-old surmised aloud.

"Thank you for helping us. I'm Mr. Smith and this is Mr. Jones."

Cassidy raised his eyebrow at their introductions. He feigned indifference to their obviously fictitious names and looked toward the spot where he thought their boat went down. Noting his GPS reading, he wrote down the coordinates before speaking, "We'll need to report the sinking to the Coast Guard. That's required, you know?"

"There are things that are required and then there are things that are not required, if you know what I mean," Carmine said with an edge to his voice.

"Not sure I catch your drift, son," Cassidy responded.

"Listen, we'd like to keep this little event quiet," Carmine scowled with exasperation at the old man. Seeing no reaction from Cassidy, Carmine produced a wad of cash, and extracted three wet one-hundred-dollar bills. "Let's just keep this between you and us."

Cassidy read the threatening tone in Carmine's voice, and realized that he had two dangerous men aboard his boat. They were two strong men, who could throw him overboard, and take his boat if they wanted. He decided to play this low-key. "Sure, fine with me," he said as he took the cash and stuffed it into his pants pocket.

"Do you know anyone around here, old-timer, who could dive to our boat and retrieve some valuables?" Carmine asked as Cassidy headed the boat around Gibraltar Island and toward his dock in Put-in-Bay where his old truck was parked.

Cassidy silently bristled at being called old-timer. He remained calm despite his inner angst. "Matter of fact, I do. The lady that I'm seeing here on the island has a nephew staying with her. And he's got a buddy who knows a bit about diving. I'd bet that he could help you out." Cassidy decided not to tell them that the buddy also was an ex-Navy SEAL.

"Good. Since my friend and I weren't planning on spending the night, could you put us up? Maybe we could stay with you tonight?" Carmine asked as he peeled off two more wet hundred-dollar notes and passed them to Cassidy. "Then, you could make arrangements for the divers in the morning."

"Sure, I can do that. Glad to help you two out," Cassidy said as he fought to contain his grin. He'd already planned on phoning the police about them the first chance that he got. His past experiences on the island told him that it would be wiser for him to play along with them for now.

After docking his boat, Cassidy drove them to his home at one of the small farms that dotted the island. They parked the truck and walked through the moonlit night to the white farmhouse. Unlocking the front door, Cassidy ushered them inside.

"Make yourselves comfortable," Cassidy urged as he walked into his bedroom and to his closet. Cassidy found two aged robes, and returned to the front room where the two were standing in their wet clothes. "Here, put these on. You can hang your clothes on the front porch railing. They should be dry by morning."

"Thank you," Carmine said as the two started to shuck their wet clothes. Cassidy walked back toward the kitchen while Carlo stepped outside and draped the clothes over the railing.

The phone was in his hand when Carmine surprised Cassidy at the kitchen doorway.

"Funny. I didn't hear the phone ring."

Thinking quickly, Cassidy responded, "It didn't. I was just going to call to see if our divers were available."

"At this hour?"

"Sure. They work all kinds of hours. Always on call," he said. He had started to dial the Put-in-Bay police. Carmine approached Cassidy, and slowly pulled the receiver from his grip. He placed the phone back in its cradle and tapped it as he looked sternly into Cassidy's eyes. "Let's not make any phone calls until morning. Understand me?"

Cassidy evaluated the seriousness of his situation. "Sure. Now let's get you guys some food. You must be famished after a night like tonight."

Cassidy was right on that note. There had been food aboard the Sea Ray that they would have been able to eat as they headed to Detroit. Now it was fish food. "I could tolerate something light."

"Me, too," Carlo said as he entered the small kitchen.

"What can we do to help, Cassidy? It is Cassidy if I remember correctly," Carmine said.

Cassidy turned away from the phone and opened the bread box. "Yes, it is. Grab yourselves a couple of cans of pop if you'd like," he said as he pointed to his fridge.

"Thanks, I'll do that." Carmine opened the small fridge and extracted two cans of pop. When Carmine turned around, Cassidy was making a plate of peanut butter and grape jelly sandwiches, and Carlo was seated at the worn table. Carmine's eyes swept the kitchen as he noted the need for a coat of paint. The front room could have used several coats of paint, too, he thought to himself.

It took just a few minutes for Cassidy to make the sandwiches. "There you go. Eat up boys," he said as he sat on a stool and watched them devour the sandwiches. They wolfed them down in minutes and placed the empty plates on the counter as the old clock on the fireplace mantel chimed 2:00.

"You boys can sleep in the front room. I'll get you some blankets."

"I'll sleep on the sofa. You can have the floor," Carmine said to Carlo as they reentered the front room. Carmine stepped out on the porch for an evening cigarette, and realized that the cigarettes had been soaked during his unexpected evening swim. He threw the pack of wet cigarettes into the yard and leaned against the porch post as he looked around the small farm. It was bathed in moonlight and presented a tranquil touch to his evening. His mind quickly shifted to Vinny, then to his merchandise that was on the bottom of Lake Erie. They had better be successful in recovering the merchandise, or Vinny could become very nasty! He took a deep breath of the fresh air as a light breeze blew in from the west and decided that the problem would be solved in the morning.

When he reentered the house, he saw that Carlo had stretched out on a thin, brown rug on the hard wooden floor in front of the stone fireplace. Carmine sat on the ancient sofa and tested it. It sagged. It was definitely in need of major spring repair, he thought.

Cassidy reappeared with blankets and pillows and began to distribute them. "Like my sofa? Found it in front of the house of the people who own the *Gazette* here in Put-in-Bay. They were throwing it out in the trash. It still had a lot of years of use left, so I grabbed it and hauled it home."

"By the feel of it, they should have thrown it out years ago," Carmine said as he bounced twice on the squeaky sofa.

"They did. I've had it for twenty years. Still has a way to go yet," he smiled. "Have a good night's rest." He slowly padded down the narrow hallway to his bedroom. As he readied for bed he thought about the calls he would make in the morning to start the clandestine diving operation and to the police.

Next Morning
Aunt Anne's House
Put-in-Bay

❧

"I've got an idea for a story. Ever been to Key West?" John Sedler, *The Washington Post*'s Managing Editor, asked Emerson Moore, his star investigative reporter, over the phone.

"No, and I'm way overdue to make a visit there. I've been to Miami and Clearwater, but haven't made it to the Keys. You remember Sam Duncan?" the investigative reporter probed.

Sedler thought for a second. "I believe so. Wasn't he that ex-Navy SEAL who was involved with you on your Put-in-Bay story?"

"Right, and a source for several of my other stories. Sam's here on the island visiting with me and I can talk to him about Key West. He has a place in Key West, and this will give me an opportunity to see it," Emerson said eagerly as he thought about his rascally sidekick. He suspected Sam worked for the CIA, and also knew that Sam had a knack for helping extract Emerson from several tough and sensitive situations. A chill ran up Emerson's spine as he thought about their daring, underwater swim through one of the island's water-filled caves about fourteen months ago. Emerson was glad to have his talented friend with him on some of his investigative stories. "What's the story you've got in mind?"

"Well, it's been several years since a major hurricane has hit the coastline from Texas to Cape Cod. About 20 percent of the nation's population reside in areas susceptible to hurricanes. Based on what meteorologists are predicting, this year could see a number of major hurricanes hit the U.S."

"Why send me to Key West if the entire coast along the Gulf of Mexico and the Atlantic are potentially in the target area?"

Sedler paused for a moment before answering. "Based on the experts' analysis of past storms and weather patterns, their findings are pointing toward Key West taking a direct hit from one of the toughest hurricanes that this country has seen in years. I want you down there to cover the story, including what people are doing to get ready, the storm itself, and the aftermath."

"Okay. When do you want me there?"

"I'd expect sometime within the week. The hurricane season has already started. Hurricane Albert started for Key West last month, but then veered out to the Atlantic and was downgraded to a tropical storm. I need you there, on the ground and following the story closely."

"Okay. I'll plan to fly there this week."

"And, Emerson . . . "

"Yes?"

"Try to be careful on this one. If the weather gets too rough, go to cover," Sedler cautioned. Sedler didn't mind situations with moderate risk, but he didn't want his daring, Pulitzer Prize-winning reporter in life-threatening situations.

"You don't have to worry about me," Emerson replied as he noted the tone of concern in Sedler's voice. "I know how to take care of myself."

"Sure you do. That's what worries me, at times," Sedler said as he thought about some of the nearly fatal misadventures that Emerson had experienced.

They ended their call, and Emerson walked through his Aunt's house. He stepped out the front door onto the screened porch, which overlooked Put-in-Bay's harbor from the east side. The porch's roof shaded him from the warm rays of the late morning sun. It was a beautiful September day. The temperatures had been hovering in the high seventies for the past week.

The tanned, six-foot-two Emerson, with his glossy black hair and dark brown eyes sat for a moment on one of the three steps descending from the porch. He thought how much he appreciated *The Washington Post* allowing him to work from this island home where he resided with his aunt. They had supported Emerson's relocation from Alexandria, Virginia to Lake Erie's picturesque South Bass Island, one of the islands in the lake's western basin that was also the home of the island resort village of Put-in-Bay. It didn't matter where he was domiciled as his investigative reporting caused him to travel extensively and he worked effectively from his virtual office.

Returning to the island had been initially difficult for Emerson who had to overcome his nightmares from his days spent as a youth on the island, and his cousin's macabre death. The combination of Uncle Frank's death about a year ago and the unexpected tragic death of Emerson's wife and son drew Emerson to the island to offer solace to his aunt and to escape his grief-driven battle with alcoholism.

"E! You going to stand there all day and just stare at Gibraltar Island, or are we going to earn some pocket change?" the powerfully built, blonde-haired Sam shouted. His five-foot-eight, thirty-eight-year-old effervescent friend had a contagious enthusiasm about him which seemed to make him at home wherever he went. It was difficult for anyone not to like Sam.

"Coming," Emerson responded as he realized that he had been unconsciously staring at the small island and thinking about the beautiful, but married Martine who had temporarily resided there when he visited Put-in-Bay last year. Fourteen months ago, there had been a mutual attraction as she struggled to maintain her marriage with her alcoholic husband. Her husband had worked for Jacques L'Hoste, the shipping magnate with whom Emerson had confrontations. The L'Hoste estate had been turned into a bed and breakfast. Martine and her husband had moved to New Orleans where her husband had found new employment, according to one of the workers at the Ohio State University's facilities on Gibraltar Island, who kept in touch with her.

"I always catch you just staring at Gibraltar Island. You thinking about that Martine girl again?" Sam asked in a teasing tone.

"Caught red-handed. I still can feel her warm breath on my face," Emerson said languidly as he recalled the parting kiss they had shared outside of Port Clinton's Magruder Hospital.

"Her warm breasts on your face?" Sam joked.

"I said breath. Come on, Sam. You know it wasn't that kind of relationship."

"But you wouldn't have minded, I'm sure. You need to give up on her. She's like chasing a shadow. You can never catch it."

Emerson knew that Sam was right, but he couldn't give up on his dream. Maybe, one day things would work out. Emerson turned his attention to the dock where Sam was getting ready for the unexpected morning dive. Mr. Cassidy, his aunt's boyfriend, had called that morning and said that he had met two men who needed someone to dive on their sunken boat off of Gibraltar to retrieve a couple of items. He wanted to know if Sam would be interested since he was in town visiting with Emerson. Emerson had checked with Sam, and then made arrangements to meet the two men and Mr. Cassidy at the Boardwalk dock. For some reason, Mr. Cassidy didn't want to drive to Aunt Anne's house and use their dock. Emerson had found it curious, but the money that the two men were offering for the dive was very lucrative—to both Sam and Emerson, who would be going along to assist.

After talking with Mr. Cassidy, Emerson had called the New Wave Dive Center on the waterfront in Port Clinton to see if Rob and his wife, Kathie or Scuba Kat, as she liked to be called, would be able to rent Sam scuba equipment and help with the dive. Scuba Kat volunteered to help and bring the dive boat out with equipment since Rob was conducting an underwater demolition class in Toledo for the police. Emerson handed the phone to Sam at that point so that the two experts could talk about what type of equipment they might need off of the Peach Point reef, which was in the general area that Mr. Cassidy rescued the two men. Having dived around the islands for years, Scuba Kat was familiar with the reef area.

Emerson arose from the steps and walked toward the dock where Sam was waving at the approaching dive boat. The late morning sun added a warm glow to Sam's blonde hair and tanned features, which helped set off his blue-green eyes. Sam's good looks, easy ways, and roguish behavior seemed to attract females—and Sam played it for what it was worth. When Sam had called Emerson and indicated that he'd like to stop by Put-in-Bay for a visit, Emerson had been pleasantly surprised. Although Emerson thought that 10 percent of the reason for the visit was to see him, the other 90 percent was to see what kind of shenanigans Sam could get into at the island's numerous bars.

"Here comes the dive boat," Sam yelled as he saw Emerson walking on the dock.

Scuba Kat expertly eased the Tiara into the dock and shut down the engines as Sam secured the aft line and Emerson tied the bow line.

"Beautiful day for a dive, guys!" Scuba Kat said as she stepped fully into view. Sam stared in awe at her striking figure in her tight wet suit, which was unzipped about a third of the way, allowing her cleavage to show. She shook her long strawberry blonde hair for a moment and took off her dark sunglasses to reveal deep blue eyes. "Hi Emerson," she greeted Emerson as she bounded out of the boat onto the dock.

"Hi there, Scuba Kat," Emerson returned the greeting warmly.

"This guy with his tongue hanging out must be Sam," she said cheerfully.

Realizing that he had been staring at her, Sam snapped out of it. "That would be me. At your service, my fair maiden!"

"I'm Scuba Kat. And maybe I should have you call me Mrs. Scuba Kat so that you remember that I'm married," she teased. She had been used to the effect that she had on men, but the only one that really meant anything to her was the effect that she had on her husband, Rob. She knew from experience that it paid to set the boundaries with guys early on when meeting them. Even the cute ones like Sam.

"Okay. Sorry about that, Mrs. Scuba Kat," Sam said feigned hurt feelings. Then moving to his more normal rascally demeanor, Sam added, "Love your catsuit! Or should I say you look like a Gumby walker?"

"Thank you, Sam. But you and I both know that it's a wet suit!" she added firmly to the handsome ex-Navy SEAL.

"Isn't it a little too warm today for you to have your wetsuit on already?" Sam persisted.

"It is a bit warm," she responded. Teasingly, she continued, "But I didn't want to tempt you anymore than I apparently have. Underneath my wet suit, I'm wearing my little thong bikini today."

Sam rolled his eyes and moaned before responding, "You're killing me! Are you really?"

Scuba Kat grinned back and said firmly, "No, but it's fun watching your reactions!"

Emerson chuckled. "Okay, okay. We've got to get going. Anything that we need to bring?"

"You can tie that motorized dinghy on the back. We can use it to work from when we get out there," she suggested.

Sam jumped to the task and quickly secured the dinghy.

"Nice boat," Sam said as he eyed the sleek Tiara.

"Thanks. Rob's brother, John, is the sales manager at Lakeside Marine and sold it us about a month ago," Scuba Kat explained. "Our other boat was dying and this one is an absolute dream."

They untied the lines and boarded the dive boat for the short ride across the harbor to the Boardwalk's dock. As they approached, Emerson waved to the water taxi pilot, Patrick, as he motored several sailors out to their sailboats tied to the moorings. From the stern of the boat, Emerson heard someone cry out his name. He looked closer and saw Patrick's pretty blonde wife, Jill, standing next to him.

Emerson returned her hello. "Hi Jill! Patrick taking you for a cruise?"

"Exactly. Today's our wedding anniversary and he promised to take me for a cruise. I didn't know he meant Put-in-Bay harbor!" the owner of the island's Silly Goose Gift Shop teased.

"I can't think of anywhere prettier than Put-in-Bay harbor!" Patrick retorted good-naturedly.

"Or cheaper!" Jill joked as she flashed a smile at her husband.

"Happy anniversary! I'll buy you guys a drink later," Emerson called. "To share," he added as the crafts grew wider apart.

"Gee, E. Don't go overboard with your spending," Sam said as they turned their attention to scanning the approaching dock for Mr. Cassidy and the two men. They didn't see Mr. Cassidy anywhere on the dock.

Then, a voice called down from the top deck bar area. "Are you, Emerson?"

Emerson peered up at the top deck and saw a man holding a beer. "Yes, that would be me."

"We'll be right down. We were just getting drinks for the road," he yelled down.

Emerson looked at his watch. Not too unusual at this time of the morning for Put-in-Bay visitors.

A few minutes later, the two men appeared and took the stairs down to the dock level. Mr. Cassidy was not with them.

"Where's Mr. Cassidy?" Emerson asked as the two boarded the boat.

"He decided that he had some things to do and stayed home. He loaned us his truck to drive down here," Carmine said.

Emerson looked out of the corner of his eye at Sam who caught the look. They both remembered how protective Mr. Cassidy was of his old pickup. He never let anyone else drive it.

"I'm Mr. Smith and this is Mr. Jones," Carmine said.

"Well, you already know that I'm Emerson. This is Scuba Kat whose boat and equipment we'll be using," Emerson said.
"Nice equipment," Carlo muttered as he eyed Scuba Kat. He then spoke up, "I may decide to take up scuba diving. Do you give private, personalized lessons?" Carlo leered. His question was followed quickly by a moan as a result of a quick jab to his ribs from Carmine's elbow.

Scuba Kat ignored the comment. So did Emerson as he continued with the introductions. "Mr. Smith, this my friend, Sam, who will also be diving on your boat today." Emerson caught a glimpse of a pistol tucked into the waistband of Carmine's slacks.

Sam nodded at "Mr. Smith." His trained eye had also spotted the partially hidden weapon, and he realized that it was going to be an interesting morning dive.

"Do you have any idea about where you went down so that we know where we should start searching for the boat?" Emerson asked.

"We were heading out of the harbor and picking up speed when we hit something. She sunk fast on the other side of that island." He pointed at Gibraltar Island.

"Sure sounds like Peach Point Reef," Scuba Kat suggested as she looked at Emerson and Sam.

"You'd know more about these waters than Sam or me," Emerson responded.

"The old man gave me this," Carmine offered as he handed a note to Emerson. Emerson, Sam, and Scuba Kat crowded around the note to read it.

"It's the GPS location," Scuba Kat said. "This should be relatively easy. Let's cast off, guys." She turned and walked to the boat's controls as Sam and Emerson cast off the lines, and the two visitors sat aft. Scuba Kat carefully turned the boat and steered it towards the entrance to the harbor.

Within a few minutes, they turned left of the first floating red can at the harbor's entrance and approached the second can on the north side of Gibraltar. Scuba Kat slowed the boat.

Emerson stood back and out of the way of the two experts, Sam and Scuba Kat. They were gazing intently at the boat's GPS as they maneuvered it toward the location that Mr. Cassidy had noted. Emerson looked toward the stern and saw the two anxious-looking visitors staring intently into the water.

The boat eased to a stop in the morning's relatively calm water.

"It should be around here," Scuba Kat suggested as she began to scan the water for any signs that would assist in shortening their underwater search. "Peach Point reef runs almost the entire length of Gibraltar Island and then towards Peach Point on the northwest side of South Bass Island. Depending on water level it can be just below the surface to a few feet below. The deepest part of the lake here is about thirty feet."

"Oil!" Sam yelled as he saw oil seeping to the surface. "Come on, E. Let's check it out," he said as he pulled the dinghy in closer and stepped aboard. Emerson quickly followed as Sam started the dinghy's outboard motor.

They positioned the dinghy close to the oil site and began to peer over the side. Sam looked over his shoulder towards the boat to make sure that the passengers were far enough away, then he turned back and talked to Emerson in a low voice. "I don't like this. It smells, if you know what I mean."

"Exactly what I was thinking. First, Mr. Cassidy never lets anyone drive his truck; and for him not to show up for an event like this!" Emerson paused and didn't complete his thought. "You saw Smith's pistol, didn't you?"

"I spotted the pistol right away. The other guy has one, too. It's in his pants pocket if you look closely enough."

"I usually don't look closely at men's pants pockets!" Emerson replied semi-seriously.

Sam grinned in response. "Look there! You can see a stream of oil making its way to the surface. Good thing that we've got a calm day, otherwise, it wouldn't be this easy. All we have to do is to follow the stream down to the boat."

Emerson turned toward the dive boat. "We think this is it," he shouted. Then in soft voice, he cautioned Sam, "We'll need to be very careful with these guys."

"I would say that's an understatement," Sam stated as Scuba Kat positioned the Tiara next to them and threw out an anchor.

"Yeah. I see the oil, too," she said as she leaned over the gunwale and peered into the water.

"You found it?" Carmine asked hurriedly.

"We think so. There's a trail of oil streaming to the surface. Scuba Kat and I can follow it down to see if it's your boat," Sam explained.

"We'll have to take lights with us. It can get real murky down there. The bottom here is usually muddy," Scuba Kat offered. "Let's get our gear on and check it out."

Sam and Emerson scrambled onto the dive boat, and the two divers began to pull on their gear.

"The BC's already have weights inserted," Scuba Kat noted to Sam as they both attached the 3,000-PSI air tanks to the buoyancy compensation devices, the black vests with pockets for weights. "They've got an integrated weight release system."

Sam nodded his head in understanding as he checked the oral and automatic inflators on the vest to make sure that they were functioning properly in the event he needed to adjust his buoyancy.

"What's your typical visibility in Lake Erie?" Emerson asked with interest.

"It can be up to fifty feet, but it averages twenty to thirty feet. The clearest water can be found in early spring or late fall. July and August have reduced visibility because of the algae blooms," Scuba Kat explained as they hooked the first stages to the tank's valve. They secured the second stage, which contained the diver's mouthpiece, the air supply to the BC to increase buoyancy, the pressure and depth gauges and the alternate air source, or octopus, which could be used as an air supply by a diver in trouble.

"The visibility was worse in the mid 1980s, but with the arrival of the zebra mussels, the water has become significantly clearer. Those little mussels act like mini filtration systems," she added.

"Who introduced them to the lake?" Emerson asked.
"No one introduced them. They actually hitchhiked in from Europe on the hulls of some transatlantic vessels. Then they multiplied like crazy."

"Faster than rabbits?" Sam asked.

"Yes, Sam. Faster than rabbits," Scuba Kat responded exasperatedly.

Sam began slipping into the wetsuit that Scuba Kat had lent him.

"I should have brought you a flowered suit," Scuba Kat teased Sam as she placed two large green primary lights within their reach, and checked that her back up light was in her BC pocket.

Looking at Scuba Kat, Sam offered, "You know, my mother told me when I was growing up to stay away from using four-letter words. But there's one four-letter word that I do my best to keep from my vocabulary. Do you know what four-letter word that is?"

Scuba Kat looked pensive. She asked cautiously, "What would that be? I'm sure that I've heard them all."

"Wife!" Sam uttered.

Emerson and Scuba Kat groaned in unison.

Sam continued as he looked at Scuba Kat, "You must be a handful for your husband to handle!"

"I'm more than a handful," she said seductively as they both put on their neoprene booties. "But, I don't believe my husband is willing to discuss that with you, and neither am I!"

"You two are sounding like the Bickersons!" Emerson inserted into the conversation. He had been enjoying the lighthearted exchange between the two divers.

"Are we going to be out here all day? I want those duffel bags found!" Carmine asked as he fretted about how long it was taking them to get into the water.

"Just a couple of minutes," Sam shouted as they finished pulling on their fins, hoods, and gloves. In slightly less than two minutes, they had transferred to the dinghy, pulled on their masks and back rolled into the water.

Emerson stepped into the dinghy so that he could be closer to the action.

After hitting the water, Sam resurfaced with Scuba Kat at his side. He tilted his head back and lifted the lower edge of his mask. Taking a deep breath, Sam exhaled through his nostrils to clear the water out of his mask and adjusted his mask. He turned toward Scuba Kat. "Let's do it!"

Both divers submerged and began their descent as they followed the oil trail toward the sunken craft. As they approached the fifteen-foot depth, they turned on their lights and continued to follow the oil trail. The air bubbles from their tanks left a trail of their own.

It didn't take long for them to trace it to the sunken Sea Ray, which was resting slightly angled to its port side. The Sea Ray's bow sat upon a large boulder, causing it to be higher than the stern.

Scuba Kat watched the ex-Navy SEAL as he swam to the closed cabin door and began to pull on it. It opened easily and he turned to signal Scuba Kat to follow him inside. Making their way carefully through the cabin to the forward berth, they spotted the two orange duffel bags that the visitors were searching for.

On the surface, Emerson and the visitors had been scanning the water for a sign of the returning divers and the two duffel bags. Emerson glanced at his watch and saw that thirty minutes had elapsed since the two divers had entered the lake's water.

Seeing Emerson look at his watch, Carmine asked, "What's taking your friends so long?"

Giving Carmine a quick glance, Emerson replied, "Don't know. Maybe they're having trouble finding the boat."

No sooner had he said it than their attention was interrupted by a noise on the surface as the first orange bag rocketed to the surface. Sam had attached a surface buoy to it and shoved it through the forward hatch.

"There's one!" Carlo yelled as the bag surfaced.

"Go get it before it sinks!" Carmine shouted to Emerson in the dinghy. He didn't realize that the surface buoy would prevent it from sinking.

Dutifully, Emerson started the dinghy's motor and chased down the first bag. He quickly pulled it into the dinghy.

"Bring that bag over here now!" Carmine demanded.

"I'm on my way," Emerson said as he took one last look for the remaining bag. Not seeing it, he turned the dinghy toward the dive boat and within a minute was at its side.

Carmine's and Carlo's hands anxiously reached for the duffel bag as Emerson lifted it to them in the dive boat. Completely disregarding Emerson, the two visitors placed the bag on the deck and unzipped it to peek inside. Seeing what they wanted, they quickly zipped the duffel bag shut.

"Where's the other bag?" Carmine demanded.

"I'd expect that it would be along shortly," Emerson replied as he eased the dinghy away from the dive boat.

A couple of minutes later, the second duffel bag popped to the surface. Emerson retrieved it and returned it to the dive boat. He handed the bag to Carlo as Carmine watched with an evil grin. Carlo quickly unzipped the second bag, peeked inside and rezipped it shut.

When Emerson started to tie up to the port side and climb aboard, Carmine said with a very direct tone, "Tie the dinghy to the stern."

"I don't think we need to do that yet," Emerson responded.

With a menacing tone, Carmine repeated himself, "I said, tie the dinghy to the stern."

When Emerson looked at Carmine, he found himself staring into the barrel of a pistol equipped with a silencer, which Carmine had produced. "I'd strongly suggest that you do what I say."

Emerson thought for a moment about trying to flee with the dinghy, but he quickly realized that it was a stupid idea. He maneuvered the dinghy to the stern and secured it. He then sat back and waited for his friends to surface. Carmine and Carlo also waited. Carlo carefully withdrew his pistol from his pocket and fitted it with a silencer that he had in his other pocket.

As he sat on the edge of the dinghy and waited, Emerson's mind raced as to how he could warn his friends. It didn't race for long as the two divers broke the water's surface. Spitting out his mouthpiece, Sam asked as he swam to the dinghy's side and saw the weapons, "Was it something we said?"

"Knock it off!" Carmine stormed as Scuba Kat swam to the dinghy's starboard side and grasped it.

"Seriously, what's going on here?" Emerson inquired.

"Let's just say that we don't need any witnesses around to talk about what you recovered for us today."

Emerson realized that his suspicion about these two being dangerous and possibly up to something illegal was right on the money.

"Sorry," Carmine said as he pointed his pistol at Sam and began to pull the trigger.

Scuba Kat's yell interrupted Carmine's action.

"There's the Coast Guard patrol boat!"

Startled, Carmine and Carlo swung their heads to look where Scuba Kat was pointing. When they did, Emerson suddenly felt himself being pulled abruptly backwards by his belt and into the water. He was pulled downward by Sam as bullets cut through the water in search of a victim.

The deeper they went, the more that Emerson's lungs ached for air. The suddenness of his submersion had not permitted him to take a deep breath to fill his lungs. In a moment their descent slowed and Emerson felt a mouthpiece pushed towards his mouth. It was the octopus, or auxiliary air supply from Sam's first stage.

Inserting it in his mouth, he took a breath of the air and exhaled through his nostrils. Attached to Sam now as a baby by an umbilical cord to its mother, Emerson had no choice but to follow Sam to the lake bottom where the sunken Sea Ray rested. There, Sam pulled Emerson with him onboard the boat and through its cabin entrance. He maneuvered him carefully into the raised bow section where their heads broke the water and into an air pocket.

Taking their mouthpieces out, Emerson took a deep breath and then commented to a devilishly smiling Sam, "That was close."

Before Sam could comment, Scuba Kat's head joined them in the air pocket. "Hi Guys! Sorry, I'm late!" she teased.

"Thanks, Sam!" Emerson said as he smiled at his rescuer. "I wondered what was going on when I felt myself being pulled backwards."

"Somebody's got to pull you out of trouble!" Sam responded with a twinkle in his eye. "Nice going!" Sam said to Scuba Kat as he referred to her diversionary tactic.

"I hoped you'd figure out what I was up to."

"In one millisecond!"

"Whatever it was in those duffel bags, they sure wanted to keep it a secret," Emerson observed as he looked around the bow section's air trap.

"Cocaine," Sam said.

"Cocaine! How do you know that?" Emerson asked incredulously.

"Scuba Kat and I got curious about the contents of the bags so we peeked in one of the bags while we were down here."

Emerson's gaze shifted to a grinning Scuba Kat. "So, knowing that, you just went ahead and gave them the coke?"

"Not quite. Sam, why don't you explain since it was your idea?"

Overhead, they heard the dive boat's motors start and pick up speed as it headed toward the mouth of the Detroit River.

"Give me a second." Sam lowered his mask over his face and sunk into the water. He reappeared within a few seconds and shoved the mask onto the top of his head.

"This is what we found." He held up a clear plastic bag filled with a white substance. "We emptied the duffel bags."

"But the duffel bags were full when I pulled them on board," Emerson protested not understanding.

"Exactly. We thought that they might open the bags to make sure that the contents were intact. So we stuffed the duffel bags with life jackets, which we found here in the bow, and placed a layer of bags of coke on top of the life jackets. They're short about 90 percent of their original load. Wait until they deliver the bags to whoever is expecting it." It was Sam's turn to break into a huge grin as he watched Emerson shake his head in disbelief.

"You guys!" Then a look of concern crossed Emerson's face. "Hey, what if the coke shifted and they opened the duffel bags and saw the life jackets?"

"We thought that the bags were stuffed tightly enough. Besides, if there was a problem, at least Scuba Kat and I were down here and you were up there!"

"Yeah, right! Thanks guys," Emerson glared good-naturedly at his two friends. He was glad that the coke hadn't shifted.

"Okay, boys. We'd better head topside. I've got to report a missing dive boat to the Coast Guard and we need to report our attempted murders," Scuba Kat suggested.

"With emphasis on attempted," Emerson grinned as he reinserted the mouthpiece that Sam handed him.

"That would be the good news," Sam chortled mischievously.

Submerging, they slowly swam through the cabin and to the Sea Ray's deck where they paused so that Scuba Kat could release a buoy to mark the sunken craft's location. The three then swam to the lake's surface.

"They're out of sight," Emerson observed as he wiped water from his eyes as they floated on the surface. "I just wish I could be there when the duffel bags are opened!"

"Don't we all!" Sam agreed with a sly smile.

Scuba Kat reached into her buoyancy compensator and pulled out an orange sausage, the three-foot-long and four-inch-wide distress-signaling device. Placing the tube to her mouth, she quickly inflated the sausage.

"Never seen one of those before," Emerson commented as he watched.

"Divers use these to attract the attention of passing boaters when they're in distress or left behind. Works pretty good," she said between breaths.

"One of these days, I need to sign up for scuba lessons. It's something that I've always wanted to do," Emerson said.

"Come on over to the dive shop. We'll fix you right up," Scuba Kat offered.

"I'll do that," Emerson promised.

"Yeah, then you can go diving with me," Sam suggested.

"I'm not sure that I'll ever be in your league, Sam," Emerson stated with heartfelt admiration for the skills of his friend.

"You don't need to be at my level in order to enjoy scuba diving. It's another world down there, as you just got a taste of."

Completing the inflation, Scuba Kat held the sausage by one end, extended her arm in the air and began to wave the safety sausage.

Seeing their proximity to Gibraltar Island, Sam suggested, "We could swim to Gibraltar. They've got security on the other side of the island, if I remember right." He was thinking about the clandestine mission that he and Emerson had taken one night a couple of years ago when they penetrated the island, avoided security, and broke into one of the offices in the Stone Laboratory. "Emerson would know more about whether security is still there since he lives here now."

"It's still there. You can see the guard from the Boardwalk's upper deck."

Scuba Kat disagreed, "Take too long. If we get picked up by a boat with a radio, we can radio the Coast Guard sooner and start the hunt for my dive boat."

Her comment was prophetic. A passing Tiara that was larger than Scuba Kat's Tiara saw the orange sausage which she was waving, and changed course to pick them up. They quickly explained what had happened, and Scuba Kat was given access to the large cruiser's radio so that she could report what had happened.

While she was calling in her report, the Tiara's crew followed Emerson's directions to his aunt's dock on the eastern side of the harbor. After they docked, the three dropped their gear and went into his aunt's house to change into dry clothes.

Leaving Sam in his room on the second floor, Emerson changed quickly and scurried down the stairs with one of his front-button shirts in his hand for Scuba Kat. She had remained in the screened front porch and had slithered out of her snug wet suit. She was standing there in her brief, bright pink bikini when Emerson walked in. She looked absolutely gorgeous with the contrast of her tan and the pink suit.

Scuba Kat turned when she heard the porch floor squeak from Emerson's footsteps.

"Thank goodness it was you. I wouldn't want to cause any more discomfort to your friend with me standing here in this suit," she teased knowingly.

"Sam certainly has an eye for a pretty woman," Emerson commented as she pulled on his shirt over her taut body. "That shirt will never be the same now that you've worn it," he joked.

Scuba Kat smiled in response to the compliment.

It was at that moment that Sam walked into the screened porch and saw Scuba Kat smiling. "What did I miss?" he asked mischeviously.

"Not a thing. Not a thing," Emerson said as he winked at Scuba Kat.

They spent a few minutes talking about their immediate plans, and then drove the golf cart into town. They dropped off Scuba Kat at the Boardwalk where she was going to arrange for transport back to the dive shop. Emerson spotted Mr. Cassidy's truck in the Boardwalk's parking lot. Since the keys were in the ignition, Emerson eased himself behind the wheel and he sped down Catawba Avenue, followed by Sam in the golf cart, to Mr. Cassidy's farm on the island's south side to check on Mr. Cassidy.

They drove up the farm's driveway and halted in front of the farmhouse with its large front porch. They strode quickly onto the porch and burst through the unlocked front door. There, on the floor, was a squirming and bound Mr. Cassidy. An overturned wooden kitchen chair was nearby.

Sam pulled a knife from his pocket and slashed Cassidy's ropes while Emerson carefully removed the piece of duct tape from Mr. Cassidy's mouth. He almost wished that he hadn't, as Mr. Cassidy unleashed a torrent of expletives. Emerson was surprised. He had never heard the cantankerous senior, who was dating his aunt, use such colorful language.

Stretching the cramped muscles in his back as he calmed down, Mr. Cassidy was helped to the chair, which Sam had set upright. Rubbing his arms to ease the cramping, Mr. Cassidy directed Sam, "Sam, go in the kitchen and look under the sink. You'll find a good bottle of Irish whiskey there."

"All Irish whiskey is good whiskey," Sam commented good-naturedly as he walked into the small kitchen and opened the cabinet door beneath the sink.

"Pour me two knuckles' worth," Mr. Cassidy ordered. "I need a pick-me-upper after all of this!"

"Tough morning for you—all tied up and all," Emerson commented as Sam returned and watched as Mr. Cassidy quickly downed the double-shot.

Mr. Cassidy's tongue emerged from his mouth and quickly wiped his lips in search of any last traces of whiskey. He eased back in his chair and began to recant what had transpired. He explained that the two gunmen had tied him up that morning after he had prepared breakfast, and then they drove off in his pickup truck.

"They didn't try to kill you?" Sam asked as he recalled the attempt on their lives.

"Nope. Why would they do that?"

Sam and Emerson then related what had happened with them after they had retrieved the duffel bag

"You don't say," Mr. Cassidy said in amazement. "That's the trouble with this world today. It's getting so that you can't trust anybody! Sorry I got you boys involved. But," he said as his tongue extended and he licked his lips again, "I'd sure like to see what happens to those dumb shits when the duffel bag is opened."

"So would we. So would we," Emerson repeated. "Leave it to Sam!"

Sam grinned as he relished the thought.

Returning to Sam's question, Mr. Cassidy responded, "They probably didn't try to kill me because I didn't know anything about the duffel bags."

"Or they thought you were just a sweet, harmless old man," Sam teased.

"Sweet? Yes. Harmless? Hell, no!" Mr. Cassidy said firmly.

"We're just glad that you're fine. Come on, Sam. Let's get back to Aunt Anne's house and see if there are any messages from Scuba Kat. She said she'd call if there was any breaking news."

Sam and Emerson left the shaken Mr. Cassidy and returned to Aunt Anne's house on East Point.

The Same Day
Key West, Florida
⋰

Stretching one-hundred-sixty miles southwest from Miami, there are a chain of coral islands, bounded on one side by the Atlantic Ocean and the other side by the Gulf of Mexico. At the end of the chain lies an island originally called Cayo Hueso, or Bone Island. It was named by Ponce de Leon for the bones he found there. The bones were the remains of warring groups of rival Indians who, by their custom, did not bury their dead. Over the years, Cayo Hueso became pronounced and known as Key West.

The vibrant island is the southernmost point of the continental United States, and is only ninety miles away from Cuba. Key West, which is two miles wide and four miles long, enjoys fresh ocean breezes and high air quality virtually yearlong.

The city's quaint gingerbread houses, lush tropical foliage, fragrant hibiscus and bougainvillea, sandy beaches, spectacular sunsets, and an ocean teeming with game fish, combine with the residents' "no hurry" lifestyle to create a mystical ambiance. Over the years, the allure of Key West has drawn Indians, New England sailors, Spanish conquistadors, Bahamian salvagers, Cuban shipwrights, spongers, fishermen, tourists, and pirates.

All sorts of people are attracted to this island, which is protected from the seas by a huge barrier reef. On the other side runs the powerful Gulf Stream, resplendent with game fish. One of those characters recently attracted to this island paradise, also known as the Conch Republic, was working as a security guard. He had a bit of pirating in his background, too.

The security guard emerged from the door on the west side of the large stone block building, which loomed over Front Street. The sign displayed over the door read "Mel Fisher's Spanish Galleon Treasure Sales." The front of the building contained the entrance to Mel Fisher's Museum.

The guard dropped wearily onto one of the benches lining the building's side and pulled out a cigarette. Retrieving his lighter from his pocket, he flicked it once and the blue-green flame magically appeared in front of his face. He stared into the flame momentarily before touching it to the end of the cigarette, which was now dangling from his mouth. Taking a deep breath, he pulled the cigarette away from his mouth with one hand as the other returned the lighter to his pocket. He exhaled and watched as the blue smoke dissipated in the warm, humid air.

The guard sat in the shade of the building and finished his cigarette. Feeling the urge for a cold refreshment, he rose and walked to the front of the building, which overlooked Greene Street and a small park. The east side of the building faced Whitehead Street.

His eyes were distracted by the young handsome couple walking together on Greene Street. The young man, wearing dark sunglasses, was dressed in a white tee shirt and blue jean shorts. His blonde companion looked dazzling in her white short shorts, turquoise belly shirt and long blonde hair. She was also wearing mirrored sunglasses. They seemed to be entirely focused on each other and oblivious to the world around them as they chatted amicably.

The young man had his arm around the blonde's waist. The guard grinned as he watched the couple in love walk away.

Tourists, he thought to himself and, then, thought for a moment about his murdered wife. He sensed the sun's strong rays and reached into his pocket for his sunscreen. Damn skin problem, he thought to himself as he began to apply the sunscreen briskly to his arms and chalky white face dotted with red blotches. He took one last look at the handsome couple. As he looked away his eyes swept past and then right back to the worker at a small open air restaurant.

The counterman was staring at the guard and grinning. He also had been watching the attractive couple, and had noticed the guard watching them. The guard returned the grin and walked down the massive stone steps in front of the museum and its courtyard. He crossed the street to the counter, and sat on one of the stools.

"Nice couple," he commented to the counterman.

"Yes, she is very attractive," the dark-skinned Arabic worker replied with a slight accent. "Can I get you something?"

"Yeah. I'll take a cherry slushy," the guard said as he leaned forward.

Within moments the worker had returned with his drink. The guard noticed that the worker was missing his index finger on his right hand when he slid the drink across the counter. The guard raised the cool drink, inserted the straw into his mouth and sucked up the cooling beverage.

Watching him intently, the worker asked, "You work over there?"

"Yep. Been there a couple of months now. I watch the treasure and make sure that no one steals anything."

The worker's eyes widened. "There's treasure in there?"

"Lots of it! Gold and silver coins. It's worth a mint." The guard chuckled to himself as he thought how ironic it was that he had landed the job there.

After relocating to Key West, he had applied for the job on a lark. His background check came back clean. It didn't show the robberies or heists that he had been involved with in the past. A clean past was one of the benefits of being in the Federal Witness Protection program, Pauley Pockets thought to himself with a large grin. He relished the irony of working as a security guard. He went from stealing to protecting goods.

Moving to Key West had been the idea of the U.S. Marshals who had been charged with relocating him after his wife's murder. He didn't want to go where it was hot or sunny because of his skin's reaction to the sun. The more the reason for sending him south, the marshals had argued, as it would be more unlikely that the hit-men on his trail would ever think about him hiding there.

Pauley had taken it a step further. He figured that no hit-man would think that he'd end up working as a guard for a museum. And Pauley liked the idea that, as a guard, he was armed. He momentarily patted the .38 tucked away in the holster at his waist. He smiled as he began to talk about the museum.

"Yeah. Guy named Mel Fisher found a bunch of treasure from some sunken Spanish ships and brought them up. People can take a tour of the museum and then buy some of the treasure on display. Why don't you know this? Aren't you from around here?" Pauley asked.

The counter worker looked around furtively before responding. "No, I'm new to this area."

New to this country, too, Pauley thought as he listened to the worker's accent.

"So, what kind of treasure do they have in there?"

"You name it, they've got it. Gold and silver bars, coins, emeralds, rings, and artifacts. Well, some of them necklaces alone are worth over a million dollars. They've got brooches worth $800,000 a piece and the gold chains, gold pendants, and emerald rings are worth a pretty penny too. Someone said they found more than $400 million and they're still bringing it up from the ocean floor," Pauley replied with pride at his own knowledge.

The worker's eyes gleamed as he tried to guess the value of the building's contents. "Surely they are concerned about someone stealing the treasure."

"Not really. We've got all kinds of security systems and back-ups. And at night, there's always two guards on duty to make sure everything is secure," Pauley said as he thought to himself how often he had thought about ways in which to rip off the store. Glancing at his watch, Pauley said, "I'd better be getting back. My break time is up. What do I owe you?"

"Nothing. It is my pleasure to pay for your drink today."

"Well, that's mighty nice of you. Thank you," Pauley said as he eased himself off the stool and began to walk back to the treasure sales. He had taken two steps when he paused and looked back at the worker. "I didn't get your name."

The worker was slow at responding. "Al, my name is Al," Asad said, giving his alias, as he rubbed the small stub where his trigger finger had been cut off. It had been healing nicely. "Maybe, I'll see you again."

"Probably tomorrow, Al. You make a mean slushy," Pauley said good-naturedly. "My name is Saul," Pauley said as he gave his local alias. With that, Pauley walked across the street, applying suntan lotion to his face, and reentered the treasure sales on the Front Street side of the museum.

Asad watched him as he walked away and began to develop a plan that could finance his retirement, perhaps, on the West Coast of the United States. His mind began to race as he turned over ideas on how to develop a relationship with the guard and pull him into a plot to steal the treasure. He knew that he would have to be careful in how he approached Pauley.

Of course, at this point, Asad was not aware of Pauley's past. Neither was Pauley aware of Asad's past.

For the last week, Pauley had been walking over to the small restaurant where Asad worked. He enjoyed the free slushies that Asad had been giving him, and didn't realize that he was being drawn into Asad's web. Asad had been very careful as he asked questions about the security of the building, and allowed Pauley to boast about his knowledge about the workings of the security system.

Asad was growing anxious about how to pose the question to Pauley, and had cautiously devised a plan. He would initiate the plan that night.

Asad was standing next to his motorcycle in an alley off of Greene Street. He had been watching Pauley's departure time and the direction that he headed home. He planned to follow him.

Pauley emerged from the treasure sales store and unlocked his bicycle from the bike rack. Mounting it, he rode down the ramp and onto Front Street. He turned right on Greene and followed Greene to Margaret Street where he turned right again. He was enjoying his ride and oblivious to the fact that a motorcycle was following him at a discreet distance.

He turned left on Angela and stopped at a house across from Key West's cemetery, where he had rented a small one-bedroom apartment on the ground floor. He pushed the bike up the front steps and locked it on the front porch.

He took a look at the cemetery, which beckoned him to take his routine evening walk. He smiled at its uniqueness and vowed to take his daily stroll. He unlocked the front door and entered his apartment. How appropriate that he lived across from a cemetery, he thought. Over the years, he had sent several people to their graves in New York and New Jersey.

From its main gate entrance at Margaret and Angela Streets, the Key West cemetery's lanes are lined with coconut and palm trees and dotted with interesting statuary. The nineteen-acre cemetery, which dated from 1847, was filled with densely packed, concrete slab–covered graves, crypts, and raised concrete box tombs. The use of concrete was an effort to make sure that the bodies didn't rise and wash out in the event of flooding even though the cemetery was in the Solares Hill area, which was eighteen feet above sea level, and the highest point on the island.

The eccentricities of the populace carry over to the whimsical epitaphs on many of the uniquely designed tombstones that abound on the island. A few of the more noteworthy carried messages like "I told you I was sick!" One widow had inscribed on her wandering husband's tombstone: "At least I know where he's sleeping tonight!"

Asad watched from the intersection and then parked the motorcycle after Pauley entered the apartment. Removing a carry-on bag from the back of the motorcycle, Asad took a deep breath and marched up to the apartment's front door where he started pounding it. He called out the name that Pauley had given him.

"Saul? Saul? Are you in there?" he asked with a sense of urgency.

Pauley recognized the voice, and was surprised when he heard it, since he had never told Al where he resided. Pauley withdrew his .38 from his holster and gripped it tightly as he cracked the door. "Hello, Al. What are you doing here? How did you know where I live?"

"I'll explain later!" Asad's words were rushed. "I'm in a jam and have nowhere to go with this. Can you hold this for me for two hours and I'll come back. I'll make it worth your while," Asad promised convincingly.

Curious as to what was in the bag and willing to help his new friend, Pauley stepped out onto the porch and looked up and down the street. Seeing no one, he took the bag and warned Asad. "Be back in two hours or the bag will be gone."

"Of course. I'll explain everything when I return. You'll understand." Asad turned and ran back to his motorcycle. He started it quickly and rode off.

Pauley reentered the apartment and carefully locked the door. He placed the carry-on bag on a small table, pulled down the shades in the small living room and returned to the table. He looked at the stained bag for a few moments and then unzipped it. Inside the bag, he saw several bags of white powder. Opening one of the bags, he dipped his finger into the powder and then tasted it. Cocaine, he confirmed to himself. He smiled as he thought about charging Asad a holding fee for keeping this stash for him.

Pauley pulled back a small rug and began to pry at the wooden flooring. Two boards pried away easily to reveal a small cubby hole that Pauley had built when he first moved into the apartment. In the cubby hole were two .45s that Pauley had purchased from two shrimpers on Stock Island, which was the next island in the chain towards Miami.

He dropped the carry-on into the cubby and resealed the floor. He pulled the small rug in place and went into the kitchen to fix himself dinner. He was humming as he worked. He hadn't hummed in a long time. Over the years, he had been teased that he only hummed before he went into action on a robbery or murder. He grinned as he hummed.

Two hours later, Pauley heard Asad's knock on the front door. He tucked his .38 in his waistband and walked to answer the door.

On the porch, Asad was replaying his serendipitous discovery of a drug transaction a few nights ago in the park next to the county beach. He had watched the sale and, as the exchange of cash for drugs was taking place, he appeared with a .45 in his hand and had taken both the cash and the cocaine. He then killed the buyer and seller and fled the scene.

While he waited for the door to open, Asad's eyes scanned the cemetery for surveillance teams. He was always watchful. He also found it particularly ironic that Pauley lived across from the cemetery. If things didn't go as Asad planned for the evening discussion with Pauley, the cemetery would have one new tenant.

"You're back!" Pauley said warily as his eyes scanned Asad for any weapons or bulges indicating a weapon. What Pauley didn't know was that Asad was equally as deadly with his hands as he was with a weapon. Seeing none, he invited Asad into the small apartment. "So, what is this all about?"

Asad took a deep breath and hoped his plan would work. "Let me have my bag."

"In due time. I know what's in the bag. I looked," Pauley said smugly.

Asad feigned surprise before he responded. He had hoped that Pauley would look and discover the cocaine. "You looked?"

"Yeah, what do you take me for, some schmuck?" Pauley asked with a growing confidence.

Asad continued to play Pauley. "Saul, I hope you didn't call the police. I can explain what happened."

"No, I didn't call the police. Not yet, that is," Pauley warned. "What I do next is dependent on how wise you are," Pauley said cryptically. Pauley saw this as an opportunity to get in on a piece of the action.

Asad slowly looked around the apartment and how bare the contents were. It was apparent that Pauley didn't have much money.

"Where's my bag?"

"Somewhere safe, Al. Depending on what you tell me, I may give it back to you." Pauley paused as a smile grew on his face, "Half-full, that is."

Asad smiled to himself. The trap was closing, and Pauley was being pulled into his web.

"But, you can't do that," Asad feigned weakness.

Pulling his .38 from his waistband and laying it on the table where Asad could see it, Pauley warned, "I think I can do just about anything I want."

Asad sat back in mock despair and then began to spin the story which he had concocted to tell Pauley. "Okay, I'll tell you what happened. I found the drugs stashed in the house where I'm boarding and stole them. The guys in the house, for some reason, became suspicious of me and I heard them talking that they were going to search my room."

"What made them suspicious?"

"I don't know. But I knew that I needed to hide them somewhere else. That's when I threw them into the carry-on bag and jumped on my bike to find somewhere to stash them. When I saw you park your bike here and enter the house, I thought I'd give you the bag while they searched my room," Asad lied. "Can I have my bag now?"

"And what are you going to do with the drugs?"

"Sell them."

"Sell them to an undercover cop?" Pauley asked. "Listen, I have experience in these matters. I'll sell the drugs for you and we'll split the proceeds. I get half for taking the risk of getting caught."

Asad again smiled inwardly. This was going better than he expected. "Do you know anyone here who you can sell them to?"

"Not yet. It won't take me long to ferret out the right people," Pauley replied as he began to think about identifying a buyer. "I have an eye for these types of things."

"Okay, then. How long until you can sell them and give me my share? I have expenses to cover."

"Give me a couple of days," Pauley said confidently. "And keep your eyes open for any more drugs at your place. We both might be able to raise a little cash on the side here, if you can get more," Pauley said as he was getting a rush from just the thought of dealing again. He was going to enjoy this. "Now, you had better return to your house so that nobody gets suspicious about you."

Asad, with faked submissiveness, agreed, "That's a good idea. This is a good thing for both of us to work together."

Asad rose and walked out of the small apartment. As he descended the steps he smelled the bougainville and looked at the nearby cemetery. Soon, he thought as he walked toward his bike.

In the apartment, Pauley had opened the fridge and grabbed an ice cold beer. He was going to celebrate his cash raising venture. One of the problems he had found with the Federal Witness protection program was that they didn't support you financially. Once they had extracted as much information as they could and used you, they threw you aside in a new location to fend for yourself. Pauley had taken a bath on the sale of the small hardware store. He needed to start raising some cash to finance his retirement. This opportunity had been delivered to his doorstep today and he planned to take advantage of it.

Pauley walked into the front room and sat in a worn overstuffed chair. He ran the ice cold bottle along the front of his forehead and allowed its cooling effect to energize him, although he was already energized by the early evening's events.

He twisted the cap off and tilted the chilled bottle to his mouth. The icy beverage felt good as he swallowed. Placing the bottle on an upturned cardboard box that he was using as an end table, Pauley sat back and thought about selling the cocaine. He had already planned to tell Asad that he couldn't get the full selling price so that he could keep most of the profits.

A few cars whisked by the front of the apartment, as Pauley continued his scheming in the growing darkness of another warm Key West night.

The Next Day
The Heron's Nest Bar
Stock Island

◈

Pauley pushed his way between two arguing shrimpers as he made his way to the bar. Pauley had learned that some of the sleaziest and roughest crowds in the Keys hung out at this bar, The Heron's Nest, which was perched on pilings overlooking a small harbor where the shrimpers docked. Loud reggae music competed with the voices of the unruly patrons in the dimly lit bar.

The crowd was a mixture of shrimpers, bikers, construction workers, retired Navy personnel, and scalawags from the lower end of the food chain.

Pauley watched for a stool to free up, and saw his chance when a biker and his washed-out blonde lady friend stood to leave. Pauley rushed to grab one of the stools. So did a tough-looking, wiry, and unshaven seaman with a shock of thick, black unkempt hair and a deeply lined face. He was wearing a dirty white shirt with the sleeves cut off and stained, beige shorts. They both went for the same stool.

Pauley, being the bigger of the two, began to muscle his way in to secure ownership of the stool. The seaman was equally determined to take the same stool, although the next stool was vacant. It was typical of situations at the Heron's Nest. No one wanted to give an inch.

Pauley grinned to himself as he continued to win the shoving match for control of the stool. He had his butt on most of the stool seat when he felt a sharp pain in his side and looked down to identify the source. Seeing that the source of the pain was a knife that the seaman had so adroitly produced, Pauley raised his eyes to look into the seaman's eyes.

"Sort of evens things up, doesn't it?" the seaman's eyes gleamed as he asked.

"You might say so." Knowing when to give in was a key to surviving for Pauley. "I'll just take the next stool." And he moved over one stool.

"That would be a wise decision," the seaman grinned with exaggerated satisfaction.

Sensing that this hard-nosed seaman could be his means for selling the cocaine, Pauley offered, "No hard feelings. I'll buy."

The bartender had noticed the shoving match for control of the chair, and had moved closer. He held a baseball bat in his hand, which was below his waist and out of sight.

Seeing the bartender, Pauley asked the seaman, "What will you have?"

"Make it a Budweiser."

Turning to the bartender, Pauley said, "Make that two." Looking back at the seaman, Pauley asked, "You a native?"

The seaman looked suspiciously at Pauley and then asked, "What's it to you?"

"Easy there," Pauley replied as he noticed the seaman's uneasiness and rottweiler-like personality. "I was just curious." Pauley then took the initiative and offered some background on himself. "I'm from the East Coast. Got myself in a bit of trouble up there, and decided it might be in my best interests to head south, if you know what I mean?"

"Not quite. What do you mean?" the seaman asked with a growing curiosity.

"I got mixed up with some gang stuff and had a few run-ins with the police," Pauley explained. "Say, where did you learn to use a knife like that? I didn't even see you go for it."

The seaman downed his beer and motioned to the bartender to bring him another. "Special Forces. Ever since I was a kid in West Virginia, I wanted to be in Special Forces. Got selected, but they washed me out."

"Why'd they wash you out?"

"Had a disagreement with my sergeant about some stuff that we were going to steal from the PX. It turned into a fight right there in the PX and we were caught. So he got demoted and I was washed out."

"Tough."

"Went back home and got a job and a woman and a fishing rod. Then I lost my job and my fishing rod."

"Didn't lose your woman, too, did you?" Pauley couldn't resist asking.

"Sometimes I wish I had. She's so mean that she'd bite off the head of a coral snake and not think twice about it," the seaman said half-seriously.

Pauley nodded his head as he listened.

"She's stupid too. I bought a used hearse one time and told her it was a camper. She believed me. We went camping in it for a whole summer before I sold it off," he chuckled as he continued with his exaggerations. "Hell, I'd swear that she's got monkey brains in that crazy head of hers. Her toenails are so long that she can climb up a palm tree faster than any old monkey. Everybody likes to take her fishing. You just let her walk in the water, and she comes out with a fish speared on each toe."

Pauley wondered which of the two was really dumber. He guessed it was the seaman, the way that he was talking.

"Then, I got into trouble when we ran out of cash and I knocked off a couple of gas stations. So, we moved down here about ten years ago. Been working shrimp boats and fishing boats ever since. Got a chance to learn all about the channels and boating here. Me and my knucklehead woman live on a houseboat off Fleming Key."

Pauley had been listening intensely and had guessed that this guy could be his link to a drug buyer. "Things are tough. You guys doing okay now as far as having enough cash?"

The seaman's eyes flashed anger as he replied. "Never have enough of that. We got rug rats now and them kids are always needing something," he growled.

"Maybe I can help you," Pauley said as he scooted his stool a bit closer. "My name's Saul."

"Folks call me J.B. What do you have in mind?" he asked suspiciously.

"I have a friend," Pauley started, "and this friend has some illegal prescriptions to get rid of for the right price. I need help in finding a buyer for him."

J.B. saw right through the question. "You're pushing drugs, huh?" J.B. asked as he cut to the chase.

Looking around before answering, Pauley said, "You're pretty direct."

"That I am."

"Yeah, it's drugs."

"What kind?"

"Coke."

"I might know a few people who could help with that. There's a guy who runs from Miami to the Keys and to Naples. He's got one of those go-fast boats. I know a guy who knows him. Let me see if I can work something out. What's it worth to me to be your go-between?"

"One thousand dollars for the introductions."

"That seems fair if all I have to do is to introduce you," J.B. thought greedily. "You know, I've got to ask you one question though.

"Yeah?"

"You undercover DEA or law enforcement? You know that you can't lie when you respond if you are. Cause then it's entrapment."

"I can assure you that I'm not. That's the last thing that I'd be," Pauley chuckled at the idea of himself being in law enforcement.

They agreed to meet at the bar again the next night where J.B. would provide Pauley with an update as to what the next steps would be.

Aunt Anne's House
Put-in-Bay
∽

The phone was ringing in the kitchen where Emerson had been cooking scrambled eggs for his aunt and himself.

"I've got it," he called down the hallway to his aunt. "Hello?"

"Emerson?"

"Yes."

"It's Scuba Kat!" the cheery voice on the other end replied. "I thought I'd let you know that our dive boat was found. We've got it back."

"Where was it found, and who found it?" Emerson gushed the questions. He caught himself as he realized that he was moving right into his questioning style. This was not a story he was working on, he reminded himself. It was a friend he was talking with.

"The Coast Guard found it adrift and abandoned about five miles west of Rattlesnake Island," Scuba Kat responded.

"Strange. What happened to our two friends?"

"It appears that they commandeered a fishing boat because two fisherman were picked up close to Gross Ile . . . "

Emerson interrupted. "That's the island in the Detroit River."

"Right," she confirmed. "A lot of wealthy people live there. I've got a couple of friends, Renee and Barbara, who work for the island's newspaper, *The Ile Camera*. Anyhow, they apparently stole the fishing boat because they knew that we'd be looking for our dive boat. So they ditched it."

"Sounds like they were heading up river then to Detroit," Emerson conjectured.

"That's exactly where they were headed," Scuba Kat agreed.

"I'd sure would have liked to have been there when the duffel bags were opened!" Emerson mused.

"Emerson, I'm holding back the rest of the story," Scuba Kat teased.

The Previous Night
A Detroit Warehouse
✍

Carmine and Carlo had parked in the alley next to the large warehouse. It was a stormy night as they ran carrying the duffel bags through the downpour to a side door lit by one solitary light. It was locked.

"Shit!" Carmine then saw another side door fifty feet away. "Try that one," Carmine ordered as the water plastered his hair to his head. The light over it had burned out earlier that evening.

Carlo rushed to the other door and tried it. It opened. "It's unlocked!"

Carmine ran to the doorway as the dark sky, filled with thunder, ominously flashed lightening close by. Seeing the lightning, Carmine yelled, "That was too close! Hurry up and get out of the way so I can get inside." He pushed Carlo out of the way and was the first to enter the doorway. Once inside, they shook as much water off themselves as they could. They gave up on their soaked shirts.

"Figures!" Carmine thought aloud. Carlo had taken heat on the drive over through the rain for forgetting to bring umbrellas. Carlo was always the fall guy.

Carmine had been deep in thought about their misadventure in Put-in-Bay, and had been pleased by their good fortune in being able to recover the duffel bags. He wasn't pleased that they had left four witnesses alive, and was working through a number of scenarios including one in which he and Carlo would return to Put-in-Bay and hunt down the three. They would start with that old man, Cassidy, and take him out after he gave them the addresses for the others.

Still angry about being drenched by the rain, Carmine looked down at the orange duffel bags that they were carrying. He couldn't imagine what would have happened if they had shown up empty-handed.

"Let's go," Carmine said. They walked through the filled warehouse to an open area near the rear and next to a windowed office. Sitting behind an eight-foot-long table and waiting for them, was slick-haired and overweight Vinny Tredosio. Two beefy and armed bodyguards flanked him.

Vinny was one of the roughest of the sub-bosses in the Detroit crime ring. He had interest, as he called it, in everything, but most of all in drugs. He had been looking forward to this delivery. It was going to be a huge payday for him when this hit the streets.

"Hey Vinny," Carmine greeted the crime overlord. "Got your merchandise here!" Carmine and Carlo swung their duffel bags onto the table. Vinny looked at the two wet bags and, then, at the two delivery boys as Carmine leaned on the table and Carlo quietly stepped back.

"Yeah, yeah. Let me see the stuff." Vinny stood and pulled the closest bag towards him as Carmine backed away and stood next to Carlo. Vinny quickly pulled the zipper and the bag opened to reveal the plastic bags of cocaine. He pulled one bag out and gave it to one of his bodyguards. "Check it out."

The guard produced a test kit and tested a small portion of the coke. Vinny sat back in his chair while the testing was under way.

"So, no problems on the run?" he questioned.

"None, whatsoever," Carmine lied as Carlo gulped.

Vinny didn't miss seeing Carlo's gulp. "You sure about that?"

"Yeah. No problems, Vinny."

"No problem, huh? You agree with that, Carlo?" Vinny probed as he stared directly into Carlo's eyes.

Carlo responded quickly, but nervously. "Yeah. Yeah. I agree, Vinny."

"It's good," the bodyguard confirmed as he closed up his test kit and passed the plastic bag filled with coke to Vinny.

"Good. Angelo, pay them."

Carmine and Carlo looked expectantly at Angelo, Vinny's bag man and his top gun, when necessary.

"Here you go, boys," Angelo said as he produced a briefcase filled with cash from beneath the table.

"Thank you. As always, it's nice doing business with you," Carmine said as he picked up the briefcase and turned to walk away. Carmine and Carlo had barely taken ten steps towards safety when Angelo's voice could be heard.

"What in the hell is this crap? Hey Vinny, look at this!" Angelo had opened the second bag and had seen something orange in the bag. The cocaine-filled plastic bags had shifted down the duffel bag's sides when Carlo had thrown the bag into the car's trunk earlier in the day. Carlo had no idea that the bags contained anything but the coke. Nor did he anticipate the events that were about to be triggered by the discovery of the duffel bags' true contents.

From out of the second duffel bag, Angelo pulled out an orange life jacket. He showed the jacket and the other jackets to Vinny.

"One friggin' minute! Come back here!" Vinny roared as Angelo dumped the contents of both bags on the tabletop, revealing only a dozen plastic bags of cocaine and six orange life jackets.

Carmine and Carlo slowly swung around and found themselves staring into the barrels of two pistols pointed at them by the other bodyguard and Vinny.

Not seeing what was on the table, Carmine asked as his head swung to face Vinny, "What's wrong?"

"This is what's wrong!" Vinny said with his eyes glazed over in anger. "What is this shit that you're trying to pull on me? Life jackets? You guys think I'm a schmuck? Huh?"

"Vinny, we don't know where they came from!" Carmine said as he glared at Carlo and Carlo walked back to the table.

"Did you check the bags when you picked them up to make sure that they weren't filled with life jackets or dirty laundry, huh? Did ya?" Vinny spewed out his questions as his anger grew and he strode around the table.

Suddenly Carmine and Carlo felt their arms being grabbed and pulled behind them by two other of Vinny's henchmen who appeared as if out of thin air. They had been concealed in the warehouse and were prepared to act if the deal broke down.

Carmine struggled as he responded, "It was all there when we picked them up!"

"Listen, you little shits. Something happened to my coke and I want to know what. Do you hear me?" he raised his Colt Cobra .38 Special with a two-inch barrel to Carmine. Vinny then walked over to Carlo.

"Carlo, I want to know if you hear me. Can you hear what I'm friggin' saying?" Vinny asked as he inserted the gun's barrel into Carlo's ear.

"Yes, yes," Carlo responded nervously. He knew what happened to people who tried to double-cross Vinny. "I hear you Vinny!" his throat was dry as he responded.

"Carlo, did you guys check the bags when you picked them up?"

"Yes," Carlo stammered. "We dumped out each bag and repacked them before we left Cleveland. They were all there, Vinny! Honest!" he wailed.

"Then Carlo, I want you to tell me if anything happened to you guys or my drugs on the way up here," Vinny demanded forcibly as he stuck the gun harder against Carlo's ear.

Still fearing Carmine's wrath, Carlo responded unconvincingly, "Nothing, Vinny. Nothing happened."

Deciding to soften his stance to get what he needed, Vinny said quietly, "Carlo, you and me, we go back a long time. Your family and my family, we were always close. So, I need to know what happened. On my mother's grave, you don't need to worry about Carmine; I'm going to take care of him."

Carmine struggled again but the bodyguard held him in an iron grip.

"Tell me, Carlo. Do you hear what I'm asking?"

"Yeah, I hear ya, Vinny." With that, Carlo unleashed a torrent of words as he explained what had happened with the sinking of the Sea Ray, the search for the sunken boat and duffel bags, stealing two boats and their flight to Detroit. When he finished, his shoulders sagged and he began to whimper.

Feeling a wave of revulsion building in reaction to Carlo's betrayal, Carmine threw Carlo a look of disgust. Carmine knew that Carlo had no idea as to what Vinny would really do to them.

"My, my. But you two boys have made this into a real mess. First, you don't follow instructions, and then you stop at some little island paradise in Lake Erie to chase some women, then you drink too much and you lose my coke! And when you think you recover it, you're too stupid to make sure whether it's all there or not!" Vinny whirls and grabs Carmine by the front of his wet shirt. "Look who I've got here, boys! This is stupid number one and Carlo is stupid number two."

Carmine stoically stared straight ahead. His demeanor hadn't changed.

Vinny let go of the front of Carmine's shirt and walked between Carmine and Carlo who was now staring down at the floor. "And stupid number two comes in here—the guy I've known since we was kids—and he don't fess up and tell me the truth. He just goes along with stupid number one."

Carlo began to raise his head. "Vinny, I'm sorry. I . . . "

Vinny interrupted and finished the sentence for him, " . . . don't know why I don't hear you. Go on. Repeat what I just said. I don't know why I don't hear you!"

Carlo repeated it slowly. "I don't know why I don't hear you."

"See if ya hear this!" Tony whirled and placed the barrel of his .38 against Carlo's ear. He quickly pulled the trigger and the gunshot exploded in the huge warehouse, echoing off the walls.

The blood-splattered bodyguard let Carlo's body fall to the floor.

"Jeez, I'm sorry Joey," Vinny said to the bodyguard who had held Carlo. "Ya got some of the blood on your face."

"No problem, Vinny. I'll wipe off what I can't lick," he smiled devilishly as his long, narrow tongue snaked out and wiped off the blood splatter within its reach.

After seeing the guard lick the blood off his face, Carmine's head snapped around and he continued to stare straight ahead. He knew that he was next. No doubt about it. He struggled to free himself but to no avail.

"Now for you, stupid number one. Should I give you another chance?" Vinny asked as he began to walk behind Carmine.

"If I was you, I would," Carmine hoped aloud and against all odds.

"Well you're not me. Wrong answer, stupid number one!" The second gunshot reverberated through the warehouse as Tony placed the barrel against the back of Carlo's head and fired. The bodyguard dropped Carmine's body to the floor.

"Boys, let this be a lesson to all of you. Don't screw around with me or you'll end up like stupid number one and stupid number two. Now, get this mess cleaned up and get rid of the bodies!" Vinny said as he and Angelo walked toward a parked Cadillac, which they entered and drove out of the warehouse.

Aunt Anne's House
Put-in-Bay

⌁

"What's the rest of the story?" Emerson asked Scuba Kat.

"You may recall that my husband is a part-time deputy sheriff here."

"Yes." Emerson was intrigued.

"He told me that they found two floaters in the Detroit River early this morning. Knowing about our little adventure, he was able to secure photos of the two."

"And?'

"They were our two boat thieves," she pronounced triumphantly. "I'd guess their buyer wasn't too pleased with the life jackets!"

"You know, sometimes life is fair," Emerson stated with a smug smile.

"Rob said they had a nasty criminal record."

"Hmmm. Since we filed our report with the Coast Guard, maybe I'll write a story for the *Post* and see if the Detroit paper picks it up."

"Well, if you do, don't use my name. I don't need any drug pushers after me, especially the ones that kill people for messing with them," Scuba Kat warned.

"I'll leave your name out of it. Thanks for the call. I'll let Sam know. He's here for another day." Emerson hung up the phone and scraped the eggs from the skillet onto a plate which he then covered. He decided to go upstairs and wake the sleeping Sam. He had heard Sam come into the house late last night after a night filled with drinking and dancing at the Round House.

The Same Day
Outside of Mel Fisher's Treasure Sales
Key West

༄

Pauley walked with a spring in his step across the street as he applied sunscreen to his arms and face and thought about the prior evening's transaction. He had met with J.B. and his bushy-bearded buyer, and sold the coke for $50,000. Pauley eased himself onto a seat in the small café where the shade protected him from the bright sunny day.

Asad saw him sit down, and prepared his usual order of an ice cold cherry slushy. Setting the slushy in front of Pauley, Asad asked, "Did you complete our transaction, Saul?"

Pauley beamed with a new sense of energy, "Yeah. You need to stop by my place tonight and we'll settle up."

"Good. I'll be there."

"Hey Al, let me show you something that I got made for myself." Pauley reached into his pants' pocket and withdrew a gold chain. At the end of the chain was a white Shasta daisy and several strands of gray hair. They were pressed between two pieces of glass. Pauley held it out for Asad to see. "Dropped this off a few days ago to have it made at one of the jewelry stores."

"What is it?" Asad asked.

"The flower that my wife was wearing in her hair the day she died. See here," he pointed, "that's a bit of her hair."

"Why do you do this?"

"To remember her by."

"That is a nice thing then," Asad said, feigning sincerity. "I will see you tonight."

Dropping Pauley's check on the table, Asad went to wait on another couple who had entered the restaurant, beaming as he went. Tonight he would propose his plan to Pauley. If Pauley accepted the idea, neither of them would have to work again. If he didn't, Asad would kill Pauley that night. He couldn't afford to have Pauley walk around knowing what Asad was planning to do.

Pauley downed the slushy and left money on the table with a five dollar tip for Asad. He chuckled to himself as he walked across the street to return to his guard duty at Mel Fisher's Treasure Sales. Ever since getting involved in this transaction with Asad, he felt more like his old self. It must have something to do with the rush that he got thinking about the upcoming heist. Of course the extra money never hurt anyone, he surmised to himself.

He planned to tell Asad that evening to keep his eyes open for other opportunities where the two of them could work together. Pauley had no idea what Asad was planning to propose that evening.

Neither Asad nor Pauley were aware that their conversation had been observed from a bench outside of a small gift shop across the street. The observer spotted a pay phone nearby and quickly strode to it. Inserting coins, the observer dialed a number in New Jersey.

The phone was answered on the second ring.

"Yeah?" the gruff voice asked.

"Is this line secure?" the Key West caller asked.

"You never know. You never know," he repeated.

"The Mrs. and me are on a cruise ship. It's kind of like my retirement cruise. Anyhow our ship stopped here in Key West. Saw something interesting that I thought you and the boys might be interested in," the caller stated with a sly smile.

"A good-looking blonde in a bikini?"

"Better than that," the caller smiled.

"Okay, then. Two good-looking blondes in bikinis?"

"Nope. It's the pocket man," the caller said cryptically. "You know, the one that you guys were trying to locate for that friend of ours upstate. He had a special interest in the pocket man."

It was the turn of the man in New Jersey to smile as he realized that the caller was referring to Pauley Pockets. "I know who you mean. Where did you see him?" He was leaning forward in his chair as his interest piqued.

"I saw him talking to some guy and thought he looked familiar. Then I saw him pull out that suntan lotion. You know how his skin is sensitive to the sun. That's when I knew it was him!"

"Hmmm."

"And you're not going to believe what he's wearing."

"Do tell."

"A security guard's uniform and he's packing a .38."

"A security guard's uniform! Where is he?"

"Here, in Key West. I saw him walk into a place that had a big sign over it. I can see it from here. It reads "*Mel Fisher Treasure Sales*." He must be a guard at a place full of treasure!" the caller exclaimed.

"Imagine that!" the New Jersey man said in awe. "They put the fox in the henhouse!" He paused for a moment and grinned evilly. "I wonder if he can resist the urge."

"What are you planning on doing about him?"

"I think I'll have a couple of the boys fly down and pay him a friendly visit." After a moment, he added, "A very friendly visit." He chuckled sinisterly.

"There's the wife," the caller said as he saw his wife walk out of the gift shop and scan the street for her wayward husband. He waved to attract her attention and, seeing his wave, she started towards him. "Got to go!"

"Thanks for the call. If this turns out to be him, we will be sure to show you some appreciation. The big guy will be very pleased if we track him down and give him a special greeting from the big guy."

"See ya!" the caller rang off.

The man in New Jersey dialed a number. It was answered quickly. "Hey Roda," the man in New Jersey said as he teased Marioda. He was the only one who could get away with calling Marioda by that name.

"Yeah?" Marioda replied warily.

"Why don't you and Ricci come visit with me in about an hour? You two have just won a vacation to Florida, compliments of the big guy. We want you to visit an old friend of ours who's on his deathbed. Only thing is, he don't know it yet!"

Marioda understood what the message was. "Sure. We'll be there in an hour."
Marioda hung up and went to find Ricci.

The man in New Jersey replaced the receiver and sat back. He reached into his desk drawer and pulled out a Cohiba cigar. Running it under his nose, he breathed in its fragrance and inserted it in his waiting mouth. Lighting it, he took a deep puff and released the smoke into the air.

He watched as the smoke climbed lazily, and thought about the phone call he would be making from a secure phone to let the big guy know that they may have found Pauley Pockets. Pauley had been the only one to successfully testify against Joey Rankito and live. As for the others who had tried, well, the graveyards were full of them. They never made it to court. The day of reckoning for Pauley Pockets was coming.

Emerson pushed back his chair from the table next to the window overlooking Catawba Avenue. He had eaten a bit too much of the evening's special prime rib buffet. It was delicious.

He looked across the table at Tim Niese, the blonde-haired owner of the Grand Islander Inn and the Islander Inn on South Bass Island. Tim's father owned Tipper's. Emerson and Tim had met and had become friends. Part of it may have been due to their shared love for the Caribbean, especially the island of St. Martin. Emerson and Tim had been to several of the same islands and enjoyed recalling their days on those paradises. Tim's hotels also reflected his love of the islands as they were decorated with a Caribbean theme.

"Great prime rib tonight," Emerson commented.

"As always," Tim, the consummate promoter, responded with a warm smile. "I have a difficult time trying to decide if I like the Friday night seafood buffet better than the Saturday night prime rib special."

"Decisions. Decisions," Emerson teased.

Suddenly, they heard a screeching of tires outside and horns blaring from the street.

"What in the world is going on?" Emerson asked as he looked through the open blinds and saw a green Army truck pull up abruptly on the lawn in front of the restaurant.

"Let's check it out. Looks like Dale's truck," Tim suggested.

They paid their bill and joined the growing crowd surrounding the vintage truck. Behind the wheel of the truck was a deeply tanned, silver-haired man with movie star good looks and wearing mirrored sunglasses. A cigar protruded prominently from his clenched lips. Emerson's eyes swept to the back of the truck where a movement caught his eye. Behind the mounted .30 caliber machine gun, which was swinging in his direction, was Sam.

Emerson shook his head from side to side at Sam and then looked at Tim.

"Wild, huh?' Tim asked.

"This island never ceases to amaze me," Emerson said.

"Emerson, I've lived here most of my adult life and I can tell you the same thing. It still never ceases to surprise me!" Tim took a drink of his island water and set it down. "Let's go and I'll introduce you to everyone's favorite village councilman, Dale. He and his wife, Kathy, run Buck and Ollie's Bed and Breakfast."

They approached the rear of the truck where Sam loomed over them behind the machine gun's barrel.

"Just stop right there," Sam warned.

From around the other side of the truck, appeared its roguish owner with his unlit cigar clenched tightly between his teeth. "This one could be the worst of the bunch!" he said.

"Put your hands up!" Sam commanded. "You've heard of Homeland Security. We're Island Home Security. Dale, you search him for weapons!"

Dale approached Emerson and began to frisk him as Tim stepped aside with a grin and watched.

"There's something a little strange about this," Dale said as he ran his hands quickly over Emerson in search of any weapons.

"That you're doing what Sam tells you?" Emerson asked.

"Nope. I pat down the men, and Sam pats down the women!" Dale chortled.

"Go figure," Emerson grinned. "Nice meeting you, finally. I've seen you riding through town on that four-wheeler of yours with that trademark cigar of yours. You always look like Mr. Cool to me! You're an island legend!"

It was Dale's turn to grin. "I'm not so sure about that."

"I've seen you driving the bus from Miller's Ferry at Lime Kiln Dock into town."

"Got to keep busy," Dale responded.

"Say, there's one question that I've wanted to ask you now that we've met," Emeron said.

"Sure, fire away!" Realizing what he said, Dale's head snapped around and he shouted to Sam, "Not you!"

"I know, but I've got you covered," Sam snickered.

"Do you ever light that cigar?" Emerson asked.

Dale looked around before answering. He said softly, "I'm not allowed. My wife would kill me if I did. It's just part of the look." He grinned mischievously.

"You know something?" Not waiting for an answer, Emerson continued, "You and Sam are two peas in a pod!"

"Did you say someone's got to pee?" Sam yelled down.

"No, I didn't," Emerson replied as he and Tim saw that Sam's face appeared to have a red discoloration. They leaned in and peered up at him.

"What happened to you?" Tim asked as he recognized the red discoloration. Sam's face and neck were covered with red lipsticked kisses.

"I cannot tell a lie. Dale did this to me!" Sam kidded.

"I did not," Dale responded firmly and even more quickly.

"Fess up, Sam," Emerson urged.

"Okay. Okay. I was over at Tim's Islander Inn and it was like MTV Spring Break. There was this gauntlet of ten girls that I just had to walk through, and they did this to me. I just had to suffer through it!" he smiled.

"Suffer! Oh sure!" Emerson responded.

"I'd better get back. I left Josh, my son, in charge of the pool party." Looking at the lipstick-covered Sam again, Tim continued, "Sounds like I'd better go and check on what's going on at the pool party!" Tim excused himself and left.

"I think he's just going to walk through the gauntlet himself!" Sam yelled after him. "You ever see him walk that fast before?"

"Nope. He's moving up to warp speed!" Dale snickered.

"Sam, did that really happen to you over there?" Emerson asked curiously.

"No. But don't tell Tim. About half an hour ago, I ran into some ladies celebrating a birthday at the Round House and talked them in to doing this to me. Then I walked around the corner and bumped into Dale and his truck."

"Yeah. He was real interested in the truck, so we started talking and just sort of hit it off," Dale added. "Then, I took him for a ride."

Turning to Dale, Emerson mentioned, "I've seen you driving that truck around the island and in the Sunday parades. Can you tell me about it?"

"I've had it for a few years. It's a 1952 Dodge M-37 Command Truck or Weapons Carrier. Found it at an auction and brought it up here to have a little fun. Caused quite an uproar with the Put-in-Bay police.

"How's that?" Emerson asked.

"Our police chief about had a fit the first time he saw it, and pulled me over. He wanted to confirm that the gun wasn't in working order," Dale explained.

"And when we saw your aunt's golf cart parked here, we figured that we'd have a little fun with you!" Sam added.

"And so you have," Emerson commented. "Sam, are you still heading down to Key West tomorrow?"

"Yeah, I've got to get back to my place there and then drive up to Miami. I've got a meeting scheduled there."

"You have a place in Key West?" Dale asked.

"If you want to call it that. It's just a small trailer that I retreat to for some R and R," Sam replied.

"Nice. You know that Put-in-Bay is called the Key West of the Midwest?" Dale asked. "We're virtually sister cities."

"Seems appropriate to me. Two great places," Sam responded.

"Don't I recall that some of the Put-in-Bay seasonal workers, especially singers and bartenders head down there in the winter months?" Emerson asked.

"Yep. The seasons compliment each other. Their off-season is our in-season and vice versa. Pat Dailey sings down there quite often in the winter months. If I could sing, I'd be there, too!" Dale said mischeviously. After pausing a moment, he remembered something more that he wanted to add. "In fact, they've declared February as Pat Dailey month in Key West, and there will be a Put-in-Bay day at Sloppy Joe's Bar on Duval Street one Sunday in February."

"I'll have to make it a point to be there," Sam interjected with a huge smile.

Turning to Sam, "Speaking of Key West, I heard that there's a storm brewing off of Cuba. If it looks like it's developing into a hurricane, I could be down there pretty quick to work on my story assignment," Emerson advised. "Maybe I could stay with you."

"Let me know for sure when you're coming. I'd let you stay in my tiny trailer, but you'll probably want to stay at the Crowne Plaza. It safer there than the trailer. Lots of times trailers have their roofs blown off and worse during hurricanes," Sam offered.

"Sounds good to me."

"Dale and I need to get cruising since this is my last night on the island," Sam said mischievously. "No telling what kind of trouble I might get into!" Sam said as he produced a handful of beads from the bed of the truck and grinned with a twinkle in his eyes at Emerson.

Dale covered his eyes. "I see nothing! I see nothing! I am only the driver for this wild man!"

"Don't stay out late," Emerson teased as he walked toward his aunt's golf cart.

Dale jumped into the truck's cab and drove around the corner and east onto Delaware Street, which was the main street for action on the island.

As Emerson drove down Catawba toward the harbor and began to turn right on Bayview, he saw Scott Buttrey, the owner of Mossback's, standing at the corner and in front of his restaurant and bar with the large windows opening on Catawba Avenue. Buttrey lived in the *Islumate* house across from his aunt's house. The steamboat style *Islumate* house was widely known for its detailed workmanship and designated as a national historical landmark.

"Busy night?" Emerson called.

"Very busy!" Buttrey shouted back. "Just stepped out to inhale a breath of fresh island air. Got time for a beer?"

"Not tonight. I'll try to stop by soon—and we can catch up."

Emerson waved as he turned the corner and headed for his aunt's house. He planned on going online to follow the latest weather news regarding a storm that was developing. In the morning, he'd be driving Sam out to the island airport to catch a flight with Dairy Air to Cleveland and his connecting flights to Key West.

That Same Night
Pauley's Apartment
Key West

⤚

Pauley looked at his watch again. It was nearing ten o'clock and Asad had not shown. Pauley walked to the front window again, and lifted the side edge of the curtain so that he could peer down the street toward the direction that Asad had come from in the past. No Asad in sight.

He let go of the curtain and went into his small kitchen to pour himself another glass of water. He downed it and looked at his watch again. Only a couple of minutes had passed from the last time he had looked. He couldn't understand what was keeping Asad.

Around the corner from Pauley's apartment, Asad sat on his motorcycle. He looked at his watch again and grinned as he imagined the tension that he was creating for Pauley. It was all part of his strategy to enhance Pauley's perception that he needed Asad to not only make money, but to also present him with opportunities to build his self-esteem. Asad had noticed how confident Pauley had been when he had waited on him earlier in the day.

Asad dismounted and began to slowly walk toward Pauley's apartment. As he stepped onto the porch, the apartment's door swung open to reveal an edgy Pauley. "Where in the hell have you been?"

Asad smiled inwardly. "Running late. I got involved in another money-making opportunity," Asad teased enticingly.

Pauley's agitation disappeared at the comment. "More drugs for us to sell?" he asked eagerly.

"Not drugs this time. Something bigger. And big money."

"What is it?" Pauley asked with growing interest.

Seeing that his trap was working, Asad played a delaying tactic to allow the secret to gnaw at Pauley. "Later. Let's talk about you selling my drugs for me."

Pauley frowned. He wanted to know more about the new opportunity. Sensing that he would get nowhere by probing, he began to relate the details surrounding the drug sale.

"I met a shrimper. His name is J.B. Scrawny little guy, but tough. He introduced me to our buyer. Big guy with a black beard. Reminded me of Blackbeard the pirate," Pauley sniggered at his feeble attempt at humor.

"The big guy was a tough negotiator. Said he had expenses and the guy he sold to in Miami was tougher to deal with when it came to buying coke. So we had to settle for $40,000. I paid $1,000 to our shrimper contact and here's your half of the remaining $39,000," he lied as he passed a brown paper bag with the cash to Asad.

Pauley had skimmed $10,000 off the selling price, but he wasn't going to announce it to Asad. That was the way that Pauley was used to doing business and he was quite pleased with himself.

Asad looked into the bag and wondered whether Pauley had told him the truth. But then again, he didn't care. All he wanted to do was to pull Pauley farther into his web. Asad looked at Pauley and smiled. "Good," was all that he said.

"So, what's the new deal that we're working on?" Pauley asked eagerly.

The use of the word 'we' was not lost upon Asad.

"I've got an idea that could pay handsomely for both of us," Asad began.

Pauley leaned forward with acute interest. "Yes? Go on."

"It would require that we both relocate. We couldn't live here any longer."

"If it was worth it, I could do that. I've had to move a couple of times here recently. So, that's no problem with me," Pauley replied, anxious to know more.

"It involves stealing some very valuable objects. Something you'd be interested in? If not, I won't go further," Asad baited.

"Stealing's no problem for me. Between you and me, I used to be involved with some big heists up in Jersey. I ran with the best of them," Pauley confided proudly.

Asad was pleasantly surprised by Pauley's revelation. Perhaps this would be easier than he expected. He leaned toward Pauley. "Two days ago, you saw me after I took a tour of Mel Fisher's Museum, and when I entered the treasure sales side of the building."

"Right, I remember that. We talked briefly as you looked at the counters filled with jewels and silver and gold coins for sale," Pauley acknowledged.

"It was a quick walk-through. I saw the video about Mel Fisher's search for the treasure."

Pauley interrupted. "You know he lost his son and daughter-in-law during the search for the treasure?"

"Yes, I saw that. Terrible!" Asad continued, "I quickly toured the museum and the second floor with the history about slave ships, but my real interest was in the Treasure Sales store."

"Yes, go on," Pauley urged as his curiosity grew.
Asad sat back in his chair and played his strong card. "We're going to steal all the jewels and coins in the Treasure Sales Store where you work."

Stunned by the boldness of the idea, Pauley sat back in his chair. An eerie silence filled the room for a couple of minutes while Pauley turned over the enormity of the heist, and Asad closely watched Pauley.

Pauley broke the silence.

"That would friggin' set you for life!" he said carefully.

"My exact thoughts," Asad concurred. "We would both have to disappear from Key West."

"Yes, I now certainly understand why we would," Pauley said knowingly as he thought about losing the oversight of his so-called protectors in the Federal Witness Protection program. He'd get so lost that no one would find him, he thought with an eager smile. "How do you see us doing this?"

"That's what I want to talk to you about. You're the inside guy on this. That increases our odds of pulling this off. I'm a thinker and action guy. Since you've got experience, you're probably the better of the two of us to plan this out," Asad pitched. He didn't want to give away all of his thoughts on the plan. He preferred to pull Pauley in further by allowing him to think that he was going to run the operation. Asad was planning a few surprises for Pauley after the robbery.

"First, there would have to be some sort of diversion. Something that would slow the police down when they responded to this," Pauley thought aloud.

"I've done some preliminary checking. There's only one electrical line servicing this island. It comes in from Stock Island and then underwater to Key West. I'll blow it up! That'll knock out the power to the island and kill the alarms at the Treasure Sales," Asad offered.

"Not a bad idea, but the Treasure Sales has a backup generator. With me being there, I'll just shut down the alarm system. I'll have to take out Billy, the other guard." Pauley thought again and then said, "That blowing up of the electrical service. It's not going to slow the police down enough. We need something bigger!"

"Bigger? Like what? You want me to blow up a building?" Asad fumed.

Pauley didn't answer. His eyes were drawn to the television, which he had muted when Asad arrived. There was a chart of an approaching storm. Pauley's eyes widened and he grabbed the remote control, quickly turning up the volume.

"This might be it! This might be it!" he repeated excitedly as the weatherman continued.

"*. . . may be on track to hit the lower keys in the next few days. Key West is definitely a high risk area. From there, Charley is expected to move northward and possibly come ashore somewhere between Fort Myers and Tampa. Our preliminary . . . *"

"We'll use the hurricane as our cover!" Pauley exclaimed as he muted the TV.

"The hurricane?" Asad asked, not comprehending the magnitude of a hurricane's power.

"It's like being in the middle of a wind tunnel where winds are going between one-hundred-forty and one-hundred-sixty miles per hour. Everything is flying around —trees, roofs, shrubs, boats, and cars! The streets will be deserted. People will have been evacuated. The police will be hunkered down inside," Pauley proclaimed with glee.

"And how will we get around?" Asad asked with concern.

"We'll break in as it starts to hit. Then, when the eye moves through, we'll follow it and make our escape."

"The eye?"

"Yeah, it's the center of the hurricane. It's real calm and peaceful!"

"Are you suggesting that we escape by driving out?" Asad remembered the long bus ride from Miami through the Keys.

"Nah. We can't take a chance on the eye not following the road. We'll escape in a boat and follow the eye out of here to land. Hurricanes always head for land. It should be somewhere north of us on the coast. Maybe Naples, Ft. Myers or Tampa," Pauley boasted with his newfound knowledge. "I know just the guy who can help us with the boat," Pauley added as he thought about his drug dealing shrimper friend, J.B.

Eyeing his prey like a stalking tiger, Asad asked, "You really think this plan will work?"

"Yeah, providing we get the weather to cooperate. We'll need the hurricane to decide that it'll go through here. It's not like we can hold a gun to its head and make it do what we want it to do. They kind of have a mind of their own."

"So you ever been through one of these hurricanes?"

"Nope. But when I was in Jersey, we had several moving along the eastern coastline up to the northeastern states. We got a taste of it, and it was bad enough."

"What about our safety?" Asad questioned.

"Should be no problem. That Treasure Sales building is made out of cut stone. It ain't going nowhere."

"So how many guys do you think we will need on this?"

"Definitely someone who knows the channels out of here and is experienced with riding out storms. This shrimper I know—I am sure he has been out in all kinds of weather. We'll probably need someone else to help with trucking the stuff from Fisher's to the boat. Let me think on it and I'll get back to you. I'll need to take a closer look around Fisher's and the dock next to the Hilton," Pauley said as he recalled that the Hilton, which was across the street from Fishers, had a dock next to it just a short distance from the street and the Treasure Sales store.

"Good. So we have a deal, then?" Asad asked as his dark eyes blazed intently.

Extending his hand to Asad, Pauley said firmly as he gripped Asad's hand, "That we do!"

"Good. I will talk to you soon." Asad then excused himself and left Pauley to turn over the events of the evening. Asad smiled slyly to himself as he stepped off the porch and headed to his motorcycle. He was already planning how to part Pauley from his share of the stolen treasure.

Two Days Later
Pauley's Apartment
༔

Asad edged closer to Pauley as he began to sketch out his ideas on a sheet of paper at the kitchen table.

Pauley drew a small box on the table. "I ain't no artist, so you'll have to bear with me," he started. "This is Fisher's. I checked it out thoroughly the other day. The back-up generator is located in the basement near the vault. It's not well-protected, as no one would expect an inside job on this. It's just a matter of me throwing the switch to make sure it doesn't come on. There's the matter of the vault where they store the gold chains, coins, and emeralds. With the power out and the backup generator not turned on, we should have enough time to break into the vault. I'll need to make sure that I get on the night shift when it's necessary."

"What about the tools for breaking into the vault? How will you get them down there without anyone knowing?" Asad probed.

"That's the hard part. We won't be able to do that until the day we decide to break in. There's a ramp next to the building where we can back a van up to the entrance to Fisher's."

"Won't people be suspicious if they see a van parked there?"

"I thought about that. But, if we're in the middle of a hurricane, people won't be out and, if they are, they'll just think that we were taking valuables away for additional protection. I don't know, but I don't think it'll be an issue. I should probably try to get some graphics for the side of the van that say Mel Fisher's Treasure Sales."

"Saul, maybe we all should wear a uniform so that we look official," Asad suggested.

"Yeah, that's a good idea, but I don't know how we can do that on such short notice," Pauley paused and then looked at Asad. "Did you spend all of your money from the drug sale?"

"No, why?"

"You better give it back to me. We're going to need it to help pay for equipment and other miscellaneous stuff. And, I'll need to buy guns for us, just in case we run into any trouble."

"And I'll need some semtex or something so that I can blow up the power line coming in from Stock Island. I'll get you my cash," Asad promised. Asad was pleasantly pleased with the Pauley's planning skills. They were better than Asad had hoped.

"Back to Fisher's. Once I break into the vault, we'll truck the treasure up the ramp in the basement to the first floor and then out the door to the van."

"Can't we use the freight elevator that I saw when I took my tour?" Asad didn't like the idea of trucking treasure from the basement up a ramp to the first floor.

"When the power is off, it won't work. Trust me. At my age, I'd prefer to use the elevator." Pauley couldn't see any way around trucking the treasure. "Once we fill the van, we'll drive it down the ramp and across the street to the dock next to the Hilton. There, we'll unload the van, and transfer our take into the boat my shrimper friend will get for us. Then, we'll follow the eye of the hurricane out of Key West and hopefully up the channel towards Naples, Ft. Myers, or Tampa."

"It's that easy?" Asad questioned with concern.

"That would be the best case. There are a couple of unknowns. What if the hurricane decides it's not going to cooperate with us and goes a different direction? I can answer that," Pauley said with an air of confidence. "We'll have alternative getaway routes. You always need those."

"Any more thought on how many men we need to pull this off?" Asad asked to see how thoroughly Pauley could think things through.

"Yeah, Al. I was thinking about that. We'll need my shrimper friend and at least one crewman on the boat that the shrimper steals. There should be a number of boats to choose from as everyone should have evacuated the area due to the approaching hurricane."

Asad nodded his head.

"Then we'll need someone to drive the van and someone to help load. So there's two plus yourself and me. About four of us, I'd guess."

"How about equipment?"

"Besides the van, which we can steal or rent if we have to, I'll probably need cutting tools and a few hand trucks," Pauley responded. "I can get those."

In the Air
Approaching Key West International Airport

∾

The small twenty-passenger plane began its descent as it approached the Key West Airport in the late afternoon. Clear, blue-green waters surrounded the mystical island, the anchor for the long emerald chain of fossilized coral and limestone islands. The subtropical islands stretched south from the Florida mainland like a jeweled necklace, and Key West was Florida's crown jewel.

Emerson had enjoyed the flight from Tampa. His face had been pressed against the plane's window as he was mesmerized by the alluring enchantment of this island paradise bounded by the Atlantic Ocean and the Gulf of Mexico. His eyes focused on the wide array of boats at rest in the harbor, the church spires, the Key West lighthouse and a few four-story buildings as the plane flew low over the luxuriant green island on its final descent. The plane flew parallel with Smathers Beach and Roosevelt Boulevard, and banked left in a slow descent as it made its final approach to the airport. Emerson had a bird's eye view of the salt ponds to the north and south of the runway.

The plane bounced once before settling on the single, 4,800-foot-by-100-foot grooved asphalt runway and taxiing up to the terminal, where its engines were shut down. During the descent, the plane's interior had grown quiet as the passengers eagerly scanned the approaching island. Once the plane was on the ground, the quiet was replaced by a sense of exuberance and a natural high, as the passengers shared their excitement about being in Key West, and began chatting about their plans for their coming days.

Looking out his window from his seat in the eighth row, Emerson waited patiently for those seated in front of him to disembark. When he could, he stood and stretched. It had been an enjoyable ride in the plane that reminded him of a narrow cigar-shaped tube, but the seats weren't as comfortable as the ones he was used to flying in. Emerson grabbed his laptop and made his way to the front of the plane. Grasping one of the rails on the stairs to the tarmac, Emerson paused in the doorway and looked at the white airport terminal, which was trimmed in aquamarine. "Welcome to Key West" was lettered in bright red on the building, and greeted the travelers as they departed the plane.

Walking to the baggage claim area, Emerson picked up a few island brochures and looked around the area for Sam Duncan. He didn't see Sam as he grabbed his suitcase and walked out to the curb.

A bearded man with long black, curly hair had been watching Emerson in the baggage claim area. When Emerson walked outside to the curb, the shirtless, three hundred-pound man, attired in worn bib overalls and wearing a pair of black shoes with flames on the toe, followed Emerson at a distance out to the curb. He leaned against a wall, which offered shade from the bright sun overhead, and quietly watched Emerson.

It had been just a few minutes since Emerson last looked at his watch, but he looked again. He had been waiting for thirty minutes and, wiping droplets of sweat from his brow, he anxiously looked at each vehicle as it passed, to see if it was driven by Sam. He couldn't understand where Sam was. He was usually punctual.

A deep voice from behind him asked, "Would you be waiting for Sam Duncan?"

Emerson turned and identified the source of the deep voice as the large man with the wild hair who he had noticed earlier in the baggage claim area. "Yes," he said warily. The stranger emitted an aura of danger to Emerson. "How did you know?" he asked cautiously.

"That means you must be Emerson Moore," the stranger noted smugly.

"Yes," Emerson confirmed. "And how did you know that I'm waiting for Sam and my name?"

"Sam's tied up and sent me to pick you up."

The "tied up" comment was not lost on Emerson. He squinted his eyes in the sunlight as he peered at the stranger.

Warming up a bit, the stranger introduced himself. "Welcome to the Conch Republic! I'm Harley Rupert, a sometime friend of Sam's. I'm supposed to take you to your hotel. You just got one bag?" he asked as he grabbed Emerson's suitcase.

"That and my laptop here," Emerson responded as he began to think that maybe his first impression had been wrong.

"Don't got much room for luggage."

"With a name like Harley, is that because we're riding on your Harley?" Emerson teased as he couldn't resist the urge to ask.

Harley paused in mid-stride and said in a harsh tone. "For a newspaper guy, you're not very good at making cute remarks, are you?"
Emerson was taken aback. "I was just trying to be friendly," he said uneasily.

"Save it for your buddy, Sam. He was supposed to meet me too, but didn't make it to his meeting with me. You can just be pretty glad that he called me and asked me to get you. And for your information, I ride a Suzuki! We'll have to tie your suitcase to your back so we can ride it into town."

Emerson frowned as he saw that this conversation was going in the wrong direction. He countered, "Listen, I don't want to put you out. I'll just grab a taxi into town."

Harley continued walking, carrying Emerson's suitcase.

"I said that I can take a taxi into town," Emerson repeated as they walked toward a deserted part of the parking lot. Emerson was getting nervous as he followed this giant woolly bear.

Harley paused next to a vehicle. "Here's my Suzuki," he chortled as he stopped by a white, weather-beaten, dented 1998 Suzuki Sidekick with a soiled white soft-top. "I was just funning you!" Harley let out a large guffaw at the look of consternation on Emerson's face. "You need to loosen up a bit, boy! Hop in!" he instructed as he easily threw Emerson's suitcase into the vehicle's rear.

Emerson climbed into the small Sidekick and watched as Harley eased his large frame into the driver's seat. There wasn't much room to spare. Emerson wanted to make a comment about trying to pour five pounds into a four-pound sack, but thought it'd be wiser to leave it unsaid.

"It's the Crowne Plaza La Concha, right?" Harley asked as he inserted the key into the ignition.

"Right."

"You're on Duval Street. Good location."

"Sam picked it for me."

Harley easily backed the little vehicle from its parking space and shifted into first.

"So Harley, do you live here in Key West?"

"You're a reporter, aren't you?"

"Yes."

"I don't need to be telling a reporter anything," Harley said sternly.

"It's not like I'm interviewing you. I'm just curious." Emerson was beginning to be exasperated with the whole way this was starting with Harley.

Harley raised his bushy eyebrows, and shot Emerson a quick glance as he replied, "You might say that I just live all around the Keys. Does that satisfy your curiosity?"

"Not really." Emerson paused and then asked the massive giant, "How do you know Sam?"

"Oh, we have, what you could say, an on-again-off-again friendship. Sometimes he gets in my way and sometimes I get in his way," he said cryptically.

Emerson wondered if the two of them were involved in CIA work, but decided not to probe further. Besides, he was distracted by the beautiful beach and the palms as the Suzuki went down South Roosevelt Boulevard.

A mile passed and Harley noticed Emerson still staring at the beach. "Nice, isn't it?"

"I'll say!"

"Smathers Beach. It's the biggest beach here in Key West followed closely by the beach over at Fort Zachary Taylor," Harley offered. He noticed two young women in bikinis rollerblading on the sidewalk next to the beach. "Scenery isn't too bad, either!"

Emerson grinned.

The tiny vehicle wove its way through a residential area with its condominiums, and then began to drive by Key West's renowned housing, which featured a wide variety of architectural designs. It was a mixture of Victorian Greek

Revival, Italianate, Queen Anne, Bahamian and Creole cottages, and two-story homes. They made a right on Bertha Street and then a quick left onto Atlantic Boulevard as they drove past the county beach.

Emerson's eyes took in the pastel-painted tropical houses trimmed out with white gingerbread and surrounded by lush vegetation. Many of the alluring tin-roofed homes had white picket fences on their small lots, which were filled with white, pink, and lavender oleander, and laurel trees. The dark-stained front doors and dark green shutters on many of the one- and two-story houses provided an aesthetic balance to the brightest of whites, which many of the houses were painted.

There was a spiritual-like quality in the air as the quaint homes oozed tranquility.

"What's with the chickens?" Emerson asked in surprise as he noted chickens and their chicks roaming the yards and the sidewalks.

"Key West has a large population of chickens. Cats, too. They pretty much go where they want to go. Nobody bothers them, and they really don't bother us—other than their droppings on your favorite poolside chair," he grinned.

As they turned right onto legendary Duval Street, Harley said, "On the left, you can see the Atlantic Ocean, and at the other end of Duval is the Gulf of Mexico. If you look real quick as we're turning, you'll see the Southernmost Point of the United States. It's only ninety miles to Cuba from here."

Emerson's head whirled around as he took in the sights. He loved the architecture, which was resplendent through the area. They continued driving down Duval, which was lined with art galleries, seafood restaurants, and quaint hotels with wicker chair-filled balconies overlooking Duval. As they neared the northern half of Duval, there was an increase in the number of tee shirt and souvenir shops as well as the crowd—and it was a festive crowd.

The Suzuki stopped at the traffic light at Duval and Fleming, and Emerson saw the Key West Island Bookstore about a block down Fleming. He made a mental note to visit it to secure some background data on Key West and its hurricanes. Emerson found himself being pulled into the city's ambiance.

Harley pointed to the vibrant coral-pink hotel with its six floors and rooftop observation deck and lounge towering over the intersection. "There she be. The Crowne Plaza La Concha. Don't know if you knew that Hemingway and Tennessee Williams stayed there and wrote. Williams wrote *A Streetcar Named Desire* while he stayed there. Thought you'd be interested since you're a writer."

"No, I didn't know. I'm staying there because I was told that it was the tallest hotel in town and centrally located for my story. And it's supposed to be one of the safest places to be in Key West if a hurricane hits." Emerson noticed that Harley seemed to be warming up to him.

The light changed. They slowly drove past the front of the hotel and turned left into the narrow alley leading to its main entrance. A tall, thin doorman wearing a beige pith helmet, beige military-style shirt and shorts greeted them. "Welcome to La Concha! May I assist you?"

"I've got it," Emerson replied frugally as he walked around the rear of the vehicle where Harley was lifting Emerson's suitcase out of the vehicle. The doorman noticed a car pulling in behind Harley, and went to greet and help the new arrivals.

"Thank you, Harley. Will you be seeing Sam soon?" Emerson asked as the two shook hands.

"Damn straight I will," Harley replied with a mysterious twinkle in his eyes. He turned and loaded his massive frame into the vehicle.

"Tell him to give me a call so that we can get together tonight."

Harley gave a barely perceptible nod and drove off.

Emerson entered the airy, marble-floored, two-story lobby filled with palm trees and tropical plantings. How elegant, Emerson thought to himself as he checked in at the front desk and secured a room on the sixth floor. As he passed the concierge desk located next to the main entrance, he picked up several brochures about Key West on his way to the elevator.

When he saw the entrance to Starbucks next to the elevator doors, he stopped in to grab a coffee to go. His eyes scanned the selection of sweet cakes in the glass-enclosed display, and his stomach growled at him. Deciding that he'd fight the temptation and save his appetite for dinner, Emerson walked to the rear exit carefully, balancing coffee, laptop case, and suitcase. He was equally concerned about spilling coffee on himself as well as his baggage.

Standing in front of the elevator, he awkwardly depressed the call button, and when it arrived, took it to the sixth floor. His room number was 654, just down from the elevator. He opened the door and entered the white-painted room, offset by tropical-colored drapes and vibrantly hued island paintings.

He set his laptop on the desk and suitcase on the floor, and pulled back the drapes for his first view from his room overlooking the Gulf of Mexico. He drank in the tropical splendor and blue ocean as he sipped his coffee and wondered how long it would be until he heard from Sam. He didn't have to wait long.

The phone rang.

"E, welcome to Key West or the island of OZ as I call it from time to time. It's home to liars, and tireds, and bares —oh my!"

"Sam, you're incorrigible," Emerson responded to his friend's greeting.

"Seriously, we've got all kinds here. Just wait until we take a walk down the street. I'm in the lobby. Why don't I take the elevator and pick you up on your floor. Meet me at the elevator doors and we'll go to the rooftop lounge for a cool drink and a great view of this island paradise."

"Okay with me. I'll be waiting at the elevator doors!" Emerson ended the call and walked out of his room to the elevator. In a couple of minutes, the doors opened to reveal Sam decked out in a colorful tropical shirt, tan shorts, and sandals.

"Hey, E!" Sam greeted Emerson as Emerson stepped into the elevator for the one floor ride to the top. "Sorry I couldn't pick you up at the airport. I was in Miami for some meetings and got a late start back. Then I had a complication."

"A complication?" Emerson asked.

Sam beamed effusively as he warmed up to telling his story. "I stopped at this little Cuban restaurant on the way back here and grabbed a bite to eat. Way too many red peppers and super hot sauce for me! More than my stomach could handle!"

Emerson grinned as he listened. He knew that Sam had a relatively sensitive digestive tract when it came to very spicy food.

"It actually hit me just before I crossed the Seven-Mile Bridge."

"What hit you?"

"I had to drop a serious load, and fast. I pulled into a rundown gas station, which was my first mistake. When I ran—and I mean ran—into its solitary restroom, I found that the toilet was backed up. I couldn't go anywhere else with all the pressure building in me, if you know what I mean."

"What did you do?" Emerson asked chuckling at his friend's plight.

"The only practical thing that I could do. I took the lid off the tank, stood on the toilet seat and dropped my load in the tank. And just in time! I couldn't have held it another minute! Any port will do when you're caught in a storm!"

Emerson groaned as he pictured Sam hanging his butt over the tank and then moaned at himself that he had even tried to picture what that would have looked like. "I'll bet the owner was surprised when he checked the restrooms."

"That you can count on. I'd guess that he'll be checking his restrooms more often to make sure that they're in working order. Could you just imagine the look of surprise on his face when he removed the tank lid?" Sam asked with a twinkle in his blue eyes.

Emerson shook his head at his prankish friend.

The elevator doors opened on the seventh floor to reveal sunny, bright blue skies.

"Wait until you see the view!" Sam said.

They walked through the door to the outdoor rooftop patio with its breathtaking view of Key West. Emerson's eyes scanned the cornucopia of lush tropical vegetation interspersed with the glistening tin roofs of two-story homes, several church spires, and the flat roofs of local businesses.

They wandered to the west end of the rooftop patio where Emerson gazed at the large whitewashed church at the corner of Duval and Eaton.

"That's St. Paul's Episcopal Church," Sam offered as he saw Emerson staring at the church. "It's the oldest church in Florida south of St. Augustine. Been destroyed three times, twice by hurricanes and once by a fire. But they've always rebuilt it."

"It sure stands out," Emerson commented as he gazed at the massive structure.

"If you get a chance, you'll want to check out the stained glass windows inside. Besides telling a story about the Bible, they also depict key events in Key West. They have windows honoring the richest man in Florida, Key West's William Curry. They even have a window about a guy who worked as a chauffer. It's real interesting!"

Emerson noted the harbor, the Gulf of Mexico, the towering roofline of the grandiose, red-bricked Key West Museum of Art and two huge cruise ships docked at Mallory Square.

Seeing that Emerson was staring at the two cruise ships, Sam offered an explanation. "They're leaving a day early. Hurricane Charley is heading this way."

"Good for my story, but bad for the folks here. I saw a number of TV news vehicles in the parking lot when we pulled in. I guess we're all here for the big story."

"You news guys are like a swarm of bees. You swarm in to do your stories, and then swarm away to the next big story. It's kind of fun watching you media guys." After a pause, Sam asked, "Hey, how's your room?"

"Quite nice, actually. Thanks for suggesting that I stay here."

"It's a safe place if old Charley makes a direct hit here. La Concha can withstand a Force Five hurricane. That's why it makes a good command post for the media. They like to use this rooftop to get some shots of incoming storms. You'll see them combine shots from here with shots on the beach or around town after the storm passes," Sam explained.

A waiter appeared and took Sam's order for a cold beer, and Emerson's order for a margarita. The late afternoon heat was stifling.

"How did your ride in with Harlan go?"

"You mean Harley?"

"Yeah, but his real name is Harlan."

"Fine. Kind of a different type of guy!"

"How so?" Sam asked.

"He's a difficult one to read. How close are you two? He was rather cryptic when he talked about your relationship."

Sam grinned slyly. "Not particularly close. Sometimes I'm not sure which side he's on. He works for the good guys, but he also runs with the bad boys in the Keys. There have been rumors than he's involved with drug running, but no one has caught him yet. From what I've heard, his life would make mine look like the New Testament!"

"So, why are you two so chummy?" Emerson asked.

"This is not for publication, understand?" Sam asked cautiously.

"Understand."

"We trade information."

Emerson's eyebrows raised. "Oh?"

"Don't worry. What I give him doesn't jeopardize me. But I need what he gives me. He's got some good contacts in South America that can provide me with information when I need it. I don't push him hard for information, but he can come up with insight that I can't otherwise get if I'm paying a visit to that part of the world."

"He seems dangerous. I can't quite put my finger on it," Emerson observed.

"He is dangerous—and don't let his large size fool you. I've seen him move quickly, more quickly than I'd expect for someone that big," Sam said with honest admiration. "He's the kind of guy who'd go swimming bare-ass-naked with coral snakes. Sort of like me!" Sam added with a touch of macho glee.

Ignoring the comment, Emerson probed, "You trust him?"

"To an extent. I've never really been able to figure out if he's one of the good guys. Then again, if he's running drugs, I guess he'd have to be one of the bad guys. But, this isn't the first time that I've had to work with the bad guys," Sam said with a wink. "Did you notice a smoky smell about him?"

"Not really."

"He plays the edge so tight that he's been close enough to hell to smell the smoke," Sam grinned.

Emerson shook his head. "You'd better be careful with him," Emerson cautioned. "There's something about him. My gut is telling me to be wary of him."

"Don't need to warn me. I've always been able to take care of myself. You're the one that I always end up rescuing!" Sam said with a twinkle in his eyes.

"Back to the storm. What's the latest you've heard?" Emerson asked.

"There's a hurricane Charley and a tropical storm Bonnie. Charley's heading into Cuba and the radio reports thought it'd hit here next."

"Do you think Charley will hit here?" Emerson asked seriously.

"Nah. We've got the grotto!"

"The grotto?"

"Yeah. I'll show it to you tomorrow. It was built in 1922 by Sister Mary Louis Gabriel next to St. Mary Star of the Sea Catholic Church. She built it to protect Key West from the hurricanes, and in some mysterious way it's been working for all of these years. Imagine the devastation that could be caused here if we got hit by a hurricane. The storm surge alone would cover Key West in minutes. The highest point is only eighteen feet above sea level."

"And knowing all that, you still keep a place down here?"

"The grotto is protecting us," Sam responded confidently. "Besides, I've actually attached floats to the underside of my trailer. That gives me a small chance of it floating away if there was a problem. People laughed at me when they saw me attaching the floats. But again, I doubt that I'd need them."

"Combining your faith with practicality?"

"You know me!" Sam grinned. "Enough talk for now. Let's grab a bite to eat. I'll take you over to Kelly's. It's a restaurant owned by movie star Kelly McGillis. It's in the old headquarters of Pan Am Airways when it first started its business with flights to Cuba from Key West.

"Sounds good to me," Emerson replied. "You know the area better than I do."

"Of course I do!" Sam flashed his winning smile at Emerson. "Maybe we can get a table on the second-floor deck next to the Banyan trees. It's like eating in a treehouse."

"Let's do it."

The two paid for their drinks and left La Concha's rooftop. It was an eight-minute walk down Fleming Street and then right onto Whitehead Street.

Entering the white-clapboard building that housed Kelly's Caribbean Bar, Grill and Brewery at the corner of Whitehead and Caroline, they paused to look at the displays of Pan Am memorabilia, which highlighted the founding of Pan Am by twenty-eight-year-old Juan Trippe at the site.

The airline's first flight from Key West to Havana to deliver mail for the post office had an inauspicious start in October 1927. Trippe had to secure the services of a pilot who had just landed his Fairchild seaplane in Key West, to fly the airline's first airmail flight to Havana. In January 1928, Pan Am started its first commercial flight with seven passengers aboard a Fokker F-7 bound for Havana from Key West.

The purchase and delivery of the Fokker Trimotors, with their longer range capabilities, enabled Pan Am to relocate its operations to Miami later in 1928.

Looking at the photos of the Trimotors, Emerson commented nostalgically, "Reminds me of the old Ford Trimotors that used to service Put-in-Bay. They were great planes. In fact, I saw one flying over the islands this summer. A group was offering flights from Port Clinton over the Lake Erie islands on a restored Trimotor."

Emerson thought back to his visits to Put-in-Bay as a teenager, and the fun he had in watching the old Ford Trimotor planes, the tin lizzies of the air, land as they ferried residents and visitors to the island. The plane with its corrugated-metal skin would slowly descend as the pilot throttled back on the three seven-cylinder, 235-horsepower Wright Whirlwind engines. Even with the engines throttled back, they were noisy, and Emerson and his cousin would playfully cover their ears as they watched the planes at the Put-in-Bay Airport.

The plane would taxi near the metal hangar where the pilot would turn off one engine and idle the other two, so that he could make a fast takeoff to Middle Bass Island, the next stop, once the new passengers boarded and cargo was loaded.

Sam nodded his head at Emerson's comment.

As they moved toward the hostess station at the rear of the entrance, they looked at the old Pan Am flight uniforms and stewardess memorabilia.

"Welcome to Kelly's. May I seat you?" an attractive hostess asked as she greeted them with a warm smile.

"Upstairs on the deck, if you have a table available," Sam requested as he took in the pretty young brunette.

The hostess scanned her seating chart. "Yes, we have an opening. Follow me, please, gentlemen," she said as she turned and began to climb the steps to the second floor.

"I'd follow her anywhere," Sam said softly to Emerson as his eyes followed her lithe figure. He took a deep breath, which Emerson noticed.

"Are you okay?"

"Barely. Her beauty just sucked the breath right out of me." Sam ducked when Emerson took a playful swing at him with his right fist.

"Sam, you're incorrigible," Emerson teased.

"Hey, careful with those big words. Remember I don't have your vocabulary," Sam teased back. "My best asset is my good looks," he said tongue-in-cheek.

"Yeah, Yeah. Here we go. It's getting deep around here," Emerson countered as they were seated next to the railing overlooking the garden patio.

A waitress appeared momentarily as they were looking at the wide selection offered by the menu. Emerson ordered a Key West Golden Ale.

"And sir, what would you like?" the waitress asked Sam.

With a grin, Sam replied, "The only kind of hurricane that I ever want to encounter. Give me a hurricane containing alcohol!"

The waitress scampered away as Emerson asked, "And just what goes into that?"

"A couple of ounces of light rum, apricot nectar, strawberry nectar, and grenadine. Then, you add a touch of passion fruit syrup and lime juice. Mix in some ice and you're all set!"

"Sure sounds like you've had a few!" Emerson teased.

Sam grinned.

Picking up his menu and looking at it, Emerson joked weakly, "It says here that the drink is named Hurricane Sam!"

"Wouldn't surprise me a bit," he retorted. "I've been know to blow into places and leave a disaster in my wake."

"Care to tell me about it?"

"Can't. Top secret, you know!"

The waitress returned with their drinks and took their meal order. For appetizers, they both ordered the crispy, coconut shrimp, which was lightly coated in a coconut tempura and served with a pineapple dipping sauce. For his main entree, Emerson opted for the Bouillabaisse Caribbean, which contained lobster, shrimp, local fish, chicken, clams, mussels, and Andouille sausage in a citrus broth flavored with red onion, fennel, roasted red peppers, and tomato-herb rouille.

Still feeling queasy from his lunch escapade, Sam ordered the Shrimp Fettuccine, which was shrimp sautéed with garlic and white wine, tossed with fettuccine and a Caribbean alfredo sauce.

Emerson sat back in his chair and took in the tropical ambiance from the deck, which was bounded by huge Banyan trees. He gazed down at the people seated in the garden patio area, which was surrounded by tropical flowers and plants. "Not very busy tonight."

"Not with the hurricane headed this way. People have been packing and heading out of here over the last few days. Remember, there's only one road in and out of this place. That's the downside to this island paradise when it comes to a serious storm."

Emerson said as he raised his ale. "This is what I call relaxing."

After finishing off the coconut shrimp, which the waitress had delivered, Sam suggested, "Let's talk about what you need to accomplish while you're here."

"Right. I'll need to spend some time at the library researching past hurricanes here."

"It's over on Fleming," Sam mentioned. "There's a guy in the archive department who really knows the island's history. You'll want to talk to him."

"Then I'd like to talk to the folks at the police and fire departments to get their insight into hurricanes and their impact on the area. It'd be interesting to get their perspective. I'm sure that they have some sort of disaster preparedness plan."

Sam nodded his head.

Emerson continued. "I'd like to meet with some of the fishing boat captains to talk with them about what they do to protect their boats if a hurricane hits."

The waitress reappeared and served their entrees.

"Delicious," Emerson exclaimed as he savored his bouillabaisse Caribbean.

"Great food here. It's one of my favorite places in Key West," Sam said as he scooped up a forkful of the shrimp fettuccine. "I know a couple of the guys over at the police department. I can help you in meeting with them."

"Good."

"I'll make a couple of phone calls in the morning. One other thing that you'll want to do."

"Yes?"

"With you being a writer of sorts, you'll want to visit Ernest Hemingway's House. It's right here on Whitehead."

"Sure, sounds great. I'd like to see his place. Have you been there?"

"Nope. Doesn't really float my boat, if you know what I mean," Sam responded.

In between chitchatting, they finished their meals and the waitress appeared at the table with the bill. "And who gets this?"

"Give it to him," Sam answered. "And could you get me a crowbar so that we can open his wallet?"

The waitress grinned.

"Come on, Sam. I'm not that tight!"

"E, you're tighter than my Aunt Betty's girdle!"

"Yeah, yeah! Sure I am," Emerson kidded as he extracted cash and laid it on the table. They stood and took one look around their treehouse paradise before descending the stairs to the main level.

They walked toward the steps leading to Whitehead Street and paused. Sam suggested, "Let's take a walk down to Mallory Square and watch the sunset. You won't believe the size of the crowd, even with the hurricane approaching. And they have great street performers."

"Let's do it," Emerson agreed.

They turned right as they left Kelly's and proceeded down Whitehead Street, which paralleled Duval Street. As they came to the corner of Whitehead and Greene Streets, Emerson's eyes rested on a huge stone building with a cannon in front. The signage identified the building as Mel Fisher Maritime Heritage Society Museum.

"That looks interesting and sounds familiar."

"Mel's the guy who went on a mission to find the wreck of a Spanish galleon. He never gave up and would start every day by saying 'Today's the Day.' Took him fifteen years of saying that, but he found the treasure."

"Talk about perseverance!" Emerson said with admiration. "I think I saw something about that on the History Channel. Wasn't the treasure value significant?"

"I seem to recall that it was in the neighborhood of $400 million. Worth more than King Tut's treasure," Sam added.

"I'd like to go in there and take a tour tomorrow," Emerson suggested.

"You need to check out the Treasure Sales. It's over here on the other side, on Front Street," Sam said as they walked around the corner to where they could see the sign hanging over the doorway. A security guard was sitting on one of the benches next to the doorway as he took a break from his duties. "They've got emeralds, gold and silver coins, and gold necklaces for sale in there. They're worth a mint."

Noting that the building sat up higher than the surrounding buildings, Emerson commented, "Looks like someone did some high water defense planning when they constructed that building."

"Yep. It's set about six-feet higher than street level. Got to protect the contents!" Sam concurred. Looking across the street, Sam continued as he pointed, "That's the Hilton, then there's a dock between the Hilton and the Museum of Art and History."

Emerson stared at the massive three-story, red brick and terracotta architectural beauty that was built in 1891. It was also elevated off the ground to protect it from flooding. The building had an unique history. It had been the Custom House, a post office, a court house, and a government center. Then the bottom dropped out in the 1930s when the city's bankruptcy crisis resulted in its closure and boarding up. Today, the building stands in its restored splendor thanks to the Key West Art & Historical Society, which had embarked on a nine-year, $9 million restoration project to restore the brick building.

The museum featured vivid paintings of old Key West by Mario Sanchez, information about the pirates who lurked in the Keys, and displays about Ernest Hemingway's days in Key West, including his bloodstained World War I uniform.

"If you get a chance to visit the museum, you can see the room where the decision to go to war with Spain was made after the Maine was sunk in the Havana harbor in 1898," Sam offered.

"Interesting," Emerson commented as they walked down the sidewalk and towards the back of the Museum where the Hilton complex sprawled along the waterfront.

From the bench next to the door of Mel Fisher's Treasure Sales, the guard watched the two tourists, Emerson and

Sam, as they walked. He eased himself off the bench and walked around the corner of the museum to see Asad and get a slushy. It only took him moments to reach the small stand. Asad had seen him approaching and had his slushy waiting.

"Hurricane might be moving this way," Pauley said nonchalantly as he sat on the stool and fidgeted with the chain and the glass that protected the Shasta daisy and the strands of his wife's hair.

Seeing his boss nearby, Asad replied, "That's what I hear, too."

"I just got my hours changed to the evening shift," Pauley said as he began to noisily slurp his slushy.

Asad nodded his head in understanding and laid a check on the counter as he busied himself. He hoped that the weather would work into their plans. He was anxious to get moving.

Ten Minutes Later
Sunset Celebration
Hilton Complex—Mallory Square

On the Hilton Pier, the thin and long-haired performer known as the Catman was putting his trained cats through their paces to the delight of the gathered crowd.

"The guy's name is Dominique LeFort. He's been here for years and takes in homeless cats, then he trains them for his shows. My favorites are Oscar and Cossette," Sam explained.

"You must have a lot of time on your hands if you know his cats by name. You're coming down here way too much," Emerson retorted.

"Whenever I get in town, I make it a point to come down here for the sunset celebration. There's nothing in the world that compares to it!"

"Not even Put-in-Bay's sunset celebration?"

"Close, but this has so much more with all the street performers."
"Yeah, but we've got a bagpiper out on Peach Point who pipes down the sun."

"There's a bagpiper here, too. We'll bump into him shortly, I'm sure."

They turned their attention back to Dominique and his cats. Emerson watched in amazement as the Catman worked the cats through their tricks. The one cat had jumped through a burning hoop and another had walked across a tightrope. Emerson was astonished as the Catman would call to one of the cats in its locked cage and the cat would extend its paw to unlatch it; then bound out of the cage to its trainer's side.

With the setting sun as his backdrop and surrounded by a large crowd of tourists dressed in tropical colors, the gray-haired trainer issued his commands to the cats in French, and rewarded them with treats for each trick performed.

Emerson was especially drawn to this performer's talent and his unique command to one of the cats as he cried out, "Oscar. Nes pas. Oscar." Feeling a gentle tug at his sleeve, Emerson turned to kook at Sam.

"He's the main attraction here, but let me show you some of the other street performers."

Working their way through the carnival-like atmosphere complete with vendors selling tee shirts, jewelry, paintings, and photography, they wandered along the waterfront, stopping to watch performances by a bagpiper and a balance wire act.

After a few minutes of listening to the bagpiper, they moved on and encountered Silver Man, a street performer sprayed entirely in silver who posed as a statue. Standing on a bench with a bucket in front of him for donations, Silver Man would surprise children and teenagers with sudden moves when they approached him to insert a cash donation between his fingers.

Often, he would let the money drop to the ground as the crowd watched the children pick up the cash and try to reinsert it between his fingers. At times, he would robotically produce a lollipop for the child and entice the child to draw nearer so that he could make a funny face or some other antic. The pretty young women, who approached him, were his favorite targets. He would entice them closer to him so that he could give them appreciative looks or a quick kiss on the cheek—much to the crowd's amusement.

"Fun," Emerson remarked as he and Sam walked away.

"The crowd is usually larger, but with the hurricane threat, you're going to see it dwindling. I notice a difference already," Sam remarked cautiously.

Scanning the sky, Emerson saw darkening clouds with a red glow on the leading edge from the south. "Looks like things are getting ready to turn worse."

"Yeah. It won't be long." Sam added as he saw some birds flying low, "The birds are a hell of a lot smarter than we are. They usually flee first during the calm before the storm. We should be seeing rain in a day or two when the first outer rain bands hit us. You can always tell when a hurricane is approaching by that red glow on the leading edge of those clouds. It's a warning signal" He pointed toward the direction that Emerson had been looking.

As the sun set behind Sunset Key, it cast its orange tentacles into the western blue sky. The onlookers applauded the sunset and began to filter back toward their hotels. Many had heard the governor's order for visitors to evacuate the Keys, and planned to leave after watching one last spectacular sunset.

Emerson and Sam wandered over to Duval Street and back to the La Concha Hotel. As they turned down the entrance drive to the hotel, they could see the hotel's parking lot—and it was filled with TV news vans with satellite broadcasting dishes.

"There are some of the vehicles I was telling you about. Looks like this will be a real media event," Emerson surmised.

"They usually flood the area just before a storm."

"Looks to me like we've got more of a media phenomenon here than a weather phenomenon."

Sam looked over at the parked vehicles. "Yeah, you guys seem to travel in packs, sort of like wolves looking for a victim or sharks sensing blood in the water."

Emerson shrugged his shoulders in response.

"How about if I pick you up at ten tomorrow morning and take you to meet with the police department? I'm sure that I can get you in. I'll make a few calls first thing in the morning," Sam offered.

"Sure. Sounds good to me." Emerson stopped and twirled around to look at Sam who was walking toward the parking lot. "Hey Sam," he called.

Sam stopped and turned. "Yes?"

"Any chance of seeing your place while I'm here? I know you didn't want me to stay there because it was small."

"Sure, we can stop sometime tomorrow. It's a small mobile home off United Street. It's not much to see and not real pretty inside. Just a place for me to crash when I'm in town or need a chance to recuperate. The weather down here speeds up my recovery time."

Emerson realized that Sam was talking about recovering from injuries he incurred in his clandestine work and didn't probe further. "See you in the morning!"

"See ya!" Sam called as he resumed his walk to his aquamarine colored Jeep Wrangler with a white canvass top and beads hanging from the rear view mirror.

Emerson walked into the lobby and returned to his room where he sat at his laptop. He rubbed his eyes briefly as began to work on his initial story ideas and search the Internet.

The Next Morning
Key West Police Department

~

At the sprawling fire and safety complex off Roosevelt Boulevard amidst beautifully landscaped grounds, Emerson had been meeting with the community relations officer for the last twenty minutes. They started the discussion with the complex's ability to withstand hurricane level winds, and moved on from there.

"Our goal is to respond effectively, make the greatest use of our personnel and to protect the lives and property of our citizens." Danny Ortiz, the community relations officer who was seated across the desk from Emerson, explained. "When the governor requires an evacuation and issues an evacuation order—as he just did, it's broadcast on the local media and in the newspaper, *The Key West Citizen*. We've got the city's radio broadcast station at 870 AM set up to broadcast pertinent information to our citizens."

"Are you set up for this year-round?" Emerson asked as he took notes.

"In a sense, yes. But especially during the hurricane season, which runs from June 1st through November 30th. We go into an informal Condition 5 at the beginning of the season. Condition 5 exists when there's a possible threat of a storm. Whenever a named tropical storm forms or is anticipated in the western Caribbean or the Gulf of Mexico, we go to a more formal Condition 5," Ortiz explained.

"Let me go back to your comment on the evacuation. How do you make sure that people are aware that they need to evacuate? What if they aren't watching TV?"

Ortiz smiled. "I can tell you don't live here. When it's hurricane season, people watch TV and stay abreast of breaking weather developments. To ensure that people are aware, the police department also will drive through the area and use our loudspeakers to make announcements. It's typically something like: 'Attention all residents. You are ordered to evacuate your homes and report to shelters. Turn your radio to a local station for shelter and emergency information.'"

"That was pretty good!" Emerson grinned.

"Should be. I'm one of the guys who's been designated for that role," Ortiz grinned before continuing. "Once we go into an emergency condition, the chief will designate a shift change from our regular six-hour shifts into our twelve-hour Alpha/Bravo shifts. Moving to Alpha/Bravo signifies that we are about twelve hours away from a storm making landfall. That's when we really step up and try to get people into the designated shelters."

"What do you guys do when it hits?"

"We get out of the way of everything. There's nothing much that we can do when it hits other than to secure our own safety. The chief will order all patrols to a shelter or the station until an 'all clear' is announced."

"Aren't you concerned about any crime during this time?" Emerson asked.

Ortiz started in disbelief at the question. "Mr. Moore," he began, "when it's so bad out that the police are ordered to seek shelter, I don't think that there will be any criminal out there focused on stealing anything. He's going to be doing everything he can to save his own butt! After it abates, that's a different story. But that's when we're out there assessing damage, calling it in and patrolling again.

"If we're hit by a hurricane, we will leave our shelters while we're in the eye to do a quick damage assessment, but it's not like we have a lot of time. It's dependent on how fast the hurricane is traveling."

"Yeah, it wouldn't be a good thing to be caught out there when the eye moves on," Emerson agreed.

"After the hurricane poses no further threat or after the emergency order is curtailed, we begin to survey the city, chart the areas of severe damage and locate any casualties. We then notify either the on-duty incident commander or an investigator so that appropriate investigations and notifications can occur."

Ortiz pulled a master checklist out of a file and displayed it to Emerson. "You can take a look at this if you like. It shows you the actions that we go through ninety-six, thirty-six, and twelve hours before a storm hits."

Emerson glanced at it and then sat back. "I heard that since the grotto was built, no hurricane has hit Key West."

"Well, yes and no. On September 25, 1998, the eye of Hurricane George passed directly over Key West, but its winds were blowing below sixty-three knots. That's the measurement between a tropical storm and hurricane. Nevertheless, we did have damage here in Key West as a result of it."

"Cause any flooding?" Emerson asked as he picked up his pen to again take notes.

"Sure did, as do many tropical storms. South Roosevelt Boulevard between the airport and the Atlantic has flooded. One time, we actually had six feet of sand from Smathers Beach clogging up South Roosevelt Boulevard. We had five feet of standing water at Eaton and White Streets. Duval Street tends to drain towards Front and Greene over by the Hilton and Mel Fisher's Museum. So you'll get a tendency for some flooding at Front and Greene."

"I'm going to try to visit Fisher's this afternoon if I get the chance. It seems to be interesting." Emerson planned aloud.

"They've got a ton of treasure to see, and the historical information is first class. Good people over there, too!" Ortiz said.

All of a sudden a light went on in Emerson's mind. "What happens to their treasure during a storm?"

"Not to worry. First, their building is made out of stone and is very hurricane resistant. Second, it's raised so that it's not affected by the flooding at Greene and Front Streets. Third, I'm sure they secure their treasure in a vault and they also have on-site security."

"That could be an interesting side story for me to follow up on," Emerson suggested.

There was a knock at the door, and the door opened to reveal Sam and another individual who turned quickly and walked down the hall.

"Ready to go yet?" Sam asked.

Emerson looked at Ortiz who slid his business card across the table. "I think we're wrapped up. If you have any additional questions, you can give me a call."

Emerson thanked him and joined Sam to walk out of the police station to enter Sam's Jeep. As the Jeep pulled out of the complex and turned left onto Roosevelt to head back to Old Town and Emerson's hotel, Emerson asked, "And how did your meeting go?"

Sam paused as he looked at his inquisitive friend. "Not for publication?"

"Not until you tell me that I can," Emerson countered.

"Ever hear about black cocaine?"

"I thought cocaine was only white."

"It used to be just white. Back in 1998, a new concealment method started being used by Columbian drug traffickers. They were having trouble smuggling cocaine into the states because of the aggressive interdiction practices being used. They discovered that if they mixed the white cocaine with black iron thiocyanate, or charcoal, it would prevent or mask a positive reading for coke during drug detection tests, based on color. And the drug detection dogs can't smell it. From Columbia, this black cocaine issue has spread worldwide."

"Is it sold as black cocaine?" Emerson asked.

"That's one of those funny things. Marketing comes in to play. For some strange reason, black cocaine doesn't sell like white cocaine so they use a solvent such as acetone to extract the chemical and return the cocaine to its white state."

"So, your meeting focused on black cocaine?"

Sam paused and looked at his friend again. He thought for a second and then said, "In part. When you think of the our country's shoreline, the more than 300 ports of entry and a 7,500-mile border with Canada, it's difficult to stop drugs from entering the U.S."

"So then, you just nip it at its source."

"Easy to say, difficult to do. Take Columbia for example. There used to be two major cartels, the Medellin and Cali cartels. They dominated drug trafficking during the late 80s and early 90s. Today, there are hundreds of smaller and more decentralized organizations. Think of AT&T's successful break-up into the baby Bells. With them being smaller organizations, it's even harder to infiltrate them.

"They've dropped their lavish lifestyle for a more conservative, lower-key lifestyle. Now, because they've become discreet and less prone to violence, they're harder to identify and very successful. Over five hundred metric tons of cocaine pour out of Columbia each year.

"On top of that, these groups are manufacturing high-speed boats that are capable of carrying two tons of cocaine. Sometimes, they'll use a mother ship and anchor offshore at night in international waters. Then high-speed boats will run out to the mother ship and load up for drug runs back to Florida."

"Sam, you sure know a lot about this. Are you working for DEA?" Emerson probed.

Sam's roguish face broke into a grin. "Let's just say that I'm a contract employee. I market my services to a number of employers."

Sam continued. "The Caribbean has become even more of a superhighway for drug trafficking—and that's due to the shifting of resources from antidrug efforts to guard against terrorists. That alone has caused overall drug seizures to drop. There's over eight thousand miles of Florida coastline to patrol and you've got the Bahamas only forty-five miles away."

"Where are most of the drugs coming into the state?"

"Miami-Dade and Broward counties. It's coming in from South America, Central America, and the Caribbean. They're using go-fast boats, pleasure craft, cargo freighters and, of course, planes to deliver here. Once here, couriers transport the drugs throughout the state on Interstate-95 and Interstate-75, and then, up north.

"Somebody's making a killing with what they're making off the drugs," Emerson observed.

"That's one of the problems. It can be so tempting. There was story about a guy who was flying some coke over here in a rented plane. The plane had a problem, and he decided to bail out rather than take a chance of being caught with the load of coke after he crash-landed. He strapped seventy-nine pounds of coke to his leg and parachuted to the ground. Only problem was that the police just so happened to see him jump and followed his parachute down to rescue him. The plane went on to crash on the edge of Stock Island."

"So the police found him with the coke?" Emerson surmised.

"Yeah. And they recognized him. He was a member of the narcotics unit."

Emerson's eyes widened.

"See what I mean? It's too tempting. Drugs can run from $1,800 a kilo and they're about two kilos per pound. So that meant his seventy-nine pounds of coke were worth about $270,000."

"Lucrative is an understatement," Emerson observed. "What about the go-fast boats?"

"Some of them run directly to the coastal harbors. Some of the smaller ones will run out at night to a mother ship, a freighter anchored in international water, and pick up loads to deliver throughout the coast. The harder ones to spot are the ones that you don't expect to be involved in running drugs."

"Like yachts?"

"Yeah. There was a yacht that came into Key West for repairs during the early hours one morning. An informant realized what he saw when he went below deck, then placed a call to DEA. The DEA showed up, found 502 kilograms of cocaine on board and seized the vessel. They arrested the six men who were on board. There have been incidents with other yachts and runabouts. You just never know when you're going to discover something.

"There was a sting, named Operation Cracked Conch, here in Key West. A number of law enforcement agencies conducted three days of raids and arrested fifty-one for trafficking in cocaine, conspiracy, or possession of cocaine with an intent to distribute. The sting was directed at a distribution chain that ran up to Miami, but they didn't nail the guy who runs the ring. He's a slippery devil, that one. They said he'd cut your eyes out in a heartbeat if you did him dirty."

Emerson shook his head in disbelief.

"I did hear an especially interesting story today. It's about Sha Sha shoes," Sam said with an air of mystery.

"Sha Sha shoes?" Emerson queried.

"Yeah. The police stopped a car on Atlantic Boulevard the other day. While they were talking to the driver, they smelled marijuana coming from the car—so they called for a K-9 unit to search for drugs. The dog signaled them to some marijuana in the ash tray and then led them to the trunk where they found a bag of marijuana, crack cocaine and Ecstasy. They pulled it from the trunk, but the dog was still signaling that there was something still in the trunk. The officers spotted a pair of Sha Sha shoes and pulled them from the trunk and the dog signaled that they contained drugs too."

"They stuffed drugs in a pair of shoes?" Emerson asked in surprise.

"In a way, but not the way you're thinking. Sha Sha shoes have a secret compartment in the sole, which is known as the 'G-spot.' When they opened it, they found five plastic baggies of methamphetamine hidden inside."

"Do they look like regular shoes?"

"Not this pair. That's why they stood out. They showed them to me. They were the 'Rock Star' model in a baby blue leather with white stars. You couldn't miss them."

"Certainly not my style," Emerson joked.

"Here we are," Sam said as he pulled the car into a small mobile home park on United Street. He carefully maneuvered the Jeep down the narrow lane, and parked next to a small mobile home that had a covered patio in front.

The patio was screened from the lane by aged white lattice work desperately in need of a fresh coat of paint. The patio area itself was littered with three chairs in disrepair, which surrounded a worn and stained rattan table. A few potted plants dotted the patio. They were in need of water and nourishment. Hanging from the ceiling were a number of colored lights and two wooden parrots.

Seeing Emerson looking around, Sam said, "I told you it wasn't much to look at."

Caught, Emerson responded, "I was just thinking how quaint this is."

"Right. Quaint isn't the word that I'd use. It suits me just fine for what I need here. Come on in," Sam said as he unlocked the door and stepped inside.

Emerson followed and was greeted by its unique interior. To the right was a small living room complete with an easy chair and small sofa. A beat-up coffee table was covered with magazines and files. Emerson bent over to look at the magazines and the file names when Sam appeared at his side. "Uh, uh. You're not getting any story ideas here," he said as he whisked the files away.

"I wouldn't do that, would I?" Emerson teased. "Whoa, what have we here?" Emerson's eyes were drawn to one side of the room that housed the latest in entertainment technology. He knew that Sam was a "techie" when it came to the latest and greatest.

"Big screen plasma TV with sound surround for both the TV and my CD player. When I turn up the sound, you can hear it two blocks away," he grinned. "But then, I get several knocks on my door telling me to turn it down."

"Nice. What's behind that door?" Emerson asked as he looked toward a door at the other side of the living room.

"Used to be a second bedroom. But I've turned it into an office. I've got the latest in technology in there, too, so that I can do a satellite uplink to sites that you would love to know about," Sam teased.

Emerson started for the door.

"Uh, uh. Can't go there," Sam said as he placed himself between the door and Emerson.

"Oh, all right," Emerson said with feigned chagrin.

Making sure that the door was locked, Sam stepped around Emerson and into the kitchen area. "This, of course, is the kitchen and down the hall are the bath and my bedroom."

Emerson's eyes swept the small kitchen area with dishes piled high in the sink and crumbs on the counter. Two blackened bananas were in a fruit bowl, and an empty pizza box with three pieces of crust sat on the counter top.

"You know, you need a wife to help you keep this place clean."

"Oh, don't use that four-lettered word around me!" Sam beseeched.

In a serious tone, Emerson asked, "Why aren't you married, Sam?"

Sam paused for a moment as he became serious. "Actually, I just don't want a woman worrying about me when I'm away on my business. I need the freedom to leave when necessary, and sometimes, that can be a moment's notice. I need to be able to focus on my business and not worry about the effect it might have on a wife if something happened to me."

"It can be very lonely without a good woman at your side," Emerson said as he started to become melancholy, recalling his deceased wife, Julie, and his son. His love for her still continued as did his attraction to the very married and elusive Martine.

"You should talk!" Sam countered.

"But Sam, I was married. It was a good partnership with both of us making sacrifices to grow our relationship. And then we had Matthew. That boy made me understand a deeper love that a parent can have for a child. How you can forgive that child and love him despite his shortcomings."

"Sounds to me like you should get married again since you were so . . . let me see . . . what's the word that I want to use? Sensitive. Yes, that's the word. You were so sensitive to the relationship and your love."

"I might do that sometime. It was a good thing for me. A nurturing experience," Emerson agreed.

"Hey, enough of this conversation. You're bringing tears to my eyes. Let's head back to your hotel."

They locked up the mobile home and jumped back into the Jeep for the short drive to the hotel.

Parking the Jeep on Fleming Street across from Emerson's hotel, Sam asked, "How about a cheeseburger in paradise? Jimmy Buffet's Margaritaville is right around the corner."

"Sounds good to me."

They strode around the corner and into the Key West-style restaurant, which was filled with hungry reporters and music from Jimmy's songs. They sat on the second floor balcony, which overlooked the restaurant's main floor and ordered their cheeseburgers. They sat back and relaxed as they listened to the music. Emerson was especially pleased when some of his favorite Jimmy Buffet songs filled the air—*Cheeseburger in Paradise, Fins,* and *Maragaritaville.*

The waitress soon returned with their food and they began to devour it.

"The cheeseburgers here are out of this world," Emerson said as he smacked his lips.

"Everything here is out of this world," Sam said as he eyed an attractive female customer with long red hair.

Emerson followed Sam's eyes and shook his head at his friend's focus.

Finishing their beers and paying the check, they left the building.

Key West Island Bookstore
Key West
∽

Spotting the blue-and-white sign for the Key West Island Bookstore hanging over the sidewalk as he looked down Fleming from the corner at Duval, Emerson decided to pay it a visit. Emerson mentioned to Sam, "I'd like to check that out. Maybe I can pick up a couple of books about hurricanes."

"Fine with me. I've got to run some errands. Why don't we meet in your lobby at seven and I'll take you for a great fish sandwich."

"You're on! See you at seven."

Sam turned left onto Fleming to retrieve his car while Emerson crossed Duval and walked the half block to the white-painted building with large front windows that housed the bookstore.

"Hello," Emerson said as he entered the store, which was jammed with books, but vacant of customers due to the approaching hurricane.

"Can I help you?" The bearded man behind the counter asked.

"Yes. I'm looking for some books on hurricanes."

"Right this way," the clerk said as Emerson followed him to the far side of the store. "Might not be too long, and you'll have a taste of one. You just don't know about them. You staying here long?"

"Through the storm. I'm writing a story about what it's like to be here in Key West during a hurricane."

"You're a reporter?" the clerk asked.

"Yes. I'm with the *Washington Post*, although I work out of one of the islands in Lake Erie." Emerson responded.

The clerk's eyebrows rose with interest at the comment. "Which island?" he asked pointedly.

"South Bass. There's a resort town there called Put-in-Bay. It's actually called the Key West of the Midwest," Emerson said proudly about his adopted hometown.

"Know it well," the clerk replied.

"How's that?"

"I'm from Sandusky, across from Johnson's Island."

"Small world, isn't it?" Emerson said with surprise as he recalled his visit to the Confederate prison camp's cemetery on Johnson Island. His mind started to drift back to his search for LeBec's and Harrington's graves. Coming back to reality, he asked. "Get back to Sandusky often?"

"Usually during the summer months when it's slower here, I head back. I keep a boat at the Harbor Bay Yacht Club over on Huron Street. I'll boat out to Put-in-Bay from time-to-time with a couple of buddies of mine and have dinner at the Crew's Nest. You know the place?"

"Know it well. Some of the best perch on the island."

"They've got a nice docking facility, too. Not as crowded as the village docks," he paused, then continued. "Not as wild either."

Agreeing, Emerson said, "It can get cranked up, alright."

"Say, do you know Duane Smith or Kim Colebrook from Harbor Bay Yacht Club?"

"No, I haven't met them yet. There are so many yacht clubs and marinas in the area," Emerson answered.

"I'll leave you here so that you can peruse our selection." The clerk returned to the front counter and Emerson looked through the books. A few minutes later, Emerson was at the front counter with two reference books that he had decided to purchase. As the clerk was ringing up the sale, Emerson introduced himself. "I never did tell you my name. I'm Emerson Moore."

"Glad to meet you, Emerson. I'm Marshall. This is my store," he said with pride as he handed Emerson his books and change. Pointing to the pitcher of iced lemonade, he asked, "Care for a glass of lemonade? I keep it here on the counter for our customers."

"I'd appreciate it," Emerson said as he watched Marshall pour him a paper cup full and then hand it to him. Raising the blue cup to his lips, he sipped on the lemonade and savored its tart taste. "Thanks. This hits the spot. I'll take it with me if you don't mind."

"No. no, by all means take it with you. Good luck with your story, although we just don't get direct hits by hurricanes here."

"Thanks. Maybe I'll end up doing a story on surviving a tropical storm here," Emerson said as he walked out of the store. He made a quick trip back to his hotel room where he dropped the books and then headed for Mel Fisher's Museum.

Mel Fisher's Museum
Front and Green Streets

❧

Emerson entered through the massive doorway to the looming stone building housing the museum. After purchasing his tickets to tour the museum, he settled into a chair in the projection room to watch the *National Geographic* video *Treasure,* which explained Mel Fisher's quest to find the sunken *Atocha* and its treasure. Mel's perseverance in continuing the treasure search after all of those years served as an inspiration to Emerson. The guy was the proverbial optimist, confidant that he would find the treasure—and he did.

Once the video finished, Emerson began his walking tour of the museum. He spent time looking at the various displays of cannons and swords, and descriptions about life aboard ship. At one display he was able to reach in and heft a large gold bar set in a plastic holder. On the second floor, Emerson peered at the shackles used on the slaver ships to transport slaves to the New World, and read the information about the trying life of a slave.

He returned downstairs and entered the Treasure Sales Gift Shop. The security guard seated next to the doorway eyed him carefully as he entered and approached the glass counter housing the treasure for sale. Emerson walked slowly around the counter as he gazed intently at the emerald rings and pendants, brooches, earrings, necklaces, crosses, cufflinks, buttons, and coins made from gold. He also saw many silver items for sale. The price tags ranged from modest to very expensive.

Emerson returned to the security guard with the chalky white skin at the doorway. "What happens to this stuff during a hurricane?"

The guard's head jerked suddenly in surprise at the question. "Why?" he asked suspiciously.

"Emerson produced a business card. "I'm Emerson Moore with the *Washington Post* and I'm doing a story about hurricanes and surviving a hurricane in Key West."

"Nothing to write about here. We don't get hurricanes here. If there was a real concern about the security or safety of our merchandise, we would just lock it up in the vault as we normally do at the end of each day. No story here," he said abruptly as he looked quickly at the card and placed it in his pocket. He then turned away from Emerson to talk to a young boy who was tugging at his arm to ask him a question.

What a rude guard, Emerson thought to himself. Emerson looked at his watch. It was getting late in the afternoon. He decided to return to his hotel room and search the Internet. He didn't know that he was being watched as he exited the side door of the Treasure Sales operations.

Seeing the door close, Pauley took out a handkerchief and wiped his brow. The reporter had caught him off guard with his question. One thing for sure, he didn't need any reporter hanging around the museum when the storm hit. It would complicate matters.

Stopping at the corner of Greene and Whitehead, Emerson raised his head to gaze at the darkening clouds. Won't be long until the rain hits, he thought to himself. He rounded the corner onto Whitehead and decided to walk to Hemingway's House to take a look at it. He didn't expect it to be open with the evacuation order given, but thought he could at least take a quick look at it from the street.

Twenty minutes later, Emerson arrived in front of the high-walled compound in which the early colonial Spanish home was located. It was closed, as he had thought it would be. As he peered through the gate, he saw a maintenance man hurriedly taking outdoor chairs inside to protect them from any damage from falling tree limbs. Emerson called to him and was able to get his attention.

The man slowly approached him. "We're closed," the tired-looking man with slight build said to Emerson.

"I'm with the *Washington Post* and I'm doing a story on hurricanes in the Key West."

"We don't get hurricanes here. We've got the . . . "

"Grotto," Emerson finished the sentence for him.

The man smiled.

"Any chance of me getting in to take a quick peek around?"

"Can't do that. We're closed, like I just told ya. Everything's locked down." The man fumbled in his pants pocket and produced a worn, green brochure describing the house. "Here, you can have this."

Emerson took the brochure. "Thanks. Tell you what, how about if I take a quick walk around the grounds and not go inside?"

The man peered at Emerson and thought for a moment. "Okay, but don't tell anybody. You reporters are going to have it rough down here with the stormy weather. You're going to be disappointed that you came all the way down here and there was no hurricane. You mind my words. I'll take five minutes and walk you around the grounds, then you're out of here. Agreed?"

"Agreed," Emerson responded eagerly as the man unlocked the gate and allowed Emerson to enter.

"This here is the main house. It was built in 1851 by Asa Tift. He was a merchant and salvager and one of Florida's wealthiest men. It's a Spanish style," he explained as they looked at the two-story home. Pointing to the foundation, he continued, "It's got a basement cut out of the limestone and about nine feet deep. If you look around here, you'll see the house sits on a small hill."

"You call this a hill?" Emerson asked in surprise.

"Down here, anything more than ten feet above sea level, we call a hill. This hill is about sixteen feet above sea level."

"So you don't worry about flooding?"

"Not too much," he said as they walked around the house. "There's the pool. It's the first pool built in Key West. There's a saltwater well in that old smokehouse that's used to fill the pool."

Two cats scampered in front of them as they approached the pool house.

"The famous six-toed cats?" Emerson asked as he bent over to catch one and hold it. He scratched it behind its ears, and it began purring.

"Yeah. Here, let me show you." The man grasped one of the front paws and showed Emerson the six toes. "Cats usually have five front toes and four back toes. You can see here that this one has six front toes."

"Interesting," Emerson said as he stooped to release the cat. "How many cats do you folks have here?"

"Around sixty. This building here," he said as they resumed walking, "used to be the carriage house." He stopped in front of a two-story building that had a catwalk connecting it to the second floor of the main house. "Hemingway had that catwalk built so that he could wake in the morning and walk right over to his writing room on the second floor." The man cast a hurried glance at the darkening sky and said, "I think we're done with your five-minute tour. I really need to get back to my chores before the rain hits."

Reluctantly, Emerson allowed himself to be walked to the front gate where he tipped the man twenty dollars for taking the time to show him around. As Emerson walked down Whitehead street, he hailed a passing bicycle taxi, the front half a bike for the peddler and the back half a rickshaw.

"Where to, sir?"

"Key West Library," Emerson requested. He wanted to make a visit to the library for some additional research before returning to his hotel. "Busy today?"

"Not really. The tourists, where I make most of my money, are leaving the island in droves," he answered. "But, they'll be back. They always come back after tasting paradise."

Emerson settled back in his seat and enjoyed the scenery of the town and houses that they passed on the way to the library, located on Fleming Street, a few blocks away from the Key West Island Book Store, and on the opposite side of the street.

When they arrived, Emerson paid and tipped the taxi peddler before entering the library. There he spent an hour doing research before walking the few short blocks to his hotel room at Fleming and Duval.

Emerson's Hotel Room
La Concha Hotel

∾

After walking in the muggy conditions to his hotel, Emerson welcomed the rush of cool air as he opened his room's door. It refreshed him as he sat down in the armchair, and he picked up one of the books he had purchased earlier in the day.

As he scanned the first book, he stopped at the chapter referencing hurricanes, and began to intently read the chapter. He learned that the category designation of hurricanes was developed in 1972 by two meteorologists, Herbet Saffir and Robert Simpson, to estimate the severity of damage that a hurricane could cause at landfall.

The book indicated that a *Category 1* hurricane could produce winds of 74 to 95 miles per hour and a storm surge of four to five feet. It would produce minimal damage. With a *Category 3* hurricane, the winds would range from 110 to 130 miles per hour and the storm surge could be as much as twelve feet. *Category 3* hurricanes caused extensive damage. A *Category 5* hurricane would produce winds in excess of 155 miles per hour and a storm surge of more than eighteen feet. This type of hurricane would result in catastrophic results.

Emerson stopped reading for a second to think about what might be headed this way. Then he reached for the television remote to catch the weather update on Hurricane Charley and Tropical Storm Bonnie, which might turn into a hurricane. It would be extremely unusual for two hurricanes to hit the state in the same year.

A news reporter was talking.

" . . . *is becoming heavier as tourist and visitors are evacuating the Keys on U.S. Route 1 in response to Governor Bush's declaration of a state of emergency. Hurricane Charley has continued to gather strength and is hitting Cuba with its devastating power and winds of 105 miles per hour. Charley is expected to hit Key West within the next forty-eight hours as a Category 3 with wind gusts reaching 130 miles per hour. Its storm surge is expected to create serious flooding in Key West. Residents have been urged to evacuate the area or to move to the hurricane shelters.*

"At the northwest part of the state, Tropical Storm Bonnie is expected to come ashore in the Florida panhandle tomorrow . . . "

Emerson shut off the TV and sat at his laptop. He was intrigued by a number of issues and wondered how he could work them together into the story. The issues were the hurricane and the drug running. He wasn't sure how he could link them. Certainly, readers were not concerned about the plight of drug runners during a hurricane.

Miami Police Department
Miami, Florida

∽

Leaning back in his chair, which he had swiveled so that he could look out on the Miami skyline, Detective Yanni Wilharm cast his eyes uneasily toward the horizon on the west for signs of approaching storms. He held the receiver to his hear and waited for the ringing phone on the other end of the line to be answered.

"Valasquez aquí."

"¡Hola amigo! Soy su amigo, Wilharm."

Valasquez quickly switched to English. "Yanni, how are you?"

"In Florida, how can you ever be anything but great!" he exclaimed positively.

Valasquez smiled. "And what brings you to call me so late in my day?"

Wilharm looked at his watch and calculated the time differential. It was late in the afternoon there. "Going out for tapas tonight?" he teased.

"Of course. You have your beaches and we have our tapas," Valasquez grinned.

For a brief moment, Wilharm pictured the tapas that he enjoyed on his last visit to Madrid. "I'll take my beaches any day. I was actually following up on that terrorist, Asad. Did you ever trace him?"

"Funny that you phoned today. I was going to give you a call about my friend, Moshe, from the Mossad. You remember him. We had tapas with him while you were visiting."

"Yes, I remember him. And why were you going to call me about him?"

Valasquez' next comment made Wilharm sit straight up in his chair.

"Moshe's flight arrives in Miami this afternoon. He'd like to meet with you for your assistance."

Wilharm was very focused on their conversation. "Does that mean you think Asad is here?"

"Maybe. There was one ship that left Barcelona that we had tried to contact, but their radio was out. When they got into port and repaired their radio, the captain misplaced the message and the photo that was sent to him. We didn't realize it until a routine follow-up on the case showed that we hadn't received a response. After we resent the photo and message, the captain took a closer look at the photo. He didn't recognize Asad from the photo. But, when he read about the missing index finger, he told us that he had a red-haired Arabic on board as a crew member. He joined them in Barcelona."

"And the ship was headed for Miami?"

"¡Exactamente!"

"Then we'll arrange to greet the ship when it arrives," Wilharm smiled smugly to himself.

"Not that easy. The ship has already docked and unloaded her cargo. She's put out to sea again ten days ago."

"Then, we will arrange for a helicopter to fly out to her and we will capture your terrorist!" Wilharm offered.

"He's not aboard. He jumped ship in Miami. They don't know where he went. He could be anywhere in your city, your state, or your country by now."

"You'll need to give me the details on the ship and we'll work with immigration here to try and track him. We can also send the photos to all our law enforcement agencies."

"I'll have them sent to you immediately. I have your contact information," Valasquez stated.

"And why don't you give me the flight information for Moshe, and I'll meet him at his gate."

Valasquez provided the flight information and they ended their call. Wilharm's heart was racing as he played through a number of scenarios as to what Asad could be doing in Miami or the surrounding areas. He reached for the phone and called the Immigration Service as soon as he received an e-mail with a photo attachment that popped up on his incoming e-mail.

Later That Afternoon
Saint Mary Star of the Sea Catholic Church
Truman Street and Winslow Lane, Key West

ঔ

Sam parked his car on the street and he and Emerson approached the High Victorian Gothic-style stone church. They peeked in and saw the white-painted, high-ceilinged, Byzantine-style interior with a terrazzo floor and a beautiful, large stained-glass window above the altar, depicting Our Lady, Star of the Sea.

They walked to the grotto, constructed in 1922 at the direction of Sister Louis Gabriel after a series of major storms and hurricanes hit Key West from 1897 until 1919. She based the grotto on the Grotto in Lourdes, France and built it to protect Key West and its residents from hurricanes. Sister Louis Gabriel pronounced that Key West would never experience the full brunt of a hurricane as long as the grotto stood. Her pronouncement is inscripted in bronze on a memorial to her in the garden. Since the erection of the grotto in 1922, no hurricanes have struck Key West.

As Emerson and Sam approached the stone enclosure, they could see pillar candles and statues as well as a small crowd of people that had gathered to pray that the approaching hurricane would spare Key West again.

A short, tanned man, clad in a white shirt and white slacks, approached them. "Would you like to join us in prayer?"

Emerson started to respond affirmatively, but was interrupted by Sam. "Love to, but we don't have time," Sam managed weakly.

"You should make time to pray, my friend."

Emerson saw Sam's uneasiness and spoke up. "What my friend meant by his comment was that we have an appointment to make. We just stopped by to see the grotto because I had heard that it keeps hurricanes away from Key West."

Shifting his gaze to Emerson, the man continued, "It works. We're all here to pray a bit harder that it continues to work. I just lit two candles, one at the shrine and one inside the church."

Sensing that Sam was edging away, Emerson ended the brief conversation, "A little bit of prayer never hurt anyone."

"We're going to be praying real hard," the man commented. "There will be a mass tonight if you'd like to return."

"We'll see if we have time," Emerson responded noncommittally as he turned to follow Sam back to the car.

Easing himself into the passenger seat, Emerson asked, "A little nervous there, weren't you?"

"Sometimes those spiritual things spook me a bit," Sam replied. Changing the topic as they crossed through the residential side streets toward the historic seaport area, Sam exclaimed, "Wait until you see what I have in store for you tonight!"

Ten minutes later, they parked the Jeep on Caroline Street and headed toward the intersection of Caroline and Williams. As they approached the intersection, Emerson saw an open-air restaurant occupying the corner of the municipal parking lot. The ramshackle restaurant appeared to be a thrown-together, misshapen collection of fishing nets, lattice work, and hawser ropes and lines.

The irregular metal roof was supported by pier pilings, exposed two-by-fours and beams. The uneven floor was a collection of worn bricks and railroad ties. Tables consisted primarily of large wooden spools were surrounded by cane-back chairs. A solitary counter with high stools overlooked Caroline Street. Hanging from the walls were fishing gear and a vast collection of license plates from across the United States. An old pickup truck sat parked off the street and almost served as one wall of the small restaurant.

"Welcome to B.O.'s Fish Wagon," Sam announced to his wide-eyed friend. "They've got the best grouper sandwiches in Key West. I'm over here a lot when I'm in town."

"He sure is," a lady said from behind the counter. The counter appeared to be in a panel truck with the side panel raised so that you could be served—similar to what you might find at a carnival. The restaurant was in a horseshoe shape around the cooking vehicle.

"Hi Sally," Sam responded. "Two grouper sandwiches and two beers."

"Got you covered."

Sam paid and they wandered toward the backside of the restaurant. "I love sitting over here." Nodding towards a door, he explained. "That's the ladies' restroom. They all have to walk by me when they've got to go. Never know when you might meet the right one, if you know what I mean."

Emerson shook his head at his friend. "Don't you ever quit?"

"Nah. That would take the fun out of my life!" Seeing a man approaching their table. Sam stood and his face broke into a big grin. "Meet Buster Obney. He's worked here for a long time."

"Hi Sam. I'm Buster," the affable, bearded Obney, who was wearing a ball cap, said as he shook hands with the now standing Emerson.

"Emerson Moore," Emerson responded.

"Sit. Sit," Obney said as he dropped into an unoccupied chair at the table. "Sam, what in the world brings you here now? You fly in just so that you could experience the thrill of another near miss?"

Sam grinned. "I had to be here for my amigo. He's writing a story about hurricanes for the *Washington Post*."

"A reporter from Washington, eh?" Obney asked.

"Yes, and no. I'm a reporter, but I'm not from Washington. I'm from one of the Lake Erie Islands. Place called Put-in-Bay."

Obney's eyes sparked as he looked over at Sam. "This is the guy you were telling me about who had some sort of run-in with a shipping giant on the islands? Some guy who lived in the bow section of a ship that had been hauled up on a cliff?"

"Yep. That's him! The one and only, Emerson Moore!"

Emerson threw Sam a frown for playing him up.

"That sounded like one hell of an adventure. Lucky you boys didn't get killed, based on what Sam told me. Sam, is this the guy who wrote the newspaper story you showed me?"

"Exactly. I think I told you he won a Pulitzer Prize."

"Yeah, yeah. I remember," Obney commented. "You know a singer up there by the name of Pat Dailey?"

"Sure. We've met several times. He's one of the island's legends. How did you hear about him?"

"We're friends. He sings down here for several weeks each winter and comes by often. I've actually been to Put-in-Bay. Nice resort town you guys have up there."

"I like it," Emerson concurred.

"It's a small world when you look at the link between Put-in-Bay and Key West. So many of the seasonal workers up there end up down here in the off-season. It works great for everyone. You ever run into a bartender named Sully? I believe that he works at the Blue Iguana or something like that."

"Sure, I know Sully. He's now working out at the Skyview Bar and Restaurant, near the Put-in-Bay airport."

"Down here, he works over at Crabby Dick's. Nice guy!"

"We'll need to make a visit to him, if we can. This grouper sandwich is absolutely delicious," Emerson said as he smacked his lips.

"Glad that you like it. People have been saying for years that we have the best grouper around," Obney said. "I've got to go. Hang around for a while. We've got a band setting up shortly."

"Sure. Sounds like a great idea," Emerson said between bites.

"We can't stay too long. I've got to meet a friend of mine soon. Got to help him with some baby-sitting," Sam winced. "Babies! I don't know anything about them!"

"Wish I could be there to watch," Emerson teased as he took a swallow of his brew. "Why are you going to do this for him?"

"I owe him a favor for something he did for me. I just wish I could return the favor in a different way," Sam lamented.

City Mooring Field
Off Fleming Key

❦

The figure at the Zodiac's controls idled back on the power as the small craft approached the dilapidated houseboat moored in the City Mooring Field off Fleming Key.

"I don't know why I let you talk me into this. I don't know nothing about baby-sitting," Sam said with an air of growing concern as they neared the houseboat.

"Nothing to it. You just read the little crumb-crushers a story and they fall asleep, then you drink beers for the rest of the night until we return," the large bearded man advised with an air of feigned experience.

"Harley, you're going to owe me big time for this!"

"I'll make it worth your while. If I could have found anyone else, I wouldn't have bothered you," Harley replied with a smile. When he received the call from J.B. and the urgency for the meeting was explained cryptically, Harley knew that he needed to attend. The only person that he found at the last minute who could cover the baby-sitting job on J.B.'s houseboat was Sam. He had preferred not to contact Sam, but realized that he didn't have any choice. He had to cajole Sam into accepting.

"Ahoy, anyone home?" Harley called out to the houseboat.

"It's about time you got here," a gruff voice called back as a man wearing a shirt with the sleeves cut off stepped out of the main cabin and caught the line that Harley tossed to him. He quickly secured it and Harley and Sam stepped off the boat.

"Sam, meet a business associate of mine. Name's J.B.," Harley said as he made the introduction. "J.B., this is Sam, tonight's baby-sitter."

Sam began to explain, "Now, J.B. I want you to understand that I don't know a whole lot about baby-sitting."

"Hell, there's nothing to it. You just tell them you'll kill them and they'll mind you," J.B. said seriously as they entered the main cabin. "Boy, get out of the way before I slap a wart on your head!" J.B. yelled when a young boy appeared.

The six-year-old, blonde-haired boy dodged under a table. A moment later, his head appeared above the table's edge. He was wearing a football helmet. "Go ahead and try," he challenged his father, and then ducked swiftly to avoid a pan that his father threw at him.

"I'll fix you, you little hammerhead," J.B. threatened. "Stupid kid. That's why they need their mother around here more."

"Where's their mother?" Sam asked as he looked around the room for more children, but didn't see any.

"Candy's at work. That is, if she can keep a job. She is so stupid!"

"Come on J.B., she's not all that bad," Harley urged. "I've seen her before. She's a beautiful woman. And she's just a sweet as can be," Harley confided to Sam.

"I figured as much," Sam replied.

"How'd you catch her?"

"Just used my charm!" J.B. responded seriously as he picked his nose. "I've got to fight women off all the time. They can't resist me!"

"My Daddy lied," the youngster said before hiding underneath the table again. "My momma is a nice person," his little voice shouted.

"Shut up or I'll throw you overboard to the sharks," J.B. roared as he crumbled an aluminum beer can that he had just emptied, and threw it in the direction of the boy.

Harley was looking at his watch. "J.B., we need to get going so that I can meet your friend," Harley suggested and turned to walk out onto the deck.

"Take good care of my knuckleheads, now," J.B. said solemnly as he followed Harley.

"As in more than one?" Sam asked as he worriedly looked around for another child. Before J.B. could answer, there was a cry from the bedroom in the aft section of the houseboat.

"That'll be the other one. He's in his crib. Probably needs his diaper changed," J.B. yelled as he hopped into the Zodiac, and Harley quickly started the engine. The boat leapt forward as they headed to Key West for their meeting. J.B. had offered Harley a job that would reward them richly, but had been very secretive about it. J.B. wanted his two new acquaintances to explain to Harley exactly what it entailed.

"I don't know anything about changing diapers," Sam shouted fruitlessly in the direction of the departing Zodiac. He stood and stared as the Zodiac roared away. Cries from the bedroom beckoned him, but he remained standing in the doorway, not wanting to face the reality of childcare. After a few seconds and an increase in the noise level of the cries, he turned and walked into the small room. Standing with both hands clenching the side of the crib was another towheaded boy. A quick glance at the first boy showed that they most certainly were brothers.

Sam sniffed as a foul odor filled the air, and grimaced when he realized what it was. Deciding to ignore it as if it would go away, he tried to calm the crying toddler. "Hey sport, what's your name?"

The toddler continued to cry as he began to shake the sides of the crib in anger.

Sam felt at a loss for one of the few times in his life. Dealing with underwater problems, explosives, and other dangerous situations were far easier.

In the Zodiac
Off the City Mooring Field

~⑥~

"So, who's that Sam guy?" J.B. asked Harley.

"Just a guy that I hang out with from time to time," Harley responded as he shifted his massive frame in the Zodiac's stern.

"You trust him?" J.B. probed.

"Nope." Harley would have stopped the conversation at that point, but he saw J.B. staring intensely at him, and realized that J.B. wanted more than a one-word answer. "I tried to sell him drugs once, but he wasn't interested."

"Why do you hang with him, then?"

Harley was slow to respond. "He can be a good source of information for me and my friends in Naples and Miami. I trade information with him from time to time, and it helps my friends with their dealings."

J.B. knew that Harley was referring to the drug dealers who he was supplying in Naples and Miami, and stopped asking questions. He turned around and looked over the bow at the approaching shoreline.

Onboard the Houseboat
The City Mooring Field

~∽~

"His name is Mason," the toddler's brother responded as he leaned against the door frame with a mischievous smile. He suspected that Sam didn't know anything about kids, and probably nothing about baby-sitting them.

Sam looked over to the boy and said, "Thanks. And what's your name?"

Between Mason's sobbing, the older boy replied, "I'm Dix."

"Okay, Dix. You can call me, Uncle Sam. What do you think we can do to make Mason stop crying?"

"He likes to be picked up and held," he said as he tried to hide a sly smile. Seeing Sam frozen in his tracks as he looked at the crying boy, Dix added with a snicker, "Uncle Sam."

"Okay," Sam said as he ignored the snicker. He reached over the crib's rail and lifted Mason into his arms. He held him close and wrapped one of his arms under Mason's bottom. It was soaking wet and something was oozing from the loosely tied diaper and onto Sam's arm.

"He shit himself!" Dix laughed as he watched the trickle of loose stool work its way down Sam's arm.

Sam quickly set the toddler back in his crib and grabbed a nearby cloth to wipe his arm. "You shouldn't use language like that, son," he cautioned the youngster.

"My Daddy does," the boy retorted proudly.

"Well, your Daddy isn't around here right now and I'm in charge. Understand?" Sam said in a tone that meant business.

The boy looked at Sam and realized that Sam was serious. He'd have to watch his step, and carefully gauge how far he could push him.

"I reckon I do."

Mason began screaming again and Sam started to walk away.

"I told you that Mason shit himself," Dix repeated.

Sam angrily swung around and said, "I told you not to talk like that when I'm here. You're way too young to talk like that. As far as your brother goes, we'll just leave him there and see if he stops crying."

"You can't leave him like that," Dix warned.

"Why not?"

"He gets the diaper rash real bad if he's not changed right away." After seeing that Sam still wasn't motivated to act, Dix continued, "And the rash creeps down his leg and burns like hell."

Sam shot him a look because of his language and Dix quickly apologized, "Sorry. I slipped, Uncle Sam!"

Sam turned his head back to the wailing toddler. "Okay, I guess we'll just have to do something about Mason's diaper." Sam swore under his breath as he approached the crib. Harley hadn't mentioned that this favor involved changing diapers. Sam would have preferred someone else had covered for Harley, but he didn't want to jeopardize their relationship because he had to ask Harley to obtain some sensitive information that he needed.

Sam reached over the crib rail and talked quietly to Mason. "Here we go, big boy. Uncle Sam is just going to lay you down on your back and we'll get that old diaper changed."

Mason stopped his crying as he got the attention that he had been demanding.

"It'd be easier if you put the rail down," Dix said as he watched Sam having a difficult time reaching over the rail and into the crib.

"Oh, yeah. I was just getting ready to do that," Sam said unconvincingly.

He grabbed the rail and tried to force it down. It didn't budge. He tried a couple of more rough moves but to no avail.

"Here, I'll show you," Dix offered and stepped over to the crib. With his practiced hand, he quickly released the rail and it dropped to its lowest position.

Sam smiled at Dix. "That'll make a difference!"

Sam reached into the crib and began to unfasten the diaper. He unfastened the two safety pins and stuck them into the top of the crib's headboard.

"My momma's not going to like that," Dix warned when he saw where Sam stuck the pins.

"She'll never know," Sam grinned.

Slowly and carefully, he began to unravel the diaper with its oozing surprise. He lifted Mason's legs and pulled out the soiled diaper. He turned to Dix as he handed the diaper to him and let go of Mason's legs.

"You can get rid of this!" Sam said as the odor permeated the air.

Taking the diaper, Dix instructed Sam as he grinned, "You need to wipe him." Dix knew what awaited Sam. He extended a container of Wet Ones.

Sam groaned as he turned back to the crib. He grabbed a couple of Wet Ones and lifted Mason. As he did, he saw that by letting Mason drop back on the bed, the sheets were now soiled. He shook his head as he wiped Mason and lifted him from the soiled sheet.

Seeing that Dix hadn't returned, Sam held Mason in one arm and he grabbed a couple more Wet Ones. He wiped off the soiled sheets, but now the sheets were wet and he couldn't put Mason back in the crib.

"Come on, partner. We'll finish this up on the table." Sam walked into the main cabin and laid Mason on the tabletop. "Dix, get me a clean diaper and the safety pins from the headboard."

Dix returned with the requested items within seconds. But first he held out a can to Sam.

"What this?"

"Powder."

"And what am I supposed to do with this?"

"Powder his butt!" Dix advised.

"Powder his butt? Why do we need to powder his butt?" Sam said as he looked at the can in his hand, and saw out of the corner of his eye that Mason had already raised his legs in anticipation of the powdering.

"It keeps him dry," Dix responded.

Sam turned to the toddler and began to shake powder out of the can. When he turned the can upside-down, the powder in the can shifted so that when Sam shook the can, a huge amount of white powder dumped out of the can. A large amount of the powder covered the toddler's butt and the excess spread on to the tabletop while the air filled with the chalky white powder.

Sam coughed as the powder penetrated his lungs.

Dix was amused as he watched Sam's inexperienced attempts. "You should have put the diaper down first, then powdered him."

"Now you tell me," Sam groaned as he looked at the mess on the table. Picking up Mason in one arm again, Sam began to wipe off the excess powder. "Grab that waste can over there and hold it for me," Sam instructed Dix who quickly complied. They cleaned the table, and Sam set Mason back down, but on the diaper, which he had Dix lay out on the table.

After several attempts, Sam was able to position the diaper and fasten the two safety pins. As he held up Mason at the end of the debacle, the loosely fitted diaper slid off of Mason and dropped to his feet. Exasperated, Sam laid Mason back on the tabletop and refastened the diaper. The second attempt was better, although the diaper wasn't as snug as it should have been.

"What do we do now?" he asked Dix.

Schooner Wharf Bar
Historic Seaport Area

∽

Making their way through the waterfront bar, which was crowded despite the approaching hurricane, J.B. led Harley to two rough-looking men seated at a table overlooking the harbor.

"This is the guy I was telling you about. One of the toughest guys, I know," J.B. bragged about his hard-looking, bearded friend. Looking around, before making the next comment, to be sure that no one would overhear him, J.B. explained in a low voice, "He's the one who bought our merchandise." J.B. was alluding to the sale of the stolen cocaine.

Both Asad and Pauley had been eyeing the new arrival carefully. Harley had been looking them over as well.

Pauley took a swallow of his drink and stared at Harley. "So tell us, how did you meet J.B.?"

"I already told you guys!" J.B. wailed.

"We know, but we want to hear his version," Asad said coolly.

Harley recognized them for what they were. They wouldn't blink an eyelash about killing you. He scooted his chair into the table. "We met out at the Heron's Nest during a fight about a year ago. I saved his butt from a beating."

"That he did," J.B. agreed quickly.

"Over a few beers, and as the night progressed, we learned that we had a number of common interests in making tax free money. So we began doing business together from time to time."

"We've made some good money together. He's got a way of doing things. He can make jumping over of a pit of alligators look easy," J.B. declared strongly in support of Harley.

"You live here year-round?" Asad asked as his gaze bored a hole through Harley.

"Pretty much. I've lived around here for years. Done a lot of shrimping. I have some connections in Miami that I deal with from time to time, and then I have some other connections in South America," Harley responded curtly.

"Drugs?" Asad asked.

"I'd rather not say."

"I'd rather you do say," Asad said with a menacing tone in his voice.

"Yes," J.B. answered for Harley.

"I want to hear him answer," Asad said coldly.

"I'll let you draw your own conclusions," Harley responded with an equally dangerous tone in his voice. He wasn't about to be threatened by anyone.

"Been busted at all?" Pauley inquired.

"Oh, for some small stuff when I was a lot younger and more foolhardy."

"You carrying?" Pauley asked.

"No," Harley responded. He had noticed the bulges under their shirts and had figured that they were armed.

Pauley finished his drink and then asked, "You both interested in making some big money?"

J.B. responded first. "I'm always interested in making money. Big or small, it doesn't matter as long as it's green."

"How about you?" Pauley asked Harley.

"I could be. It depends on what's involved."

Pauley looked around the crowded room, and at Asad. Asad nodded his head for them to take the next step. "Let's go out to our van."

Pauley paid for their drinks and they walked out of the Schooner Wharf.

City Mooring Field
Off Fleming Key
~

"It's soup," Dix said as he poured the soup in a bowl for Sam. They sat down for a snack at the table, which still had a layer of powdery residue, because Mason had wanted something to eat. Dix handed Sam a spoon and opened a jar of baby food, which he gave to Mason. Mason's face lit up and he began to eat contently.

"Dix, what kind of soup is this?" Sam asked suspiciously as he looked into the bowl and saw pieces of what appeared to be meat floating.

"Turtle soup. My momma made it," the boy responded with a hushed giggle.

"Are you sure?" Sam asked when he noticed the funny look on Dix's face.

"Yes sir, I am," came the response.

"Okay then." Sam lifted a spoonful to his lips and slowly tasted it. It wasn't bad. "Tastes good." He downed several more spoonfuls and noticed that Dix was almost doubling over as he tried to contain his laughter.

"What's so funny, Dix?" Sam asked as he took another spoonful.

"I won't eat it. She thickens it with dead tadpoles!" he said, and rolled on the floor laughing.

Sam sprayed soup into the air and across the room as he spit it out. "I don't think that's so funny!" Sam said as he stood and looked around the room for a cup to rinse out his mouth. Spying a cup next to a chair, he grabbed it. He noticed that it wasn't empty and then saw out of the corner of his eye that Dix was giggling again. Cautiously Sam turned to him. "What's so funny now?"

Covering his hand over his mouth, Dix responded. "That's my daddy's spit cup!"

"Gross!" was all that Sam said as he replaced it and walked over to the sink. "You got any clean cups here?" Sam noticed on the counter and between the salt and pepper shakers stood a can of Raid. He shook his head as he wondered how he let himself get into this situation.

"There are clean cups on the second shelf," Dix offered.

Sam eyed the boy carefully before slowly opening the cabinet door. He breathed a sigh of relief when he saw that it appeared to be a typical shelf of clean glasses. He filled the glass with tap water and rinsed his mouth to rid it of the tadpole taste.

Dix appeared at his side. "My Momma gets mad when my Daddy cleans fish here at the sink."

Crinkling his nose at the thought and the pungent smell in the area of the sink, he said, "I would too! Why doesn't he do that outside?"

"I don't know."

Looking around the room, Sam decided to go to the kids' level and sat on the floor with his back to what appeared to be J.B.'s chair. As he stretched his hand out on the floor to support himself, he felt something small, sharp and crinkling. He looked over to see what he had put his hand on and picked up something off-white colored and curved.

Smiling, Dix provided an explanation. "You found one of my Daddy's toenails. He sits there and clips them and makes mamma mad because he won't pick up his clippings." Dix smiled when he saw Sam toss it down and walk over to the sink to wash his hands.

"Why don't you come over and sit on the sofa with me and I'll tell you some stories?" Sam suggested as he dried his hands and walked over to the sofa. He looked it over carefully before sitting. "So tell me Dix, do you know how to field strip an M-16?"

It was evident by the boy's look that he didn't understand what Sam was talking about. "A little too technical then?" Sam searched his mind and decided that the boy might be interested in some of the pranks that he had pulled over the years since the boy seemed to like pulling pranks on him. "When I was in high school, there was a time when my buddy and I had to fill up a water cooler for my soccer teammates. Coach asked us to take our break early and fill it. After we left the field and filled the container with fresh water at the main building, we returned to the practice field. That's when we saw it."

"What did you see?" Dix asked eagerly.

"We spotted a frog hopping along his way. So my buddy and I grabbed the frog and dropped it in the water container. We placed the container on the bench and watched all the guys and the coaches drink from it. It was a hot day, and they almost drank it dry."

"What happened? Did they find the frog in there?"

"Oh yeah. My buddy and I were rolling on the ground because we were laughing so hard. One of the guys got suspicious and lifted the lid. He spotted the frog and told the other guys. We had to get off the ground real quick because they were after us. Good thing I was a fast runner. They got my buddy and pounded him a bit."

"Did they pound you?"

"No. By the time they caught up to me, they had cooled down," Sam grinned.

"That was cool. Do you have any more stories like that?" the boy asked as he made himself comfortable in one corner of the dilapidated sofa.

"I've got lots of fun stories like that." Sam proceeded to his next story.

Municipal Parking Lot
Caroline and Williams
⋞

The four men approached the rear of the white commercial van Pauley had rented.

"We'll talk back here." Pauley opened the door and the four men climbed into the back of the van and sat on four chairs that had been arranged around a small table with a map of Key West. Underneath the map was a chart of the water around Key West.

"Are either of you wedded to living in Key West?" Pauley asked.

"I don't care where I live as long as the money is right. Why?" J.B. questioned anxiously.

Pauley ignored him and looked at Harley. "What's your answer?"

"Why's it important to know the answer to that?" Harley wanted to know.

"Because what we pull off might make it a little too hot to live around here. It's too small a community, and people can put two-and-two together too quickly."

With rising interest, Harley responded, "Then, my answer is the same. I don't care where I live."

"Okay, here's the deal. We're going to pull off a heist at Mel Fisher's in the next forty-eight hours when the hurricane hits and the cops are too busy with the hurricane. There's about $400 million worth of treasure there!"

"Ain't no hurricane going to hit Key West. We got the grotto to protect us," J.B. said confidently.

"Either way, we're going to do it. Interested?" Pauley queried. Pauley had noticed that Harley had pulled his chair in closer.

"You can't just sit down in the back of a van one night and say that you're going to commit a major robbery in the next forty-eight hours," Harley stated incredulously. "It takes serious planning."

"The planning is done, we need some brawn to help execute it," Asad said.

Harley didn't like his use of the word 'execute.' "Please continue then. If it makes sense, I'm in. A heist of that size is going to be worth some serious bucks. Let's hear it."

"Count me in!" J.B. was jumping at the chance without even hearing the plan.

Pauley outlined the plan as he played with the gold chain that contained the Shasta Daisy and a few lockets of his wife's hair enclosed in glass. "I'm now reassigned to the night shift at Mel Fisher's. I'm a security guard there. Al here," he referred to Asad, "will blow the electrical service to the island."

"I've already identified where the electrical service comes into the island. Once I blow it, I'll catch up to you at Mel Fisher's," Asad explained.

"When the power goes off, I'll take out the other guard, cut the alarm to the police station, and stop the backup generator from starting. Harley, you'll drive this van, which will be parked here. It will have acetylene-cutting torches in the rear. You'll drive it to Mel Fisher's on the Front Street side. When you get there, you'll back the van up the ramp to the Treasure Sales entrance where I'll meet you. You and I will take the torches inside and cut open the safe where they put everything."

"What about me?" J.B. asked.

"You have a special job," Asad teased.

J.B. took him seriously and his eyes widened at the comment.

Pauley continued. "Your job is to steal a boat that we can use for the escape. We'll ride out of here in the middle of the hurricane's eye and stay with it until it makes landfall. So, you'll you need to make sure that it's something that can withstand hurricane-like waves."

Responding quickly, J.B. said, "That's not going to happen! Like I said before, hurricanes don't hit Key West. And if it did, you wouldn't want to follow an eye up the coast because you still have the other side of the hurricane to pass over you. That could be some serious damage. And another thing, you don't know that the hurricane is going to go in the direction that you want it to go."

Ignoring his comment, Pauley asked, "Can you steal a boat?"

"Yep. I know where there's a forty-six-foot Hatteras. If it's not there, there's a thirty-six-foot Yellow Fin that I could steal. Where would you want me to take it?"

"Pier B at the Hilton. The Hilton is across the street from Mel Fisher's. Once we load the van, we'll drive it over to Pier B and load up the boat."

"Piece of cake!" J.B. replied confidently.

"You two guys are responsible for getting us to Naples where we'll split up our take." Pauley explained.

Harley's mind was racing. He saw the opportunity and thought about the best route out. "J.B.'s right about no hurricane hitting us. Maybe we get a tropical storm or just some of the hurricane's storm bands. That should make the getaway a bit simpler. We can take the Northwest Channel out of Key West and then head straight north to Naples."

"Good. You're both in?"

Harley and J.B. nodded their heads in unison.

"J.B., you need to find a boat to steal."

"I'll look first thing in the morning."

Looking around the van at the three seated conspirators, Pauley said, "When we're ready to go with this, I'll call both of you on your cell phones. Harley, you'll need to write down your cell phone number. Both of you stay loose because this can break either tomorrow night or the next night."

"We'll be ready!" J.B. said with eager anticipation.

"Harley, we'll have the van with the torches parked in this lot. I'll give you the spare keys now." Pauley handed the keys to Harley. "There'll be one change to the van."

J.B. and Harley looked inquisitively at Pauley.

"It'll have magnetic decals on the side that say Mel Fisher's Treasure Sales. Something I had made up in the upper keys. If anyone sees the van backed up that ramp next to the building, they won't be suspicious."

"If the weather is as stormy as they expect, and with that evacuation order out, I don't think anyone will be walking around," J.B. offered.

"It seems that you two guys have this pretty well planned out," Harley said with admiration.

"We've anticipated everything," Asad said dangerously. He had been fairly quiet during the entire conversation as he concentrated on watching the reactions from J.B. and Harley. If he thought for one moment that they weren't buying into the plan, he'd have killed them before they left the van. "Harley, there are a couple of things that your friend, J.B., said, when we met earlier, that you could help with."

Harley's head swung around and he eyed J.B. carefully as he asked his question. "And just what are those couple of things?"

"He said that you have some contacts who might be able to supply us with weapons and explosives."

"That's possible. What are you looking for?"

"Three or four .45s, a couple of shotguns, and rifles."

"Shouldn't be any problem," Harley commented nonchalantly. "What type of explosives did you have in mind?"

"Semtex. Can you get it?"

"That's just to blow the power station?"

"Yeah. But I want to level it, so I'll need more. Get me . . . "

Harley cut him off. "I can handle it. I know about semtex." Harley thought for a moment and brought up a topic that no one had discussed that evening. "I didn't hear either one of you talk about selling the stuff. Who are you going to sell it to? It's going to be pretty hot, and you won't be able to fence it through the regular channels."

Pauley replied to Harley's question. "That's another area where we thought you could help us."

"How's that?"

"J.B. said that you have good connections in South Florida. We'd like you to tap into those connections and find us a buyer."

"My connections don't deal with selling stolen treasure!" Harley said indignantly.

"But they might know somebody who does," Pauley responded.

Harley stared at J.B. He now knew why he was brought in on the deal. They wanted him to arrange for the sale of the stolen treasure. J.B. averted his eyes from Harley.

"Let me get this straight. You guys put together this heist, you do all of this planning and you don't know how you're going to cash-in what you steal?"

Pauley replied with a dangerous and serious tone in his voice, "It's not that big of a deal. I have my own network of contacts, but I didn't want to chance using them." Pauley knew a lot of the fences on the Eastern Seaboard, but if he went to one of them it could get back to the boys in Jersey and New York. He didn't want to unnecessarily signal his whereabouts after his last incident. If push came to shove, he'd take the risk and call one of the fences he used in the past. That was his only alternative.

"Why don't you want to use your fences?" Harley asked suspiciously.

"Let's just say that there was a disagreement between us, and that they are not very happy with me now," Pauley replied cryptically.

"Can you do this? Can you find someone to buy this?" Asad asked solemnly.

Harley paused for a moment as his mind whirled and developed an intriguing plan. "There's a guy in Miami who's the head of the South Florida drug trade. He could be interested, but of course, he'd want a deep discount to buy the goods." This could present the opportunity that Harley had been working toward—meeting the head of the cobra, the guy that was known to Harley as Frank.

Pauley replied. "We figured that. As long as it's reasonable, we'll walk away rich men." Pauley smiled as he thought about the cash he'd realize.

Harley smiled, too, but his smile didn't convey what he was really thinking. He was anxious to contact his Miami connections. "Let me see what level of interest my connection has." Harley had never been able to talk directly with the top dog. He always had to work through his underlings. This might prove to be his opportunity to talk to Frank and eventually meet him. Harley was quite satisfied where this was going and how his private plan, which he was quickly developing, might unfold. This could pay off very well for Harley.

"How soon can you let us know?" Asad probed.

"Tomorrow, I hope. Time is short, isn't it?"

"Yes, very short," Asad replied anxiously. "And the weapons and semtex?"

"Tomorrow. That shouldn't be any problem. I'll make phone calls tonight. My contacts in the upper keys have a variety of stuff that I can use."

"Here's my cell phone number. You call me and let me know what your friend can do, and we'll arrange for you to deliver the weapons and semtex," Pauley instructed as he passed a scrap of paper with his number on it.

"I'll call you around eleven o'clock in the morning," Harley said.

"Let's get moving then," J.B. said with a gleam in his eyes.

They swung open the back door of the van and J.B. and Harley headed over to the dock to retrieve the Zodiac.

"Trust them?" Asad asked as they watched J.B. and Harley disappear around the corner.

"I don't trust anybody," Pauley said. "We'll need to be careful that they don't try to rip us off and take us out of the picture when we get together to sell the treasure. That would increase their take by 50 percent."

Asad thought for a moment and spoke. "Maybe we'll turn the tables on them and take them out and the treasure buyers after we sell the treasure. If we do it right, we can have the cash from the sale and still have the treasure."

Pauley's face lit up in anticipation of doublecrossing Harley, J.B., and the buyer. "How do you see us pulling that off?

"Not sure yet. Give me a little time."

"You don't have much time!"

"I don't need much," Asad said softly as he recalled how quickly he moved in the past, at the last minute, in setting up ambushes or planting explosives when opportunities presented themselves. He had a few surprises up his sleeve, which he would use when necessary over the next few days.

"You let me know what you're thinking, then. Let's go." Pauley and Asad emerged from the van, and locking it, disappeared into the night.

Pauley was humming as he walked. He had spent too many years as the monkey at the end of the chain. Now it was his turn to be the organ grinder and tell the monkey what to do. A broad smile crossed his face as he walked.

J.B.'s mouth had been jabbering the entire ride back to the houseboat. As they approached the houseboat, they noticed that there weren't any lights on.

"Oh, oh."

"Trouble?" Harley asked as he reached inside a storage compartment and retrieved a .45.

"Don't know. No lights on. That's unusual." J.B. glanced at the old watch on his weatherworn arm. It was 11:05 p.m.

Harley cut the Zodiac's motor and allowed the boat to glide the final few feet to the houseboat. If there was a problem, someone surely would have heard the Zodiac's motor and be waiting for them.

The boat nudged against the houseboat and J.B. quietly stepped off the Zodiac and secured the line to the houseboat. He stepped to one side of the door while Harley, gun in hand, stepped to the other side. J.B. slowly snaked his hand between the screen door and its frame to the adjacent light switch. He flicked on the switch as he and Harley burst into the main cabin.

"What's going on here?" a sleepy voice called from across the room.

Harley and J.B. looked and saw Sam, blinking his eyes in the bright overhead light. Next to Sam, and still sleeping, was Dix. Sam had his arm around a sleeping Mason who was lying on Sam's chest. His diaper was hanging around his feet.

Harley secured the .45 in his waistband and relaxed. "It's just us, Sam."

"Smells like somebody pissed themselves," J.B. said as he sniffed the air.

A groan came from Sam. "I'm all wet," he said as he carefully lifted the sleeping Mason off his chest and saw that the boy had drenched the front of Sam's shirt.

J.B. strode across the room and took Mason. "His britches need to be around his waist. No wonder he pissed on you." Tugging up Mason's diaper, J.B. carried the sleeping boy to his crib in the next room.

Sam carefully arose from the sofa without waking Dix. As he stood, he pulled off his tee shirt. "Guess I won't be wearing this until it's washed."

J.B. reentered the main cabin. "My knuckleheads give you a hard time?"

"Quite the opposite," Sam said as he decided not to disclose how rough it had been. "We played some games, had a little snack and I told them stories about a U.S. Navy SEAL named Sam."

"You were lucky. They usually put up a big fuss."

"Not with me. It was a piece of cake. Kids and I get along great," Sam said with confidence.

"Ready to go, Sam?" Harley asked.

"Sure."

"Harley, I'll be in touch. Thanks for watching my kids, Sam," J.B. said and then turned his back to grab a beer from the fridge. "Did you guys leave me any soup?" he asked as he raised the lid and looked inside.

"Yes, we did. As difficult as it was, we left some for you. Have at it." Sam wanted to gag as he said it, but was able to suppress the feeling.

Stepping into the Zodiac, Sam leaned over the side and rinsed out his tee shirt in the warm water. Harley started up the Zodiac and they headed back to the Garrison Bight where Harley kept the Zodiac.

"How did your evening go?" Sam asked Harley.

"Fine."

"Want to talk about it?" Sam probed.

"Nope. Nothing that would interest you."

Harley was known to be very close-lipped about his life and what he was up to. Sam sensed that whatever it was, Harley wasn't going to share anything with him. It was probably something illegal, Sam thought.

Sam settled back in the bow and stared at the clouds rolling in and beginning to hide the stars. Probably rain later that night, followed by a day ravaged by rain, he thought to himself. He had no idea of the danger in store for himself the next day.

The Next Morning
Blue Heaven
Bahamian Village

❦

After turning on Petronia and driving through Bahamian Village with its conglomeration of brightly painted and inviting shops, they parked the Jeep. Through the sheets of driving rain, Emerson and Sam ran from the Jeep to the Blue Heaven's gated entrance and down its brick path. They quickly made their way through the deserted open courtyard dining area and onto the covered deck of the two-storied house trimmed out in blue. A weathered sign on the street side announced the restaurant's name in faded blue paint to passersby.

"Wet," Emerson said as he shook the rain from his light jacket.

"Keeps the crowd down. No waiting today," Sam grinned optimistically.

They were seated inside and the waitress gave them menus and large cups of coffee. They read the menu quickly and placed their orders.

Emerson opted for the Rooster Special, which consisted of two eggs, bacon, and Betty's banana bread. Sam ordered Seafood Benedict, a fresh fish sautéed and served with poached eggs on English muffins with lime Hollandaise sauce.

"Cool place," Emerson said as he looked around the interior.

"Did you see the shower stall in the courtyard?" Sam asked.

"Out of the corner of my eye."

"It had a sign on the side of it. It read that showers are one dollar and it's only two dollars to watch," Sam grinned mischievously.

"Only you'd notice something like that," Emerson teased good-naturedly.

"Seriously, this place is one of the top ten best places to eat in Key West. It's got a long history. They used to have cockfights here, and Ernest Hemingway refereed some of the Friday night boxing matches. If I remember when we leave, I'll point out the rooster cemetery where they buried the dead roosters."

"I'd hope they wouldn't bury a live rooster," Emerson kidded.

"Okay!" Sam growled at his friend. "You'll see the chickens and roosters that live here roaming around freely and pecking at the ground while people are eating. It's fun to watch. They've got a lot of cats walking around here, too."

Seeing Emerson looking towards the rainy courtyard, Sam suggested, "You won't see too much today because of the rain." Sam sat back in his chair and gazed toward the stairs to the second floor. "The second floor of this building used to be a bordello years ago."

Emerson shook his head. "It's amazing to learn the history of a building's uses. If only the walls could tell us their stories."

Before Sam could comment , the waitress returned with their food and Emerson took his first bite of the banana bread.

"Exquisite," he proclaimed to Sam.

"Yep, they've got great food here. They can get long lines of people waiting for a table. We'd have had to wait if there wasn't this rain and the hurricane threat. It chased all of the tourists away."

"What happens to the charter fishing boats when they're faced with threatening weather like this? With the hurricane, that is?" Emerson asked as he munched away on his breakfast.

"They tie them down. I can take you out to the marina when we're done. A friend of mine has a charter boat there. I might add that he's also an ex-Navy SEAL," Sam said proudly. "His name is Captain Steve Luoma. He captains the *Fish Check*."

"I'd like to meet him. That could be another angle to include in my story. While you were out gallivanting last night, I was in my room writing the opening portion of my story."

"My, my. Weren't you the good boy. Come all the way to Key West and then stay in your hotel room during the evening hours?" Sam was teasing, but he had also been aware of Emerson's earlier struggle with alcoholism. He didn't want to push him too far.

Ignoring his comments, Emerson continued, "I was busy pulling together my notes from the day. It's more productive to do it while it's fresh in my mind."

They intermixed their friendly banter with bites of food as they finished their breakfast and drove to meet Luoma.

Pauley's cell phone rang shortly before eleven o'clock. He had just poured himself a cup of coffee and walked into his tiny living room. Wearing only his gray boxer shorts, he walked over to the kitchen table, scratching his large belly as he walked.

"Yes?"

"It's Harley."

"Did you talk with your friend?"

"Yes, I did." Harley was quite pleased with the way the morning's events had transpired. His initial phone conversation had been from a pay phone booth on Stock Island with his primary contact, Jaime, in Miami. He told Jamie enough to get him excited. Jamie had taken the phone number and promised to call him back after he talked with his boss. Harley was shocked when the phone rang in the booth, and Frank was on the line. He wanted to know all of the details about the heist, and Harley had selectively divulged the plan. He held back the details about how they were going to break in.

"Is he interested?"

"Very interested. He has a pretty big ego, and for him to be involved in something of this magnitude would be very important to him."

"So, he'll buy the treasure?"

"Definitely."

Pauley leaned against the kitchen counter, slowly savoring his sip of coffee. He was smiling in anticipation. "Did you get the guns and explosives?" he asked.

"Pick them up this afternoon. A friend of mine is meeting me in Marathon to deliver them to me."

"You need cash to pay him?"

"I've got it covered. You can reimburse me."

"Good. Here's Al's number. Why don't you go ahead and call him. He's worried that you're not going to come up with the explosives."

"Sure. I'll call him."

Pauley gave Harley the number and ended the call. He placed the empty cup in the sink and began to hum.

The Airport
Key West

∽

The small plane was fighting a strong crosswind and the rain as it began its descent to Key West's only runway. When the wind was blowing from the wrong direction, landings were more challenging to pilots. The nearly empty plane had a rough flight since it departed from Miami as the rainstorm from the hurricane moved in. The pilot and co-pilot held firmly to the controls as the plane was buffeted from side to side by the wind.

Sitting in the third row were the plane's only passengers. Their hands were tightly gripping their armrests and their faces were strained from the flight's rigors.

Marioda and Ricci had flown from Newark to Miami early that morning and watched as the two flights to Key West were cancelled. Finally the third flight was set to go and they were the only passengers to board. No one was heading to Key West. Most people were trying to get out of Key West with Hurricane Charley bearing down on the island.

"I can't wait until we get on the ground!" Ricci complained as the plane took a sudden dip.

"There are a number of ways to get to the ground. Let's hope that it's by landing," Marioda said sarcastically.

"We'll never get a flight out of here if the weather gets worse."

"That's not a problem. We'll just tell them that we'll return the rental car in Miami. Then, we don't have to worry about flights being delayed by any hurricane. We'll sit it out and drive out of here."

"You been through a hurricane before?"

"Nope. But it's nothing to worry about. Just a little storm. Blow down some trees and damage some roofs. Just like home," Marioda said aloofly, although he had no idea what he was talking about.

After the plane taxied up to the terminal and they departed, they walked inside to the rental counter and secured their rental car and maps.

To the dark-haired woman behind the counter, Marioda asked, "Could you show me how to get to Mel Fisher's Museum?"

"I'd be glad to," she responded as she placed a map on the counter and highlighted, in yellow, the streets that they should follow to get there. "You may want to call, first. With the weather moving in, they may be closed. A lot of the places are closing."

"Thank you. That's a good idea," Marioda said with no intention of following through.

Marioda and Ricci walked through the gates and into the sheeting rain to their rental car in the lot. Finding it, they sat inside and shook the rain from themselves as they tossed their umbrellas into the back seat.

Marioda picked up his cell phone and called a number on Stock Island. The phone was answered on the second ring.

"Who is it? I'm busy." The voice stormed.

"It's a couple of your friends from up north. I believe you have a package for us."

"Who is this?"

"This is the guy who you got a call about. You were going to supply him with something he needed," Marioda said cryptically, as he referred to the waiting weapons.

"Oh yeah. I've got it here for you."

"We've just landed. Can you give us directions to where to meet you?"

"Sure." He gave them directions to a meeting place that he used often and ended the call. Marioda smiled as he pulled out of the airport parking lot and turned left onto rain-soaked South Roosevelt. It wouldn't be long now, he thought to himself, as he watched the wipers working hard to keep the windshield clear.

Charterboat Row
City Marina
༚

Sam drove out on Truman Avenue and turned left onto Palm Avenue. He only went a short distance before pulling off on the right onto a small road along Garrison Bight.

As they drove along the Bight in the sheeting rain, Emerson noticed the houseboats tied up. "What a life that must be," he said longingly.

"At least the ones over here are sheltered somewhat. The houseboats off Fleming Key are in for a bit of a ride during this type of weather." Sam found himself wondering how the two youngsters, whom he had babysat last night, were doing.

He drove under the Palm Avenue bridge and followed the drive to the AmberJack Pier #1. Standing underneath a covered shelter next to his dockage was tall, blonde-haired Steve Luoma, a native Conch and one of the best fishing captains in the keys.

Sam parked his Jeep in front of the shelter and he and Emerson ran through the rain to Luoma's side.

"All secure?" Sam asked his friend.

"Yeah. I was just checking her one more time," he said.

The *Fish Check* was a custom built thirty-seven-foot sport

fishing boat that Luoma had used for years in fishing the keys. His fighting chairs had seen fisherman land dolphin, kingfish, tuna, wahoo, sailfish, blue and white marlin, barracuda, shark, and tarpon.

"Meet a friend of mine, Emerson Moore. He's a *Washington Post* reporter doing a story on the hurricanes," Sam said as he introduced the two.

"Hi. You sure timed your visit well. I'm not so sure that you'll see a hurricane make landfall here, but you should see enough stormy weather to write about. We'll get some flooding in the low spots, too."

"I'll take what I can get. My editor is focused on a story about Key West during a hurricane. I called him early this morning to see what he wanted me to do if the hurricane's path diverted from Key West, and he said to stay here and do a story."

"There's always stuff you can write about the preparation procedures that people go through. You'll see people over at Home Depot buying up new trashcans so that they can fill them with clean water to drink. Plywood is probably sold out by now. Batteries, candles and canned food are pretty hot items too. One time, we had a storm blow through here that knocked out the electricity for several days," Luoma added.

"Great idea. We'll have to run over to Home Depot and check it out."

"Then, there's the after-storm clean up. And that can be dangerous."

"How's that?" Emerson asked.

"You've got to be careful when you're walking around. You never know what will get you. There was a guy who picked up a section of chainlink fence after a storm and was killed."

"Killed?" Emerson asked, confused.

"The guy couldn't see it at the other end. A downed, live electrical wire was touching the fence. When he picked up his end, that's all she wrote," Luoma explained. "And if the winds are strong, and you're out walking around, make sure to protect yourself. You don't know what kind of debris might be flying through the air. There's a story about one guy who braved high winds and was found dead later. He had been impaled by a two by four that had broken off and been driven partially through him."

"Dangerous!" Emerson sighed.

"The *Fish Check* all right?" Sam asked as he looked at the craft pulling at its lines.

"Should be. I'm counting on Charley missing us," Luoma hoped aloud. "We've doubled and tripled all the lines and added spring lines from the center cleat to the forward pilings.

"We cleaned up everything around our dock space and tied whatever else needed to be tied" He pointed to *Fish Check*'s bridge. "We raised all the Isen glass."

"Isen glass?" Emerson asked, not understanding what Luoma was talking about.

"Sorry. That's the plastic windows on the bridge. When they're raised, they help create less wind resistance. If we really thought a hurricane was going to hit, and we decided to keep the boat here, we'd avoid any problems with the top-hamper." Anticipating that Emerson wouldn't understand, Luoma explained, "That's anything that increases the windage above the superstructure like Bimini tops, antennas, and outriggers."

The noisy horn of a small truck, which had pulled in close to the shelter, interrupted their discussion. "Steve, I'm out of here unless you need me for anything more!" yelled a voice with a very British accent from the truck's small interior.

"We're set. Thanks, Gary." The little truck drove off in the pouring rain. "That was Gary. He's my first mate."

Emerson and Sam nodded their heads.

Luoma continued with his explanation of hurricane preparedness as Emerson took notes. "Again, if a hurricane was headed here, we'd also protect the engine compartment. You'd secure any openings with duct tape and close the water intake seacock. You'd remove your electronics, and tape over the faces of any electronics that you couldn't easily remove."

"Then there's the one most important thing that we do here when we're in for a bad blow," Luoma said with a serious look.

"What's that?" Emerson inquired.

"Make sure that the insurance premiums are paid up," he smiled. He looked at Emerson. "Come back after the storm and I'll take you out to the reef for some good fishing."

"Thanks. I'd like that," Emerson said.

"Okay, Steve. I'd better take our reporter friend on out to Home Depot so he can interview some folks there," Sam said as the rain increased in intensity.

Looking at the rain beating on his boat, Luoma said quietly, "This could last for a couple of days. Good luck with your story, and do come back for that fishing trip."

"That's a promise," Emerson said as he turned to join Sam who had already raced through the rain to start the Jeep's engine.

Key West Police Department
North Roosevelt Boulevard

∽ঔ

"Mr. Kagan, he can see you now," the receptionist called to the visitor who had dashed from the cab through the drenching rain and without an umbrella into the police headquarters building five minutes ago.

"Thank you," Moshe responded as he turned away from the front entrance, where he had been staring through the glass doors at the rain. It had been a rough flight from Miami on the chartered plane the Miami Police Department had secured to fly Moshe to Key West.

As he watched the deluge outside, he had replayed the events of the last couple of days. Wilharm's people had been effective in running down leads on Asad. A review of the I-9's, one of the federal government forms required for completion during the hiring process at any business, had produced information about a recent new hire in a Key West restaurant, who was of Arabic origin. Follow up investigation revealed that this hire was missing his index finger—that was all Moshe needed to hear. He immediately requested assistance in making travel arrangements for a trip to Key West. When he was warned about the approaching hurricane, he ignored them. His focus was squarely on catching Asad.

Moshe followed the receptionist down the hall to meet with the chief of police. When he entered the chief's office, he saw a rather harried-looking chief. With the hurricane bearing down on the island, he understood where the chief's focus was. It certainly wasn't on meeting with Moshe.

"Good flight down?" the chief asked as he rounded his desk to shake hands.

"As good as one could expect under the circumstances. We ran into some turbulance," Moshe said as he thought about one particular steep drop the plane unexpectantly had taken on the flight from Miami.

"Actually, I didn't expect you to fly here today. The tourists are heading out of here as fast as they can," the chief said with a look indicating that he had been through evacuation drills before.

"I don't want to take a chance of Asad slipping away from us. It was important that I make the flight," Moshe responded seriously.

A knock at the door interrupted them.

"Come in," the chief called.

The door opened to reveal a tall man wearing a suit, who walked confidently into the office.

"Moshe, this is someone who I thought it would be important for you to meet," the chief said.

The stranger handed Moshe a business card. Moshe's eyes were riveted on the card and he looked up at the other visitor with a look of surprise.

"Why don't you come with me to my office so we can let the chief get back to his hurricane preparedness plan. We've got quite a bit to discuss."

Moshe thanked the chief and eagerly followed the stranger to his office.

City Mooring Field
Off Fleming Key
∽

The small houseboat was feeling the rain's intensity as the seas began to kick up. J.B. and his wife, Candy, had been packing what few very important personal items they had, in preparation to go to a shelter on the island.

J.B. had argued with her that there was no need to go for shelter, but she wanted to be safe.

He and his wife had been arguing when J.B.'s ringing cell phone interrupted them. J.B. whirled and angrily grabbed the phone. "What do you want?" he yelled.

"Temper, temper."

Calming down when he recognized the voice, J.B. said, "Sorry about that. I was in the middle of something."

"We're on for tonight," Pauley replied softly.

J.B. responded, "Okay."

"You can get the boat as we discussed?"

J.B. walked into the bedroom so that he could talk privately. "Yeah. I scouted out a couple. I've got my eye on a Hatteras."

"Good. I don't want any slipups," Pauley warned.

"You won't get any from me," J.B. countered.

"I want you to call me on my cell phone once you're underway with the boat," Pauley reminded J.B. Pauley heard the edgy tone in J.B.'s voice. Perhaps it was the stress of the evening's plans.

"Later." Pauley hung up.

J.B. walked back into the main cabin. "Okay, let's get you and the kids to shore. I've got some business to attend to."

Candy looked intently at him. "Business in weather like this?" She looked deep into his eyes and saw a glazed look that she had seen on several occasions in the past. It was a look that usually resulted with him getting into trouble with the police. She was nervous.

"Yeah, I've got business to do," he smirked secretively.

Candy didn't know why she stayed with him, as she thought about the two jobs she worked. He was always getting in trouble with employers or the police. Nothing seemed to work for them. And she was getting tired of the verbal abuse. He had never hit her, although he had come close on several occasions.

"I'm working on something big. If this pans out, we won't have to work again," he sneered at her. "I'll probably be gone for a while, but I'll let you know where I am so that you and the kids can catch up to me. Maybe I'll have us a big, new house and you'll have plenty of money."

"Sure I will," she said with exasperation. She had lived through his get-rich schemes before.

"Feel like working up a little sweat before we go?" he asked his wife cryptically.

"The only sweat I work up around here is when I have to chase you for the grocery money," Candy rebutted. "If you're thinking about anything else, forget it!"

"Aw, Hon," J.B. started.

She ignored him. "Is whatever you're doing legal?" she asked hesitantly.

"Don't worry about it!"

That cinched it for her. It was probably illegal. He could end up in jail if he was caught.

"Get the kids and let's get moving. I've got things to do!" he ordered.

She resigned herself to the tasks at hand and walked into the kids' room. Mason heard the yelling, and was standing silently at his crib rail. "Where's Dix?" she asked.

"Here I am, momma," a voice called out from underneath the crib. Dix had sought a safe refuge from his father's rantings. He was wearing the old football helmet for protection—just in case.

"Let's get you boys ready. We're going ashore to one of the shelters," she said with an air of tranquility. She didn't want to upset her boys any more than they were.

"Is it a hurricane, Momma?" Dix asked as he crawled out from under the bed.

"Maybe. For sure, it's a bad storm," she said as she steadied herself in the rocking houseboat. The storm's intensity was building—just like the intensity of their marriage. Trying to dispel any fear that Dix might have, she suggested, "We're going on a camping trip with a bunch of people. We'll be in a storm shelter and we're all camping out there."

Dix's face broke into a big smile as he raced to get ready for this new adventure.

It took a few minutes for them to pack some clothes and for her to take what few valuables she had.

"Let's get going," J.B. called from the runabout that he had started next to the houseboat.

She and the kids ran out into the driving rain and boarded the boat for the rough ride to shore and the safety of a shelter.

An Hour Later
Garrison Bight

∾

The strengthening wind threatened to tear the leaning palms along the road from their secure footholds. The rain was still sheeting as a man wearing a yellow slicker parked a borrowed green Chevy S-10 pickup truck in one of the parking spaces. He turned off the ignition and looked from side to side to make sure that no one was around, as he reached into his pants pocket and pulled out a pillbox, which he opened. He withdrew a small white pill and popped it into his open mouth. Swallowing the pill quickly, he returned the pillbox to his pocket. He was going to rely on the effects of the PCP to help him make it through the night's activities. He would need to be as alert and energized as possible. He sat for a few minutes more as he looked around and made sure that there were no witnesses to his planned theft.

Starting to feel the effects of the PCP, he opened the truck's door and stepped into the drenching rain. Still seeing no observers, he made his way along the dock and to the large Hatteras which strained against its lines. The lines had been doubled in anticipation of the high winds, and had been tied high to the pilings to allow for rising water. The pilings were about six feet above the gunwale.

J.B. had selected a forty-six-foot Hatteras Sportfisherman with 820-horsepower diesels. With a fifteen-foot beam and a 650-gallon capacity fuel tank, it could easily attain a top speed of thirty-five knots. J.B. knew that this boat was used frequently as a charter boat since it had great stability and layout. She could easily handle three- to five-foot seas and could be pushed to handle bigger seas.

She had a master stateroom amidship with a head, shower, and double berth. The one stateroom forward was a vee-berth cabin and also had a head and shower. The salon had huge windows around it and a built-in L-shaped settee. The entire interior was trimmed out in teak.

J.B. carefully boarded the craft and made a quick check to be sure that no one was onboard. Not that he expected anyone to be onboard in worsening weather like this.

As he climbed the ladder to the flybridge, he slipped on the wet ladder. He dropped two rungs before catching himself, but not before incurring a cut to the bottom of his chin.

He ignored the pain and quickly finished his climb to the flybridge. When he sat down on the captain's chair, he noticed that a thick red liquid was trickling slowly on his wet slicker. He rubbed his chin and when he pulled his hand away, it was red, too. Swearing at the cut, J.B. looked around and found a soiled rag, which he grabbed. Ignoring the dirt, he applied the soiled rag to his cut to slow the bleeding.

With the other hand, he began rummaging around underneath the console in search of a hidden spare key that the owner may have left on board. In a matter of minutes, he found it taped to the wiring harness and pulled it free. Inserting the key in the ignition, he fired up both engines and listened carefully in the drenching rain for the comforting rumble of the 820-horsepower diesels.

He smiled to himself and checked the soiled rag to see that the bleeding had stopped. Tossing the rag to the deck, he climbed down the ladder backwards and unfastened the lines securing the craft.

He also opened the in-deck bait well and the large fish box at the stern, to be sure that they were empty. And they were. They would soon be filled with treasure, J.B. grinned greedily to himself.

He checked to be sure that the bilge pumps were running smoothly in anticipation of the heavy seas they would face after loading the sturdy craft. J.B. took a quick look around to be sure that he wasn't being watched and untied the lines. Very carefully, he climbed back to the bridge. He slowly pushed forward on the throttle and the craft eased through the sheeting rain and out of Garrison Bight.

The twelve-foot-high chain-link fence surrounding the electrical substation had a four-foot-high cut on the far side. A pair of footprints led through the mud and wet sand from the nearby grove where a motorcycle was carefully hidden. Crouched in the torrential downpour was a soaking wet Asad. He was carrying a small bag that contained the semtex that Harley had given to him when they met earlier in the afternoon.

Asad had packed the semtex around the electrical cable and the control transformer. He was cautiously inserting the detonator and its attached timer. The timer was set for forty-five minutes so that Asad would have time to travel to Mel Fisher's.

Asad stood and gathered some nearby debris to cover his handiwork. Although he didn't expect anyone to be walking around in this weather, he still took the precaution. He retraced his steps to the cut wire and noted that his footprints were being covered by a layer of rainwater. So he wouldn't worry about them.

Carefully, he parted the cut fence wire and stepped through. He produced some strands of wire that he had previously cut, and quickly wove them through the cut fence wire so that the cut would be harder to notice. He walked back to the hidden motorcycle and mounted it.

It started easily and he edged it out of the grove and down the narrow service road. From the service road, he merged into the light traffic and headed back toward Mel Fisher's. He had one stop to make on the way. He had something to do that he hadn't disclosed to Pauley or the others. He gritted his teeth as the wind-whipped rain struck has face like sharp darts.

❧

Emerson was looking past Mallory Square and over Sunset Island at the blackening sky, which was intermittently filled with brilliant flashes of lightning, Emerson felt a growing disappointment as he realized that the hurricane was going to bypass Key West.

"That's the worst of the storm," Sam offered as he huddled as close as possible to the wall and the slight coverage from the rain that the small overhang provided. "And it looks like it's going to stay out there."

"Yes, it does," Emerson lamented. "They told me at the front desk that most of the reporters left early this morning when the news broke that Charley may come ashore in the Tampa area. No big story for me here."

Ignoring his last comment, Sam noted, "You never know about those hurricanes. They can turn on you at the last minute. It may be headed for Tampa now, but you just don't know for sure."

Sam swung his head around and suddenly stopped as he stared at a solitary boat passing the Pier House. "Would you look at that idiot! This isn't the time to be out in a boat!"

Emerson looked to where Sam was staring and also saw the Hatteras moving slowly, but steadily through the choppy waters.

"Must be an emergency," Emerson thought aloud.

A few minutes later, they watched the boat as it motored past Mallory Square and approached the Hilton Dock.

"Looks like he may be pulling in to tie-up," Sam suggested.

"Let's go talk with them. It'll give me a chance to follow up on that flooding down at Greene and Front," Emerson said as he began to turn and head toward the elevator.

"When we're done, I'll drive you around Key West and see if there's anything else that grabs your attention for a story. With this wind, we should have plenty of downed branches, trees and power lines," Sam said as he followed Emerson.

The White Van
Municipal Parking Lot

≺᠍

The parking lot was deserted except for the solitary white van, which was being approached by a man who was tightly holding onto the hood of his yellow slicker to protect himself from the driving rain. He stepped to the lee side of the van and produced a key from his slicker's pocket. Inserting it into the passenger's door lock, he turned the key quickly and unlocked the door.

Harley jumped into the van, closing the door behind him and scooted over to the driver's seat. He inserted the key in the ignition and sat back to take a deep breath in the dry comfort of the van.

Spotting a towel on the floor, he wiped his wet face and dried his wooly beard as best as he could. Somewhat more comfortable, Harley opened his jacket and reached under his oversized tee shirt and into his bib overalls to extract his concealed handgun. He was wearing a Texas Strong Side, a leather-belted holster with attached pockets on the opposite side for two magazines. He carefully checked over the Beretta 8-40 Cougar Inox, ejecting the magazine and reinserting it. He hefted the gun for a moment and smiled confidently to himself as he reholstered it under his shirt.

Nothing like being prepared, he thought to himself. He had learned a long time ago not to trust any of the drug dealers that he dealt with. You never knew when a deal would go bad.

Pumping the accelerator, he reached for the ignition key and turned it. The starter turned over, but didn't fire. He had to try two more times before the van started. Turning on the windshield wipers, he watched as they struggled in vain to clear the rain from the windshield. He put the van in gear and eased out of the parking lot. Within seconds, he was slowly driving down Caroline, with the rain beating a tattoo on the van's metal roof, and toward Whitehead Street.

After turning right onto Whitehead, he turned left onto Greene Street and followed with another left onto Front Street. He pulled under the covered portico of the Hilton, which was across the street from Mel Fisher's, and waited for the signal to drive across the street and to back up the ramp at Fisher's.

Pauley paced nervously between the empty glass display counters in the Treasure Sales store, pausing anxiously to open the door and peer outside to see if the white van had pulled into its prearranged parking spot at the Hilton. Even though he finally saw the van park across the street, he was still on edge.

"You all right tonight?"

Pauley's heart jumped out of his chest as he was startled by the other guard's voice.

"Yeah. Yeah. I'm okay, Tommy," he answered unconvincingly.

"You've been like popcorn on a hot skillet, the way you've been jumping around here tonight," the guard said as he sat in a nearby chair and rubbed his balding head. "It's the hurricane threat, isn't it?"

Pauley thought quickly. "Yeah, that's it. You know, I've never been in weather like this," he answered.

"Nothing to worry about. No hurricanes hit Key West anymore."

Before he could respond, Pauley heard the motorcycle pull to a stop on the ramp outside of the door and shut off its engine.

"Now, who in the hell would be out on a motorcycle in weather like this?" the other guard asked as he rose to his feet and walked by Pauley. He opened the door and found himself staring into the dripping wet face of Asad. He was so surprised that he took a step back and right into the descending butt of Pauley's handgun. It struck him in the temple and he dropped to the floor.

"It's about time," a sweating Pauley said as he bent over to pull the guard away from the doorway.

"The weather is bad," Asad said with an evil gleam in his eye as he helped drag away the guard.

"Semtex ready to go?"

Asad stopped and looked at his watch. "About five minutes from now."

"I'll give the signal," Pauley offered. "You can tie him up here and gag and blindfold him."

Asad bent to his task with the rope and material that Pauley had produced from a small bag, which he had hidden under the counter. Pauley opened the door and stepped onto the cement ramp and waved to Harley.

As Harley turned the van lights on, he was startled when the passenger door swung open unexpectedly. His right hand started for his hidden gun, but relaxed when he recognized the soaking wet J.B.

"Whew! This is some blow that we're having!" J.B. said as the van started out and he shook some of the water from his slicker.

"Will we still be able to use the boat in this weather?" Harley asked curiously.

"Shouldn't be a problem. I actually saw a hint of clearing sky to the southwest," J.B. responded as the van stopped and began to back up the ramp.

The van slowly crept up the ramp and under the covered overhang. Pauley motioned for it to stop and J.B. and Harley ran to the rear where Pauley was already opening the back to unload the equipment that had been purchased over the last few days.

"The boat's all set?" Pauley asked as the three of them eased an acetylene torch with its oxygen cylinder and acetylene cylinder on wheels down a wooden ramp, which they pulled out of the rear of the van.

"No problems!" J.B. said confidently. "It's a piece of cake when you know what you're doing."

Asad joined them and heard J.B.'s response.

"Anyone see you take the boat?" Asad asked urgently.

"In weather like this? No one in their right mind would be out," he replied as the four of them looked at each other in reaction to his comment. They all laughed.

"The only ones out in weather like this are the ones who're going to get rich!" Pauley grinned.

"That's for damn sure," J.B. responded greedily.

A ringing phone inside the building interrupted their conversation.

"Who'd be calling now?" Asad asked with concern.

"Got me. I'll find out!" Pauley ran inside while the others continued unloading the rest of the cutting tools and the hand trucks.

A few minutes passed and the three had entered the building when Pauley rejoined them. "It was Kim Fisher. He's the president of this place. Wanted to be sure that we were doing okay here in the storm."

"What did you tell him?" Harley asked as he wiped sweat from his brow.

"Told him that everything here was under control," Pauley said as he took one last look through the door and paused. "Oh! Oh!"

The three swung around towards Pauley. Asad quickly filled his hand with a Kimber .45. "What is it? Police?"

"What would you guys do without me?" Pauley started. "You forgot to put the signs on the van!" Pauley stepped outside and opened the driver's door. From behind the front seat, he picked up the two large magnetic signs that read Mel Fisher's Treasure Sales. He attached them to both sides of the van, then scurried back to the building. "You want people snooping around? Good thing that I'm running this heist!"

"Yes. It is a good thing that you are," Asad said with an air of mystery.

"What about that?" Harley asked as he pointed.

All eyes followed to where Harley was pointing. It was a security camera. They looked around the room and saw four more cameras. All had their red recording lights on.

"This is crap!" J.B. yelled as he looked directly into the closest camera.

"Not to worry, boys," Pauley started. "There's no film in the recorders. I took them out when the other guard went on break. You probably didn't notice, but there were cameras on the outside, too."

Asad's relief was physically visible. "That's one of the benefits about having someone on the inside, isn't it?"

"Yes it is, Al," Pauley replied with a bit of cockiness.

Just then they heard an explosion in the distance and the lights flickered, then went out.

"Out of my way!" Pauley yelled as he raced toward the rear of the salesroom. He opened a hidden panel and pulled down a lever. "That kills the generator and the main alarm system to the police station," he said as he gulped down deep breaths of air. "I'm not used to this running crap!"

The four of them reached up to the hats that they had previously placed on their heads, and switched on the lights. The beams provided erie shafts of light in the store's black abyss. They also switched on portable auxiliary lights, which they planned on leaving at strategic points along their route in the building so that their evening's work could be completed safely.

The phone began to ring again.

"Now what?" Pauley asked as he quickly walked around the counter and to the ringing phone. "Yes?" he answered.

The other three waited anxiously as a voice on the other end threw out several questions.

"I don't know. The lights cut out and the backup generator didn't start. I've got an electrician on the way to figure it out. It may take him a while to drive over here, but I'd expect that we get the generator fired up shortly and reestablish our power and the alarm system. I can call you back when we're up."

Pauley paused as the voice on the other end continued talking.

"Okay, if that's what you would like to do. I'm sure that Mr. Fisher would appreciate your extra viligence. Thank you."

Pauley hung up the phone and turned to the other three. The light from the three other hats centered on Pauley's face, which had turned even chalkier looking after the phone conversation.

"Well?" Asad asked impatiently.

"It was the police. They're concerned that our alarm is out."

"Are they coming here, now?" J.B. asked with consternation as he began to look around the darkness.

"No, but they're going to call every fifteen minutes to be sure that there are no problems here. And they confirmed that the vault alarm is still working."

"Vault alarm?" Asad asked incredulously.

"I didn't mention it to you before because it's no big deal. It runs on a battery back-up independent of everything else here. But I know how to get around it."

"I hope you know what in the hell you're doing," Harley said. "This is worth a lot to all of us."

"Don't sweat it!" Pauley replied. "Let's get downstairs."

They wheeled the hand trucks and the torch down a ramp to the basement. As they went, they placed the auxiliary lights at strategic points to light their return trips since they would be pushing loaded hand trucks to the van.

Inserting three keys into a massive steel door, Pauley unlocked it and swung it open on its well-oiled hinges. "There she is boys!" Pauley said as they shined their lights on the massive vault.

"I hope you know what you're doing!" J.B. said nervously.

"I've done this a few times in the past, boys," Pauley said with an evil grin as they approached the vault. "See there," he pointed to two magnets that were touching across the closed doors. "If you pull them apart, it sets off the backup alarm at the police station."

The group looked at the magnets on the doors. From one, a wire was attached with the other end disappearing into the wall.

"Just cut that wire," J.B. suggested as he pointed to the wire.

"And set off the alarm? Is that what you want to do, J.B.?" Pauley asked with frustration.

"Then, how are you going to get in there without pulling them apart?" J.B. asked.

"I'm going to cut the bolts holding the magnets in place."

"Yeah, and then they're going to fall and hit the ground—and the alarm goes off," J.B. agitated.

"Not really. First, we're going to tape these two magnets together." Pauley produced a roll of duct tape and secured the two magnets together. Then, he pulled out four pairs of welder goggles. "You all better put these goggles on," he cautioned as he slipped on his goggles.

"It's not a smart thing to stare into this light without eye protection. You can be momentarily blinded by the arc light," he warned. Before he could ignite the cutting torch, the phone started to ring. Pauley swore and then said, "I forgot about the fifteen minute calls." He slipped the goggles to the top of his head and reached for the portable phone. "Yes?" he answered.

After a pause, Pauley said, "Everything is fine here. You really don't have to call. We're locked down good here." A pause followed as he listened to the caller. "Okay then. I'll talk to you in another fifteen minutes." Pauley set down the portable phone. "Goggles on, gentlemen."

He pulled on a pair of protective welder's gloves, fussed with his equipment and ignited the cutting torch. He turned to the magnets and began to cut the bolts holding the magnets in place.

J.B. thought the magnets were beginning to dangle dangerously. If they hit the floor, he was concerned that the alarm could be set off by the impact and the jarring of the two magnets would separate the contacts even though they were taped together.

Pauley switched off the cutting torch and removed his goggles. The magnets were on the verge of dropping. Pauley's gloved hands carefully grasped the magnets and pulled them loose from the remnants of the bolts. "Nothing to it, boys," he said proudly as he carefully laid the two attached magnets on the floor to the left of the vault.

"Now for the big door." The ringing portable phone interrupted the beginning of his next phase. He quickly answered the phone and assured the police that all was well. He was able to talk them into adjusting the calls to every thirty minutes.

Sliding his goggles back on, he bent to pick up the cutting torch and ignited it. The bright light filled the room as it began cutting through the vault's steel doors. It was a time-consuming process.

After fifteen minutes, Asad left to go upstairs to the sales area. He slipped his goggles to the top of his head as he walked into the sales room. He unlocked the door and stepped out into the wet evening's air and breathed deeply. He thought how well everything was going to plan as his eyes scanned Front Street and the Hilton for any potential problems. He leaned against the stone building's wall and relaxed momentarily before returning to the action in the basement.

When he entered the room containing the vault, he saw that the doors had been cut open and the other three were inside the vault. An atmosphere of excitement and greed permeated the vault as Asad joined them and began stuffing emeralds into one of the canvas bags that had been brought down on the hand carts.

"Fill them up, boys," Pauley urged with unbridled glee although the encouragement wasn't necessary.

J.B. was happily whistling to himself as he thought ahead to the street value of the stolen gems and treasure.

"I've got a full load," Harley said as he started to wheel his hand truck out of the vault and to the truck.

"Oh no, you don't," Pauley warned. "You think we're stupid. You'd wheel that up, jump in the truck, and be off with yourself, leaving us here to fend for ourselves."

"I wouldn't do that. The thought didn't even cross my mind," Harley protested with a sly grin.

"Listen, I've been around the block, pal! We all stick together now."

Harley, frustrated that they had misread his intent, looked at each of the three. Their faces were frozen with hard-looking stares. "No problem for me. Let's get the others loaded then." Harley rejoined them in filling more bags and loading up the other three hand trucks.

Once they finished loading the hand carts, they followed each other as they pushed them up the ramp to the first floor. The loads were so heavy that two of the thieves had to push a single cart to the first level. Once the first two carts were there, they returned to the basement and pushed the remaining two carts to the first level.

Pauley cautiously opened the sales room door and stepped outside onto the ramp. He looked around to make sure that no one was around, and held the door wide open so that the other three could push their hand trucks to the rear of the van. Harley opened the van's rear doors and he and J.B. began throwing bags into its rear while Asad returned to the doorway and pushed Pauley's hand truck to the van.

The portable phone in Pauley's hand rang as his eyes once again scanned the area for any potential onlookers. He reentered the building where it was quieter and answered the phone. "A bit late this time, aren't you?" Pauley teased as he looked at his watch and saw that forty-five minutes had elapsed since the last call.

He listened to the caller and then responded, "I don't know what's keeping that electrician. Maybe the streets are too badly flooded."

The other caller continued and then Pauley suggested, "I'll give the electrician a call. You know, I bet it's getting real hectic for you guys. Why don't I just check in with you every hour so that you don't have to check on me. Remember that we still have the back up battery-powered alarm working."

They reached an agreement and Pauley pocketed the portable phone.

"Everything okay?" Asad asked solemnly.

"Leave it to me. I've got everything under control." Pauley looked at the others and said, "Let's go back downstairs for another load."

They returned to the basement vault and loaded up again with Pauley pointing out which items to load. He was careful to pick the items that were the most valuable.

They returned to the first floor, and while the others loaded the van, Pauley looked at the time and made another call to the police as they had previously agreed. The team of thieves returned to the vault for the final load and transported the other guard to the basement with them where they left the blindfolded guard trussed in a chair.

As they left the vault with their final load they also toted their cutting equipment and picked up the lights that they had stationed along their busy path. All of the equipment and lights were loaded in the van.

As Pauley began to pulling the door to the Treasure Sales business closed behind him, Asad appeared next to him.

"I need to go back inside for a moment," Asad said with a menacing look.

"Why?" Pauley asked.

"Trust me. I just need one minute."

Pauley opened the door and Asad stepped inside, pulling a knife as he entered. Pauley thought for a moment and realized what Asad had in mind. Bursting into the room and racing to the basement, Pauley was too late. Asad was standing over Tommy's body, which was slumped lifelessly in the chair. Asad turned to stare grimly at Pauley as he wiped the blood off of his blade on Tommy's shirt.

"Why did you have to do that?"

"He might have talked. We need every advantage that we can get," Asad said grimly.

Pauley knew that he was right, but he had liked Tommy. Asad and Pauley left the building and Pauley locked the door. He went over to the loaded van and the waiting accomplices.

The rain was abating as Pauley looked across the street to the lane next to the Hilton, which they would drive down to get to the waiting getaway boat. His eyes were drawn back to the portico in front of the Hilton where a vehicle was parked. It hadn't been there the last time they had delivered a load. The hairs on the back of Pauley's neck warned him of eminent danger.

Just then, they heard an explosion in the distance.

In Front of Mel Fisher's Museum
Greene and Front Streets
∽

It had been a frustrating evening for Emerson and Sam. When they left the hotel, they found that a tree had blown over and crushed Sam's jeep in the parking lot. It was too heavy to move, so they decided to walk in the rain.

When they started down Whitehead, they were blocked by fallen electrical lines that were sparking dangerously.

"I wouldn't take a chance of going through there," Sam warned. "We can circle around and go over to Duval and then down Greene Street."

"Okay by me," Emerson said as he adjusted his hood and slipped his covered notepad inside his slicker.

They retraced their steps to the La Concha and walked down Duval Street to Greene and turned left. As they began to walk down Greene, Sam pointed to Sloppy Joe's Bar at the corner of Duval and Greene. "That's another of my favorite places down here," Sam said. "That's where they have Put-in-Bay Day every year. A whole bunch of your islanders visit this little island to escape that winter up there."

"From what I understand of those wintry days on Put-in-Bay, who'd blame them for slipping away to another island paradise?" Emerson asked as raindrops hit his face.

Within a few steps they began to pass the warm, inviting light and music coming from Captain Tony's Saloon on Greene, Sam stopped walking. "I'm drenched. Let's stop for a shot."

"Drenched? How can you be drenched? We just started walking!" Emerson asked with mild surprise.

"Just a bit thirsty, you know what I mean?" Sam smiled meekly. "Just a quick one. It's going to be a long night."

Sam didn't realize how prophetic his comment really was.

"Oh, all right."

The two entered the bar and ordered their drinks. Halfway through the drinks, the lights went out and the music died.

The handful of customers in the bar muttered among themselves about the sudden loss in power. The light from outside the open doorways provided enough light for everyone to see.

The bartender yelled, "I can still pour shots and we've got bottled beer, so none of you leave. Refills?" he asked as he looked at Emerson and Sam who were seated at the bar.

"Yes!" Sam replied eagerly.

"Not for me!" Emerson answered. "Power go out here often?"

"Just depends on how bad of a storm we get hit with. It doesn't usually take them too long to get the power back on," the bartender said as he poured another shot for Sam.

Turning to Emerson, Sam explained, "You know, this was the original Sloppy Joe's where Hemingway hung out. He'd come over here every day at 3:30 after he had written most of the day. This is one of my favorite places to drink when I'm in town."

"Now, why don't I find that surprising?" Emerson asked his roguish friend as he looked at the few hundred bras hanging from the ceiling.

Seeing where Emerson was looking, Sam said unconvincingly, "Now those have nothing to do with me coming here nor do their donors. I come for the conversation."

"Right!" Emerson grinned at his friend.

"I always make it a practice to drink only on days ending with the letter 'Y'," Sam chuckled as he raised his filled shot glass in a salute to Emerson and quickly threw it down. He smiled as it warmed him.

"I'm ready for anything now! Thanks Ray!" he called to the bartender who was carrying a roll of duct tape.

Seeing the quizzical look on Sam's face, the bartender explained, "I've got to duct tape my cats to the ceiling. That's to keep them from blowing away!"

"That would be more interesting than what you already have dangling from the ceiling!" Emerson teased.

"I'm not sure I agree with that comment, E!" Sam rebutted.

Leaving the dry sanctuary of Captain Tony's, they walked down to the intersection of Greene and Whitehead where they observed the rising floodwaters at this low intersection. Turning right onto Whitehead, they made their way down to the intersection with Front Street and then cut over to Mallory Square.

"Quite different now!" Emerson observed as he looked around the deserted celebration area.

"As you would expect," Sam added.

They walked along the square and towards the Hilton. As they rounded the Hilton's annex, they saw a large boat tied to the dock behind the Hilton's main building. The craft was straining at its lines.

"That's the boat we saw from the rooftop. Now, what idiot would have left his boat out in weather like this?" Sam wondered aloud.

It was the only craft in sight. The others had been moved to safer dockages.

"It takes all kinds."

"Let's make sure that she's secure," the ever-helpful Sam suggested as they neared the solitary boat. They quickly checked its lines and ensured that the boat was secure.

"Maybe he was caught offshore and made a run for here," Emerson suggested.

"I don't know. I just don't know. Something doesn't smell right about this," Sam said as he looked around the deserted area and they walked toward Front Street and the front of the Hilton.

"Rain stopped," Sam said as he threw back the hood on his yellow slicker and was quickly followed by Emerson.

"You think the worst is over?" Emerson asked.

"Maybe."

As they emerged from the side of the building and onto Front Street, Emerson pointed to the water flooding the intersection at Greene and Front Street. "It's much higher now."

"What in the hell?" Sam paused and then grabbed Emerson's arm. "Step back here."

"What's wrong?" Emerson asked as he stepped with Sam into the limited concealment offered by the Hilton's landscaped front entrance.

"Just what do you think those guys are doing?" Sam asked as they saw the men across the street loading bags inside a white van and pushing wheeled oxygen and acetylene tanks into the van.

"The sign on the side of the van says it's one of Fisher's vans," Emerson noted as he scanned the van's signage. With growing suspicion, he muttered, "But why would security guards need cutting torches? See something else unusual?"

"Yeah. Security guys with only one guy in uniform."

"That's a bit strange, wouldn't you agree?"

"Definitely."

They watched as the men closed the doors to the van and grouped at the rear of the van as the uniformed guard closed and locked the door to Mel Fisher's Treasure Sales after an Arabic-looking man emerged from the building.

"What do you want to do?" Emerson asked.

"Let's go talk to them."

"Just what I was going to suggest."

They walked out of their semi-concealed area and past the parked black car under the portico. They were oblivious to the two people sitting quietly in the car. As they crossed the street, they heard an explosion.

"What was that?" Emerson asked.

"Got me," was Sam's response.

On the ramp, Pauley was staring intently at Asad. "What did you do?"

"What do you mean?" Asad glared angrily at the condescending tone in Pauley's voice.

"The explosion. We agreed to only blowing up the electrical power station. What did you do?" Pauley demanded.

"Just a little insurance for us," Asad grinned cryptically.

"Answer me!" Pauley shot back.

"There's nothing like hitting them where they don't expect it. I planted two timed explosives at the hospital. The second should . . . "

He didn't get a chance to finish his explanation as a second explosion sounded in the distance.

"That was it," Asad grinned.

"I should kill you right now," Pauley stormed as he reached for his holstered handgun. Before he could withdraw it, Harley interrupted.

"We got company!" Harley said pointing to the two figures walking across the street and starting up the ramp. Harley slipped behind the side of the van as the other three walked over to the Front Street side of the van.

"Hi there! We're from the *Washington Post*. We're working on a story about the hurricane down here," Emerson said as they boldly approached the van and the three men. Sam noticed that one of the men was missing.

"Shit! Reporters!" Pauley muttered quietly as he recognized Emerson from his visit to the Treasure Sales.

"Oh, hi. I talked with you the other day when I was in. Do you remember?" Emerson asked as he recognized Pauley.

"Yeah, I remember," Pauley replied coldly.

"We noticed that you were loading bags from the store and wondered if you were taking the treasure somewhere for safekeeping."

Before Pauley could respond, Asad flashed his gun from under his shirt and pointed it at the two new arrivals. "Yes, we are taking it somewhere for safekeeping and you can help."

Seeing the gun in Asad's hand began to anger Pauley, but then he warmed to the idea. Pauley said, "Yeah. We could use some help unloading the van."

"Wrong approach," Emerson whispered to Sam.

"I'll say," Sam agreed. "Distract them and I'll go for help."

"Since we're going to be helping, mind if I look inside?" Not waiting for an answer, Emerson slid open the van's side door and reached inside for one of the bags.

The three thieves' attention was focused on Emerson and they raced to restrain him. As they did, Sam whirled around and started to run. He took one step. One step into a brick wall. He stumbled backward and onto the ground. He found himself looking into the barrel of Harley's Beretta.

"Well, what a surprise! How you doing, Harley?" Sam asked from his prone position on the ramp.

"I'd say better than you at the moment," Harley responded as he held the pistol on Sam.

"You know him?" Pauley asked Harley.

"Yeah. He's worked with DEA. I've sold him information from time to time and he's tried to bust me, but could never quite do it, could you Sam?" Harley asked in triumph. "Looks like you're the one who got busted." Harley's deep laughter filled the air as he chuckled at Sam's predicament.

"I'm not so sure about that," Sam winced in pain from a bruise to his ribs caused by his fall. He rose to his feet.

"Whatever!" Harley retorted with a mocking look.

"Let's get moving," Pauley said as he pointed his drawn revolver at Emerson. "Harley, you drive and we'll walk behind it with these guys. And don't get ideas about driving off and leaving us. Al, tell him why."

Asad smiled wickedly as he pulled a remote detonator from his pocket. "You drive off and I explode the semtex packed underneath the van. It's that simple. Understand?"

Harley nodded his head and stepped into the driver's seat. "J.B., you want to ride with me?"

A wide-eyed J.B. replied, "No, I'll just walk." For once in his life, he made the right decision.

"A good choice," Asad laughed.

The van eased down the ramp and pulled onto Front Street with the others following. Before it had gone five feet, two shots rang out. The first shot penetrated the windshield, narrowly missing Harley's head. Harley brought the van to an abrupt stop and jumped out of the van. The second shot was intended for Pauley, but missed him and hit Sam in the shoulder. Blood flowed freely from the wound as Sam and the others ran behind the van for what protection it offered.

Asad slowly poked his head from around the van and toward the Hilton's portico where it appeared that the shots had originated. A bullet struck the side of the van uncomfortably close to Asad's head. He recoiled quickly in reaction to the near miss.

"Who in the hell is that?" Pauley asked as he saw Emerson tending to Sam's wound as best as he could.

"Don't know. I couldn't see them," Asad worried.

"Okay, let's take inventory. Three of us are armed with handguns. Anybody have anything else?" Pauley asked rapidly.

The others responded negatively.

"J.B., you carrying?"

"Nope. Nobody said anything about expecting trouble on this," J.B. responded nervously.

"I could unpack the semtex and we might be able to use it someway," Asad suggested as he thought about the explosives under the van. "There are the shotgun and rifles in the back, but they're underneath the treasure. We piled the treasure on top of them."

"Let's see what they want," Pauley suggested.

Before he could ask, a yell came from beneath the portico. "Hey Pauley. You up to no good again?"

Pauley leaned against the van in surprise as he recognized the voice and anger began to well up in him. His blood pressure also began to rocket.

Asad looked at Pauley. "Saul, they're calling you? Your name is Pauley?"

"Yeah, yeah. It's Pauley. It's a long story. I'll tell you about it sometime," Pauley edged past Asad to the rear of the van and yelled, "What brings your sorry ass down here, Marioda?" Pauley was gripping his pistol tightly as he thought about his opportunity to avenge his wife's death, He completely forgot about the treasure heist as he focused on his adversary.

"You do! And I owe you one big time for me having to come down here in friggin' weather like this. Could I come down when it's nice? No, I have to come down when the weather is bad so I can't enjoy the beach! Bet you don't go to the beach that much, Pauley, with that sensitive skin of yours. You're probably keeping all the stores down here in business with you buying up all that sunscreen!" Marioda gloated.

"There's nothing saying that you can't just turn around and go back home," Pauley shouted, as his mind raced for ways in which to draw the two gunmen into the open. He knew they were here to fulfill the contract on him.

"Can't do that, Pauley."

"Is that your shadow, Ricci, with you?" Pauley called.

"Hi Pauley!" Ricci yelled.

"So what do you guys want? You're interrupting our transaction!" Pauley said.

"You making a withdrawal?" Marioda responded with glee. He knew he had them trapped. Without allowing them to respond, he continued, "Pauley, your time is up. We're here for you."

"Joey sent you, huh?"

"Yeah. He wanted us to deliver some flowers to you."

"Because he loves me so much?" Pauley yelled sarcastically.

"No, they're for your funeral. He wanted these delivered to you in person. So, here we are!"

Pauley was sweating even though he wasn't warm. Another hour and they would have been out of there without bumping into these guys.

"What about the rest of us?" Asad asked.

"We're just here for Pauley. We don't care about the rest of you or what you're doing. We've got an assignment and we're going to kill Pauley."

Asad glanced seriously at Pauley.

"We might be able to take these boys out," Pauley suggested with a serious look on his face.

"And how do you propose we do that with what little armament we have?" Asad questioned.

"We'll rush them," Pauley said as he tried to step back into his leadership role.

"They've got position on us. We wouldn't make it without two or three of us getting killed," Asad said as he quickly assessed the situation. "I'm not ready to be one of those two or three."

"We can't stand here behind the van all night. If they don't kill us, we'll be caught when people start returning. We don't have a choice."

"I don't know about that, we might have a choice," Asad replied ominously.

Asad looked at Harley and J.B.

"Harley, you go around the front of the van and my friend here, Pauley, and I will go around the rear. Don't move until I tell you to. And Pauley, since it's your friends out there, you go around the van first."

"Guess who'll be target number one!"

"Like you said, we don't have a choice," Asad said mysteriously.

Pauley and Asad positioned themselves behind the rear of the van. Pauley was peering around the corner when he felt cold steel against the back of his head. "Drop it," Asad ordered.

"What? What do you mean, drop it?"

"Do what I said, and do it now."

Reluctantly, Pauley dropped his handgun.

"Why should the rest of us risk our lives when they're just after you?"

Pauley unleashed a series of expletives at Asad. Betrayed, he thought to himself. He hadn't expected that from his partner.

Asad yelled around the corner of the van's rear, "Hold your fire. We're coming out!"

Holding the gun tightly against Pauley's head, Asad stepped from the back of the van with Pauley in front of him. "I want to understand one thing clearly. Once you're finished with Pauley, you leave and don't bother the rest of us, right?"

"Right. Our thing is with Pauley," Marioda yelled.

"Okay. Here he is." Asad said as he pushed Pauley away from himself and into the open. As he did, he pulled the trigger, sending with a lethal shot to the back of Pauley's head.

Pauley's eyes widened in fear and his mouth gaped open as he felt himself propelled forward. He knew that he would never realize his dream of retiring with the wealth from this heist. As the bullet from Asad's gun exploded in his head, he felt his body pummeled by a bevy of shots from Marioda and Ricci who wanted to be absolutely sure that he was dead. As he fell, the gold chain with the glass enclosing the Shasta daisy and a few locks of his wife's hair fell from his hand, shattering as it hit the pavement. Within minutes, the broken pieces were washed down a nearby storm sewer.

Asad, who had stepped back behind the van, was grinning as he watched J.B. and Harley rush over to view Pauley's dead body. They were joined by Marioda and Ricci. Ricci kicked Pauley's body. "He's finished."

Marioda's stern face changed into a broad smile as he looked down on Pauley. He spat on him. "That's from Joey, you turncoat."

Marioda and Ricci were still staring at Pauley's body when Asad expertly placed two shots in each of them, killing them instantly. Their bodies fell upon Pauley's body.

Harley and J.B. stared in shock at Asad. Harley wrestled whether he should take a shot at Asad. He had been holding his gun loosely at his side and quickly calculated that Asad could shoot him before he could even raise his gun.

"What was that all about?" Harley asked uneasily.

"Can't leave any witnesses. What if they get back to this Joey guy and read in the paper about the heist here. Don't you think they would come after us? Don't forget that they got a good look at the three of us. I did it to protect us." Asad said quickly as he tried to calm their uneasiness.

J.B. spoke first. "Yeah, I understand," he said nervously. "You did it to protect us. Thanks, Al. I always knew that you were the real brains here. Saul or Pauley, whatever his name was, really didn't get it, did he?"

Asad smiled. "He got it in a way he didn't expect from me." Asad stared hard at Harley. "And what about you?"

"I'm in," he said quickly and with feigned submission. Harley knew that he'd have to watch his back after seeing that Asad couldn't be trusted. "You didn't have any choice."

"No, I didn't," Asad agreed solemnly.

Asad was quite pleased with himself as he rounded the van. His pleasure didn't last long. He found himself staring into the barrel of Pauley's pistol, which was now in the hands of a very unsteady Sam.

"Hold it right there, partner!" Sam said from his sitting position on the street. He said it as well as he could despite his loss of blood. When Emerson had carefully grabbed the dropped weapon, they had had a whispered argument as to which of them should bring Pauley's discarded pistol to bear on the others. Because of his ex-SEAL background, Emerson reluctantly agreed that Sam should confront Asad.

"Let's see if I can unscramble this messy egg that we've got here," Sam said.

Asad realized that he was now holding his handgun loosely at his side and if he started to bring it up, Sam would fire before he could. "Now what?" he asked with a menacing tone.

"Drop it," Sam ordered.

Behind Sam, another voice spoke calmly. "You drop it, Sam."

Sam kept his gaze on Asad as Emerson turned to discover the source of the voice. It was Harley. And he was pointing his Beretta at Emerson, but had his eyes focused on Sam and his gun.

"Drop it, Sam, or I take out your newspaper buddy. It's your choice. You get Al, and I get your pal. Then we can see whichever one of us will survive the second shot."

Weighing the odds, Emerson made a quick decision. "Better do as they say, Sam. It was worth a try," he said gloomily.

Sam dropped the gun.

"Kick it over here," Asad commanded Emerson who stood and kicked the gun to Asad. "That's more like it. We don't have time for this kind of stuff." Asad picked up Pauley's gun and stuck it in his belt as he walked over to Sam and kicked him sharply in the side with such force that it broke two of his ribs. Sam moaned and rolled over to lie on the road. Standing over Sam, Asad pointed his gun at Sam's head. "I know how to take care of people like you."

Emerson looked around as he desperately tried to think what he could do. He knew that Harley's gun was trained on him. He decided to risk a shot from Harley and tackle

Asad. With a burst of energy, Emerson launched his body at Asad.

As he hurtled through the air at Asad, Emerson heard Harley's gun fire, but the bullet missed him. Emerson's body collided with Asad's, knocking Asad to the road. Ignoring Harley, Emerson grappled with Asad and struggled for control of Asad's pistol. The scuffle was short-lived as Emerson felt Harley's gun barrel against the back of his head.

"You've got two choices," Harley's deep voice boomed. "Either stop or I'll pull the trigger. Make your choice, now!"

Realizing the futility of any additional effort, Emerson ceased fighting and stood to his feet. He was followed by Asad, who approached Emerson from the rear and drove a fist into Emerson's kidney. "That was a stupid thing to do!" Asad said as Emerson bent over in pain.

"And now for your friend," Asad said as he began to walk toward Sam, who had not involved himself in the fight since Harley had him covered.

Before Asad could pull the trigger, Harley interrupted, "Let me do that. I owe him for a few times that he's stiffed me over the years."

Asad hesitated as he wrestled with allowing Harley the privilege of taking Sam out. "Okay, then. He's yours." Turning to Emerson, Asad ordered him with his pointed gun, "You can come with me and help me drag those three bodies into the landscaping."

Emerson assessed the situation again and was thinking about making a run at Harley. He was tensing his muscles when Sam murmured, "Don't try it! You don't have a chance. Do what they want you to. I'm not worried."

"But Sam," Emerson began.

Sam interrupted. "Do what they say. I want it that way. Now get out of here before they kill you, too."

Emerson squeezed his friend's good shoulder. He ignored Sam's advice and began to charge Asad for a second time. He didn't get far as he felt himself falling. Sam had stuck out his leg and tripped him.

Asad was laughing sinisterly. "Now that isn't something that I've seen before. The friend tries to save my life—or is it the life of his friend?"

Emerson rose to his feet and looked at Sam. "Now why in the world did you do that?"

"E, you're better at words than you are at fighting. It's too dangerous for you," Sam winced in pain.

"Come on, American cowboy," Asad sneered at Emerson and pointed his gun to where the bodies lay. They walked to the other side of the van and into the street. J.B. went with them to help.

Emerson bent over to grab one of Pauley's arms while J.B. grabbed the other. Asad supervised.

Looking under the van, Emerson saw Harley's feet walk over to Sam and then saw Harley drop to his knees on the ground. Emerson and Asad could see Sam's face since his head was visible on the ground behind the van. They saw as he looked up at Harley and saw his head jerk when Harley pulled the trigger. He couldn't mask his look of surprise, and then, his eyes stared blankly into the sky. His head rolled to the other side and he lay still.

Emerson held back tears at the sight of his friend's death and stared at Asad. He muttered an oath of vengeance under his breath.

"I know what you are thinking, and I'll be waiting for you to try it," Asad smirked at Emerson. "Now, both of you, pull these bodies into the shrubs."

They bent to their task and deposited the bodies in the shrubs in front of the Hilton's portico. As they stood to return to the van, Harley appeared. "I dragged Sam's body off into the landscaping on the other side," he said proudly as he looked closely at Emerson.

Emerson targeted him for retribution also. He would bide his time and carefully plot his revenge.

"Good," Asad said as he noticed the hard look Emerson gave to Harley. "Get back to the van and follow us to the boat."

Harley returned to the van and started the engine. Putting it in gear, he followed the other three, led by J.B. down the drive next to the Hilton, and out to the dock. Emerson walked in front of Asad, who kept his gun pointed at him the entire time.

"We will need to load this as fast as we can. With the rain stopped, people are going to be coming out to check the damage. We don't need anyone seeing us load this boat," J.B. yelled from the Hatteras Sportfisherman as it rocked in the choppy water. He raced ahead to make sure that it was secure and had found everything to be in order.

"And the police will be expecting a call from Pauley. That's one call that they won't receive. Then they'll be out here checking around." J.B. called.

"We don't have any time to waste," Asad said sternly.

The van slowed to a halt next to the boat where Asad and Emerson waited. They hastily formed a line from the van to the boat, and transferred the bags to the boat.

Emerson thought several times about trying to make a break for it, or throwing the bags into the water, but decided there was nothing to gain. He'd bide his time until he could think clearly. The last fifteen minutes had been filled with shock, and his mind was clouded with the brutality of it all. He was going to miss his roguish friend.

It didn't take long for them to finish the transfer of the bags. Then Asad directed Harley and Emerson to empty the van and convey its contents to the boat. He took the two signs off the van's sides and threw them on board. He then went back to the van and crawled underneath and retrieved the semtex.

"Never know when you might need this," he explained as Harley started the van's engine and positioned it toward the small harbor. Asad then directed Harley to take a cinder block out of the van and place it on the accelerator. Harley threw the van in gear as he jumped it and rolled hard on the concrete pier deck as the van careened over the edge and slowly sank beneath the water.

Returning to the Hatteras, Harley was rubbing his shoulder. "That should slow down anyone trying to identify us," he grinned.

"I'm hoping that they start looking for us either in town or driving out of town. I don't think anyone would think we've escaped by water in seas like this," Asad beamed confidently as they boarded the Hatteras.

J.B. had climbed up to the flybridge and started the 820-horsepower diesels. The rumbling engines were a comfort to all three of the thieves.

Harley cast off the bowline, and under the watchful eye of Asad, Emerson cast off the stern line. The Hatterras moved steadily away from its berth as J.B. slowly pushed the throttle forward, and the Hatteras headed toward the northwest channel and rough seas.

Asad had Harley and Emerson store as many bags as they could fit in the deck bait well and the large fish box at the stern. The remaining bags were carried into the salon and stacked in one corner.

Seeing Asad and Emerson drop into the salon's seats, Harley asked, "Drinks? I need something wet."

"I'll take a slushy," Asad said as he mocked Pauley's daily requests for his favorite drink. Harley and Emerson looked at him in confusion. "Forget it. I'll take a water, if there's one available."

"I'll pass," Emerson said as his mind raced with plans to escape.

Harley found drinks in the galley's fridge and served them. "I'm taking a beer up to J.B." Harley left the salon and closed its door behind him.

Asad had noticed Emerson tense up and commented as he laid his gun next to him on the seat, "I know what you're thinking. And if you want to try me, do it."

Emerson relaxed. He would try it, but when Asad wasn't expecting it. Relaxing as comfortably in his seat as he could, he closed his eyes—although he tried to peer through a small slit to watch Asad in the event that he drifted asleep.

Emerson feigned sleep, but Asad didn't relax his vigilance.

The Hatteras plowed on through the four- and five-foot seas as it left the northwest channel and began its run to Naples in the darkening night as previously planned. The Gulf of Mexico was barren of any other craft that night.

Five Hours Later
South of Naples
⋘

Hearing the engines cut back and feeling the boat's forward progress slow, Asad looked around with concern. Seeing Emerson asleep, he left the main salon and approached the ladder to the flybridge. Asad climbed up to the flybridge and saw Harley and J.B. huddled around a chart. They were deep in conversation and pointing to different channels.

"Lost?" Asad asked mockingly.

Harley and J.B. turned around in unison with surprised looks on their faces.

"We didn't hear you climb up here," Harley started. "No, we're not lost. Just making sure that we head into the right channel."

"Make sure that you pick the right one," Asad said before taking a last look around. He had seen a few lights twinkling toward the mainland and hoped that they were close to the rendezvous point that Harley had arranged. "You sure about this Frank guy?"

"He's the top dog in this food chain. You'll only see him come out for the big deals, and this one he wanted to personally be involved in," Harley replied with an edge to his voice. He was looking forward to getting this over with and saying goodbye for good to Asad.

"Make sure that we get to the rendezvous point on time," Asad directed abruptly and then left the flybridge. As he turned, he saw Emerson poised to dive from the stern to swim ashore. "I wouldn't do that if I were you," Asad warned as he leveled his gun at Emerson.

Seeing his odds for success greatly diminished, Emerson stepped away from the stern and walked back to the salon as Asad motioned him inside.

"I don't like him," J.B. said. "You saw what he did to Pauley. He just offed him like it was nobody's business."

"Yeah," Harley said as he thought about how quickly Asad sacrificed the guy who had been running the heist.

"I don't trust him."

"Neither do I. We'll need to watch each other's back, J.B.," Harley cautioned.

"You can count on me."

"Good. I've got yours."

They turned back to the chart and then matched the coordinates, that they had been given, to their GPS reading. "Here we go," J.B. said as he brought the craft around and headed for the right channel. Throttling back on the power, he carefully eased the boat into the wide channel. Watching his GPS closely, J.B. turned the craft to port and entered a second, narrow channel. Moving into the channel for one hundred yards, he cut the engines and then shut off their running lights.

Harley dropped to the main deck and entered the salon where he saw Emerson staring intensely at Asad. Seeing Harley enter the salon, Asad turned to face him.

"What is it now?" he asked.

"We wait. You'll need to shut off any lights. It's too dangerous around here to let any lights show." Asad joined him in turning off the lights, which had been dimmed.

"Where are we?" Emerson asked.

"Not for you to worry," Asad glared.

Emerson's eyes swept the room as he tried to recall where the various light switches were. Maybe he would have an opportunity to disrupt their secret plans.

"It'd be better if you all join me on deck," Harley suggested.

"Let's go then," Asad said as he looked again at Emerson.

Emerson stood and walked out to the open stern of the Hatteras. He was surprised when he was greeted by the sight of J.B. standing on the flybridge, holding one of the rifles that they had transported from the van to the boat. Harley picked up a rifle that had been stored near the flybridge ladder.

With the exception of J.B., they all sat down to wait. J.B. remained on the flybridge and scanned the darkness for their guest to arrive, as he popped another PCP into his mouth. He wanted to be fully alert for the next phase of the transaction, even if it made him a bit more jumpy than usual.

In the distance, they could hear the engines of high-speed boats motoring down the main channel that they had used. There seemed to be a lot of traffic on this quiet night despite the recent passing of the storm. From their vantage point, they could make out the shadowy outlines of the passing boats as they cruised by the entrance to their smaller channel. None of them had their running lights on.

Emerson wanted to ask, but Asad beat him. "Why don't they have their running lights on?"

"Same reason we don't. No one wants to get caught," Harley went on to explain. "They're go-fast boats. They run out into international waters off the coast. There's probably a freighter from South America at anchor. They offload drugs and then they run them into the coast at a number of points. This is in the area of one of those points," Harley said with obvious experience. "It's not really a good idea for them to find you around here. They'd shoot first and then ask questions—and our firepower doesn't come close to theirs."

"How do you know so much about this?" Emerson probed Harley.

"Wouldn't you like to know?" Harley teased.

Looking at Asad, Emerson stated, "I need to use the head."

Asad nodded and looked at Harley. "You take him and watch him."

Emerson stood and entered the salon, closely followed by Harley who clenched his rifle tightly in his hand. Emerson walked into the head and did his business. When he walked out of the head, he saw Harley waiting for him. "There's something that I wanted to ask you."

"Go ahead."

"Weren't you and Sam friends?"

Harley's eyes hardened as he stared straight into the darkness. He didn't respond.

Emerson asked again. "I asked you whether you two were friends?"

Harley replied slowly, but deliberately, "At a distance." From his facial expression and body language, it was apparent that Harley was uncomfortable with the direction the conversation might be heading.

Emerson pushed. "How could you kill him like that? Sam told me that you two worked together on projects and exchanging information!"

The tough-looking Harley squirmed for a moment. "It was either him or me. You saw what Al did to Pauley. Do you think for one moment that he wouldn't have offed me? It was better that I killed Sam. I made it a quick death.

Besides, I've owed him one for screwing me with bad information on a deal that I was trying to set up. I almost got busted because of him!"

"But you guys knew each other!" Emerson said with exasperation.

Harley's face was stoic. Before he could comment, Asad opened the door and shouted urgently, "Better get out here. There's a boat coming down our channel."

They emerged from the salon and into the stern where they saw the outline of a large craft approaching them. On the flybridge, a jittery J.B. brought his rifle up and sighted it on the craft.

Suddenly, a bright white searchlight from the approaching craft filled the night, blinding the Hatteras' occupants. A loudspeaker on the craft issued a command, "This is the United States Coast Guard. Lay down your weapons and place your hands behind your heads."

Emerson breathed a sigh of relief as he quickly complied and placed his hands behind his head. His face broadened into a large smile. Harley's face broke into a smile also, but for a different reason. He knew the game they were playing. Then, Harley heard a warning yell from J.B. who was high on PCP again.

"Busted. Put out their lights!" Before Harley could yell, J.B. opened fire on the approaching craft and its searchlight. Asad began to raise his weapon to fire.

"Don't!" Harley ordered loudly. "Al drop your weapon," he commanded as he swung his rifle in Asad's direction. Asad's face was filled with disbelief as he dropped the shotgun that he had been holding.

A single shot rang out from the approaching craft and caught J.B. in the chest. J.B. dropped his rifle as he was propelled against the control panel and fell to the flybridge's deck. Bright red blood began to emerge from the wound in his chest.

"Al, it's not what you think. Trust me," Harley said quietly.

Both Emerson and Asad looked at Harley with a lack of comprehension. With the greatest amount of reluctance, Asad dropped his weapon.

"That ass should never have fired at us, Harley," the voice boomed over the loudspeaker as the craft slowed to within twenty yards of the Hatteras and glided up to the stationary vessel.

"He got nervous, that's all," Harley said as he climbed to the bridge to tend to J.B.

As two armed men jumped from the craft to the Hatteras to secure the two boats together, Asad and Emerson saw that, in fact, it was not a United States Coast Guard vessel. It was a fifty-three-foot Carver 530 Voyager and carried five armed men with another at the controls. Jumping onboard the Hatteras, one of the armed men climbed to the flybridge with a medical kit and relieved Harley of his efforts to stem the blood flow.

"Nothing much you can do for him," Harley muttered as he began to descend the ladder. He needs to be in a hospital and I'm sure that that won't happen."

One of the armed men on the deck approached Harley and shook hands with him. "Sorry about all the confusion, Jamie. He shouldn't have fired at you guys," Harley said.

The tall, muscular Jamie with the close-cropped hair replied, "You're right. He shouldn't have fired. Anyhow, I'd like you to meet Frank. He decided to come along on this trip since it was worth so damn much."

"I thought he might," Harley concurred.

"Hey Frank, would you like to join us and see what our friends have brought us to buy?" Jamie called to the shadowy figure still at the controls.

An ice-cold voice replied as the engines shut down. "One moment."

The wiry-framed Frank jumped aboard the Hatteras and walked into the light. An uncontrollable gasp of shock escaped from the Harley's mouth when he saw Frank's deeply scarred face—it looked like the first layer of skin had been peeled away. The disfiguration stemmed from burns that had not been treated properly a couple of years ago. His face was devoid of eyebrows and eyelashes, and his head was hairless.

Frank knew the effect that his appearance had on others and utilized it to its maximum effect just as his father would have used any advantage to its maximum effect. His eyes blazed at each of the boat's occupants as he looked them over carefully. When he saw Emerson, his eyes locked on him and bore right through Emerson.

"Who's this?" Frank asked deliberately as he stared menacingly at Emerson.

Emerson had been evaluating his chances of diving over the side and swimming to shore, but had put the idea aside as he realized what marksmen these new arrivals were. He felt uncomfortable under the long stare from Frank.

As he looked at Frank's eyes, he sensed some familiarity, but couldn't place it. Even the voice had seemed vaguely familiar.

Harley answered. "That's some newspaper guy that stumbled on us when we were leaving the museum. We were one short when we got to the boat, so we brought him along to help load it."

"One short?"

"Yeah, the guy who put this heist together had an accident and died," Harley said as he glanced quickly at Asad.

"Accident?" Frank asked, still staring at Emerson.

Asad spoke. "He took a bullet from some guys who wanted to rob us, isn't that right Harley?" Asad asked as he lied through his teeth. He didn't want to bother Frank with any unnecessary details.

Harley nodded his head in agreement. He knew what Asad was doing.

"So you're Harley, then?" Frank said as he pulled his eyes away from Emerson to look at Harley.

Harley stepped forward with an extended hand, but dropped it when he saw that Frank had stepped to the side.

"That's me."

"I've heard a lot about you. You do good work for me," he replied as he thought of the drug deals that involved Harley.

"Thanks. It pays well for both of us," Harley replied. Pointing to the prone figure on the flybridge who was moaning as one of Frank's men attended to him, Harley introduced J.B. "That's J.B. He's the one who got me involved and who stole the boat. He and I have done a few small drug deals."

Frank looked briefly toward J.B. and then quickly turned to Asad. "And who are you?"

"I'm Al. Saul, the guy who was killed, and I dreamed up this heist. We did all of the planning." Asad, as tough as he was, recognized that this new arrival was someone very dangerous to deal with.

Frank's head turned back to glare at Emerson. The others couldn't help noticing how riveted Frank was on Emerson.

Emerson noticed it also and his uneasiness grew. He didn't understand why Frank was so interested in him.

Asad broke the ice. "Do you know this reporter?"

A sly smile crossed Frank's face as he continued staring at Emerson. "You're Emerson Moore, aren't you?"

"Yes," Emerson replied slowly.

"You don't recognize me, do you?"

"Vaguely, there's something about you that is somewhat familiar. I just can't place it," Emerson said cautiously.

Frank caught Emerson by surprise with his next action. He swung a pointed foot around and caught the unsuspecting Emerson in the knee, dropping him to the deck. "Pick him up!" Frank commanded two of his armed men.

Grabbing Emerson's arms, they raised Emerson to his feet and held him securely. With no way to protect himself, Emerson tightened his stomach muscles as he prepared for the anticipated blows. The flurry and intensity of the blows were beyond Emerson's expectations as he found himself the recipient of a number of punches pummeling his ribs, face, and stomach. They were all delivered by an angry, red-faced Frank.

"Don't remember me, huh? You'll take the memory of me and my father to your grave—and it won't be long," Frank cursed as his rage grew.

Between blows, Emerson tried to talk. "I don't recognize you. Who are you?"

"Drop him," Frank commanded the two men holding Emerson. Emerson's body crumpled to the floor.

"Let me start by reminding you who my father was. Jacques L'Hoste!" Frank sneered at Emerson.

Emerson gasped as he realized that this was Francois, Jacques' son, who had been beating the hell out of him. "You're Francois? But you died in that tanker explosion!"

Emerson quickly recalled the incident and subsequent story he wrote two years ago about the Lake Erie shipping magnate on South Bass Island and his out-of-control son who was now standing in front of him. As a result of Emerson's actions, the father had been killed and his son was supposed to have been killed during his racing boat chase of Emerson. The chase ended in a fiery explosion when Francois and the racing boat collided with a lake freighter that was owned, appropriately enough, by the shipping magnate.

"Did anyone find my body? No, I don't think so!" Frank said contemptuously.

"We thought it was unrecoverable."

"It takes more than that to kill me!" he stormed. "I ended up onshore on Rattlesnake Island. I heard your friend call for you and saw as you rode your jet ski over to pick him up. I was in pain from my burns, but my hatred for you kept me alive. When you left the island, the guard continued his rounds and found me on the shore. Good thing for me that he was a former employee of my father."

"Did he take you off the island?" Emerson asked as he pictured the events of that night.

"No!" Frank snarled. "There were cops and investigators all over trying to find my body. He didn't want to chance it. So, he took me to his cottage on the island and treated me with his homemade remedy for burns." Frank paused for a moment as he ran his hand across his burn-scarred face. "As you can see, his home remedy didn't work very well. I stayed there for weeks while everyone searched for my body. When it was safe, he arranged for a plane to fly in and take me off the island. We then made our way to Miami where I kept my go-fast boat."

"I remember you seemed to have a penchant to race go-fast boats. Weren't they watching the boats?" Emerson questioned.

Frank grinned evilly at Emerson. He was taking much pleasure in explaining his escape from the clutches of death on Lake Erie. "Of course, they were—and my apartment there also. So, I made arrangements with the pilot who had flown me there to fly me to the Cayman Islands where I had several offshore bank accounts. I tapped one of them and began to build a new life for myself. I returned to Miami and rented another apartment close to South Beach and ran my business out of there. No one is looking for Francois L'Hoste anymore. That's one benefit that I got from these scars. They help me with my new identity."

"What happened to the L'Hoste shipping empire?" Emerson asked, intrigued by the story.

"Gone. The bastards in top management took it over when they saw the reports that my father and I had been killed. I certainly could not reappear," he said sarcastically.

Emerson paused as he remembered reading several newspaper accounts regarding the L'Hoste shipping empire. "Didn't I read that the chairman and the president of the company had sudden and mysterious deaths?"

Jamie, who had been listening patiently, answered with a devious smile, "Real sudden and real mysterious, huh, boss?"

The look that was exchanged between Jamie and Frank left no doubt in the minds of the others who was responsible for those deaths.

"What a crying shame!" Frank mocked.

"So, you moved into drug running?" Emerson mused out loud.

"I needed to finance my lifestyle! And I've done quite well by it, wouldn't you say boys?"

"Very well," said Jamie.

"He's the leading drug lord in South Florida," Harley chimed in.

Frank acknowledged his comment with a sly smile.

Asad had been quiet during the conversations between Emerson and Frank. It was his turn to speak up. "Your men can lower their weapons. I'm in charge here," he started solemnly as he tried to wrest control back to himself.

"I wouldn't say that you're in a position to be giving anyone orders," Frank glared back at Asad.

Harley interrupted. "I think what Al meant to say was that we're all in this together, and we need to move forward with the treasure transfer and close our deal."

Frank eyed Asad carefully and sensed that he couldn't trust Asad. "Okay then. Enough of this chitchat. Let's see some of this treasure."

Harley moved to the stern fish well and opened it. He untied one of the bags and passed it to Frank so he could see the contents.

Sticking his automatic in his belt, Frank withdrew two gold chains and several emeralds. "Nice. Very nice," he oohed as he examined the treasure. He dropped them back into the bag and ordered, "Load it all on board here."

Asad interrupted, "The matter of the payment?"

Frank's head swiveled slowly and his eyes bored into Asad. "We will settle up in Naples. Let's worry about getting everything there, first." He took one of the Kalisnikovs from one of his men and sternly instructed, "Go ahead and transfer the treasure."

Under his watchful eyes, they formed a line from the Hatteras to Frank's Carver and transferred the treasure aboard. They made short work of it.

After the last bag was transferred Asad stood and wiped his brow. "I guess that Harley will need to pilot our boat since J.B. is wounded. We'll follow you to Naples."

"Nope. Can't have none of that. Your boat is probably stolen. Is that correct, Harley?"

Harley nodded his head.

"They'll be looking for it. We'll need to make it disappear."

"Disappear?" Asad questioned.

"Yeah, disappear. We'll sink it right here. Better transfer anything else that you have to this boat," Frank ordered.

Seeing Asad starting for the salon, Frank ordered one of his men, "Go with him and be careful."

Harley and one of Frank's men began to lower J.B. carefully down the flybridge ladder. "He's going to need medical care," Harley indicated as a moan escaped from J.B.'s mouth.

"Still bleeding?" Frank asked.

"Yep."

"He shouldn't have fired on us," Frank said grimly.

"He shouldn't have," Harley agreed as he wondered if J.B. had been high on PCP again. He was very aware of J.B.'s pill popping habit.

They transferred J.B. to the stern of the Carver and were joined by the rest of the contingent. One of Frank's men leaped from the Carver to the Hatteras and disappeared into the cabin for a few minutes. He then reappeared and rejoined the rest of them on board Frank's craft, giving Frank a nod as he boarded.

The armed man at the controls put the Carver into reverse, and they backed into the main channel.

"I thought you were going to destroy the Hatteras," Asad said.

Looking at his watch, Frank said, "It won't be long now."

From the channel they reemerged into the Gulf of Mexico and began to head toward Naples. They had been at sea for barely five minutes when an explosion was heard behind them. Looking back toward the mainland, they saw flames shooting in the sky.

"There goes the Hatteras," Frank gloated.

They watched as the flames quickly disappeared and turned to face the bow as the Carver continued on its journey to Naples.

After a short while at sea, Frank called to the man at the controls, "Let's bring it to a stop." Turning to Jaime, who was standing toward the stern where he could keep an eye on the new arrivals, Frank asked, "Jamie, see any bait fish?"

Jamie looked overboard. After a few moments he responded, "Yeah, looks like we've got some running."

"Good." Addressing the others in the stern, Frank asked, "How would you like to do some deep sea fishing?"

Asad's mouth dropped. "At a time like this?" He didn't get it.

"Yes. I like to fish for shark, but we didn't bring any bait." Then in a menacing tone, Frank said, "But I see that you were kind of enough to bring the bait with you."

Asad and Emerson looked with a lack of comprehension at Frank. Then they followed his eyes to J.B. who lay in the stern moaning. Asad's eyes lit up.

Realizing what Frank meant, Emerson looked aghast. "You can't do that!"

"And just who is going to stop me?"

"I am," Emerson started for Frank, but was roughly pulled back by the sudden vise-like grip of a hand that clamped hard on his arm.

"I wouldn't do that," Harley urged. "He'll throw you in, too."

"Oh no, I wouldn't, Harley. I've got something special planned for our Mr. Emerson Moore!" Frank said with an evil air of mystery. "Make sure that he's bleeding. Open the wound a bit if you need to," Frank instructed Jaime and another of his men who had joined him. Jamie produced a sharp knife from his pocket.

J.B.'s eyes widened in terror as the two men tried to hold him. "You're not doing this to me!" he screamed at them as he struggled to free himself. He grabbed the hand that held the knife and tried to shove it backwards into its owner, but the two men were stronger than J.B. and pinned him to the deck.

Jaime probed the wound and freshened the blood flow as J.B.'s shrieks filled the air.

"No! Stop. Don't," he cried out futilely.

"He's bleeding again," Jaime smiled as he withdrew the blood-covered knife and looked up at Frank.

"Good. Over the side with him, then. Let's go trolling for sharks."

The two men attached lines to the struggling J.B. and began to inch him closer to the stern. J.B. was clutching wildly at them and anything within his reach as he tried to slow the inevitable. Finally, they had him positioned precariously on the stern.

"Time to go bye-bye," Frank said sarcastically. "Over the side with him!"

J.B.'s fingers clawed at the stern cleats, and he was able to grasp one momentarily until Jaime used the butt of his .45 on J.B.'s fingers. Recoiling in pain from the blows to his fingers, J.B. released his death grip and over the stern he went.

Splashing into the warm water, J.B. bobbed momentarily. He nervously turned around in a circle as he scanned the waves for the telltale sign of any approaching shark fins. Seeing none, he began to swim back to the boat, which had drifted ten feet away. The pain from his wound faded away as he focused on his survival.

Seeing him swimming toward the boat, Emerson started again to move toward J.B. to help him aboard, but was forcibly held back by Harley's grip on both of his arms.

"You can't do this!" Emerson cried out at Frank.

"Careful, or they may have you join him," Harley cautioned as he tighly gripped Emerson's arm.

Frank looked at Emerson and smiled evilly. "Hey! Look how fast he's swimming! Can you believe that he's actually catching up to us? Give us a little speed," he commanded the crewman at the controls who eased the throttle forward.

All eyes turned to J.B. who was left astern as the line tightened, and he began to be pulled slowly through the warm water. It was just a matter of minutes before the first fin appeared. It was joined quickly by two more. The fins appeared and disappeared several times as they followed their bait.

J.B. saw the fins, too. His hands were moving over each other as he tried to work his way along the line and back to the boat. He had turned on his back as he was being dragged so that he could keep one eye on his hungry visitors.

"Looks like we got three nine-foot bull sharks out there. They're probably two-hundred-pounders," Jaime shouted to Frank.

J.B. saw one of the fins accelerate and began to wail in animal-like terror as he increased his attempt to work his way up the line. He pulled his legs up tight underneath himself so that he could kick at his attacker.

The onboard watchers saw the first fin suddenly dart toward J.B. He was pulled under as the shark initiated its first bite-and-run attack. As the shark lunged in, it opened its jaws wide and then snapped them shut on one of J.B.'s legs, which had been extended in a strong kick, but had missed its mark. The stern line strained with tension as the large shark tore off one of J.B.'s legs.

"Wish we had a hook on that line," Jamie called to Frank as he saw the size of the shark. "He sure likes our bait!"

From the flybridge, Frank watched the gruesome spectacle in front of him. He didn't try to hide his perverse smile as he reveled in the depravity.

J.B.'s head and upper body reappeared above the water. His inhuman shrieks of pain rent the air like a knife, stabbing into the hearts of the onlookers.

Asad was watching the display with a macabre sense of amusement. He relished the pain that J.B. was experiencing. If circumstances were otherwise, he might enjoy working with this Frank.

Emerson felt sick to his stomach and averted his eyes. He wondered what Frank had in store for him. Emerson turned his head back to see J.B.'s body shoot under the water's surface at the same time that another fin had submerged. The bull shark hit J.B. and dragged him deep under water until the line tightened and wouldn't allow it to go deeper. The shark broke off its attack with a tearing motion and pulled away flesh from J.B.'s lower body. Another shark replaced it, and before J.B. could resurface, kept him submerged as it tore into him.

His lungs were bursting for air. J.B. couldn't take it any longer. He gave up. His lungs filled with water as the next shark attacked and J.B.'s life drained from him.

When his upper torso reappeared, its lifeless eyes stared vacantly toward the heavens.

"Cut the line," Frank instructed Jamie who produced his knife again and slashed through the line. The fins converged on J.B.'s body, pulling it under for the final time.

"Let's go. Show's over." Frank said as the boat picked up speed. Then he added, "That is, for now." He looked at Emerson when he said it.

The boat headed for Naples.

The Wee Hours of the Morning
A Naples Area Boat Repair Facility

❦

They had finished carrying the treasure from the Carver to the warehouse. Frank had busied himself with opening most of the bags and examining the contents.

"Good stuff, huh?" Harley asked Frank.

"Quite beautiful." Turning to Asad, Frank said as he examined several of the pieces. "I think we may have a problem."

"A problem?" Asad asked. "What do you mean a problem?"

Holding an emerald necklace up to the light, Frank observed, "These pieces are quite unique. So unique that they may be the only ones in existence. That makes them very recognizable, and I'm sure that the staff at Fisher's has cataloged each of the items."

"And the problem is?" Asad questioned.

"The uniqueness of some of these items make it difficult for us to sell them." Frank withdrew a gold chalice from the bag and turned it over in his hand as he examined it. "I may not be able to sell these for what I thought I could. We're going to have to talk about a very deep discount here."

Asad's look of chagrin told the story. "How much of a discount?" Asad was anxious to complete the transaction and get on his way. He had been counting on this nest egg so that he could relocate to the West Coast and disappear from everyone who was tracking him. He'd never have to worry about cash again.

"I'm thinking about ten cents on the dollar," Frank said as he noticed that his men had their weapons at their sides.

"That's unacceptable," Asad stormed.

"My father always said that it's not a good idea to try to corner a tiger," Frank warned with a sly look on his scarred face.

"It's unacceptable!' Asad stormed again.

Emerson's eyes swept the room. He didn't like the growing tension in the room.

"You're not open to my offer?" Frank asked.

Harley had seen it coming before Asad did.

"No, I want forty cents on the dollar," Asad demanded foolishly.

"Then you give me no choice. I'll take it all and you get nothing," Frank said as his men took their cue and pointed their weapons at Asad. Asad had played right into his hands.

Asad's eyes were defiant as he slowly looked at the guards and their pointed weapons. A thin smile crossed his face as he carefully withdrew his hand from his pant's pocket. "I don't think so. You're the one who may end up with nothing," Asad said confidently as he gripped a device in his hand.

"Oh, oh," nervously muttered one of the guards, who had been emptying the bags on the table, as he recognized an unexpected find in one of the bags.

Frank's head snapped around. "What is it now?" he asked forcibly as he tried to peer into the bag to see what triggered the guard's nervousness.

Asad answered for the guard. "It's a little surprise that I planted in several of the bags in the event that we had a breakdown in our negotiations." Asad slowly raised his arm and displayed a remote detonator.

Unfazed, Frank asked quietly, but dangerously, "And what do you have in your hand?"

"My equalizer. If you don't want to deal with me on my terms, I'll just eliminate the basis of our disagreement. It will all vanish in front of our eyes." Asad said slyly. "I've packed semtex in several of the bags in case we had a disagreement." Looking out of the corner of his eyes at Emerson, Asad explained, "I planted it after we left Key West." He turned his head back to Frank.

Asad had been so focused on Frank and his henchmen that he hadn't noticed movement behind him. Harley had repositioned himself behind Asad. Suddenly, Harley lunged for Asad's right hand and was able to grasp the detonator before Asad could react and depress it.

While Asad resisted Harley and struggled with him for control of the remote, two of the guards rushed them. They pulled Asad away from Harley and held him tightly as Harley grabbed the remote detonator.

Frank approached the group and took the remote that Harley held out to him. "Thanks," he said. Turning it over in his hand as he looked it over, Frank commented solemnly, "So, you were willing to go that far? You would have destroyed the entire treasure because you didn't like my offer?"

Asad said nothing. He just glared at Frank through slitted eyes.

"This puts a different light on our transactions, wouldn't you agree, boys?" Frank asked his men.

His men mumbled their agreement as Frank stared dangerously at Asad. "Bring him over to the engine repair area," Frank instructed.

They walked to a corner of the facility where engines were pulled and tested. Attached to the side of one of the two water-filled tanks was a Mercury 250-horsepower outboard engine. The repairs to the six-cylinder motor had been completed late that afternoon and the motor had been positioned and readied for testing the next day.

"Tilt it up. I want to be sure that the prop is installed," Frank ordered one of his men who tilted the black outboard forward, causing the prop to emerge at the bottom of the shaft.

"It's there!" the man responded.

"Put it back down and start the engine," Frank ordered as he saw that the gas line had been connected.

The man started the engine and the testing area echoed with the noise from the strong engine as it idled. Frank looked into the tank and said," Let's give it a little speed and see what happens."

He watched as the blades of the prop spun wickedly. Frank smiled devilishly to himself and turned to Asad who was still held tightly by the other men. Harley and Emerson were also standing with the group. "Bind him, but leave his right arm free!"

The two men were joined by Jaime who had picked up duct tape and began to wrap it around Asad. Asad twisted and turned as he tried unsuccessfully to resist their attempts to restrain him. It didn't take the guards long. Within a few minutes, Asad had been bound and the guard held one of his arms tightly so that he couldn't pull at the duct tape.

"Bring him over here to the tank," Frank ordered with an evil smile.

Again Asad attempted to resist, but his attempts were futile.

"Since you tried to destroy my treasure with the detonator that you held in your right hand, I'm going to have to punish you."

Asad stared straight ahead.

"Say good-bye to your right hand, Al. Stick it in the prop!" Frank commanded Jamie. "It's slice and dice time," Frank added as he arched his eyebrows and displayed an evil grin.

Asad jerked back his hand in reaction and tried to pull away, but Frank's men held him firmly and pulled him closer to the tank.

"Wait, you can't do that," Emerson protested as he began to rush to Asad's aid. He suddenly found himself again restrained by Harley.

"Want to join him?" Frank asked.

"You can't do this!" Emerson repeated as he struggled to free himself.

"Now, don't you worry, I've got plans for you too. I certainly wouldn't leave you out of all the fun!" Frank grinned sinisterly.

Asad's eyes widened in terror as he did his best to resist. But again it was futile as two of the guards tightly gripped his arm and extended his hand toward the whirling blade. Asad had not known terror before. He had always created it.

The hand, which Asad had closed, was pushed into the spinning "meat cutter." He grit his teeth as he fought to contain his cries of excruciating pain. It wasn't long until his shrieks of pain rent the area, and blood splattered as he fought to withdraw it to safety.

Harley and Emerson both shuddered involuntarily as they watched the event unfold in front of their eyes. Emerson was repulsed by what he saw and only wondered what sort of revenge Frank had planned for him. He shuddered again at the atrocity that he was witnessing. He anticipated his own suffering. When it came, it too would be drawn out and equally as gory.

Emerson sensed Harley's grip relaxing. He took the opportunity to break free and began to rush to aid Asad. His rescue attempt lasted all but three steps. A sudden blow of a blunt object to the side of his head caused him to stop in midstep and fall to the floor where he lost consciousness. As he was fading away, he glimpsed Harley standing over him, still gripping the barrel end of his Beretta.

"I hope you didn't damage my goods too bad," Frank sneered as he gazed at the crumpled body.

"Nah. Just a love tap," Harley grinned back. "He was getting a bit rambunctious!"

"Let's see what we have there," Frank said with a wolfish grin as he instructed his men to show him the stump of Asad's arm. Examining it, Frank said sarcastically to Asad, "My, my. Looks like you've had a little accident and your hand is gone!"

Asad, with his face twisted in pain, weakly glared at Frank as Frank approached him. Blood was pumping from the severed arteries in Asad's wrist. "Secure him over there and let him bleed to death while we watch. Coffee anyone?" he asked nonchalantly as he settled into a nearby chair. He didn't expect an answer.

Asad's arm was bound to his side as he was laid on the floor and the men watched the blood drain. In a matter of twenty minutes, he was dead.

Looking at the dead body, Frank rose from his chair and said nefariously, "Show's over. Time for the next act. Let's return to the treasure. I've got an interesting idea."

With two of the men dragging the unconscious Emerson, they walked back to the tables loaded with treasure. Frank began to run his fingers through a pile of gold coins.

The men dumped Emerson on the floor in front of the table and then circled around Frank, the table, and the alluring treasure.

After sifting through the coins, Frank directed Jaime, "Revive him."

Jamie filled a nearby bucket with water and doused Emerson.

Emerson regained consciousness, coughing several times as he opened his eyes. Fighting off dizziness after catching his breath, he began to become aware of his surroundings. Unintentially, a moan escaped from his mouth.

"Back with us again?" Frank asked the stirring Emerson.

Emerson shot Frank an uncompromising stare.

"Don't talk then," Frank said as he weighed a handful of gold coins. "Pretty, aren't they?" he asked Emerson.

Emerson was still in shock after seeing the depths of cruelty that Frank had gone to with Asad. He nodded his head in reply.

"Have a seat, Mr. Moore," Frank said as he pointed to a chair in front of the table.

"That's okay. I'll just stand," Emerson responded as he rose to his feet. He ran his hand through his head and found a raised bump from the gun butt blow.

"I said, have a seat!" Frank said as anger crept into his voice.

Emerson found himself thrust into the chair by two of Frank's men. Then, they took positions on each side of the seated Emerson.

"Bind his arms to his sides," Frank instructed as he tossed a roll of duct tape to one of the guards. Emerson began to stand in defense, but was abruptly shoved back into the chair as the two guards overpowered him and secured him with the tape.

Looking at Emerson with glee as he toyed with the gold coins, Frank asked, "Hungry? It must be hours since you last ate."

Emerson replied, "Nope. I'm quite fine."

Letting the coins fall from his hand and noisily onto the table, Frank probed, "Ever wonder what a gold coin tasted like?"

Emerson was silent as he realized where this was heading.

"Or how about several gold coins?"

Emerson held his tongue.

"Not talking, then? Well, we'll just have to force feed you a bit. Have you ever tried to digest a gold coin? How about fifty or so?"

"You're out of your mind, you crazy bastard!" Emerson yelled as he realized that there was no way out.

"Tsk, tsk. Name-calling won't get you anywhere!" Frank mocked as he walked around the table and stood in front of Emerson. He caught Emerson off guard as he quickly swung and smacked Emerson's temple with his fist. "Don't call me names. No one calls me names like that!" Frank warned.

Emerson shook his head as he recovered from the stinging wallop.

"You're not going to fill him with coins and bury him, are you boss?" Jamie asked as he worried about losing any of the coins.

"Oh no. Thank you for asking, Jamie. We're going to retrieve the coins before our friend here dies." Frank produced a sharp edged knife from his pocket. "We're going to gut you while you're still alive and swallowing the coins. I'm going to let you see your intestines pulled from your abdomen as I cut into them. Then, I'm going to search for my gold coins that you're digesting. If I don't find them there, I'll move up into your stomach and cut it open so that I can retrieve my coins. All of this in front of your eyes. Now, what do you think about that, Mr. Emerson Moore?" Frank asked with unbridled vengeance.

Bile surged up inside of Emerson as he realized the agonizing death and suffering that Frank planned. Emerson struggled at his bindings, but was unsuccessful.

Frank laughed at Emerson's predicament. "It's useless. And after we watch you suffer a while with your guts exposed, we're going to drop ants on your exposed innards and let them have at you. You won't be able to do anything as those tiny scavengers begin to devour your intestines and you feel them enter the open wounds from where we extracted the coins."

While Emerson had been unconscious, one of Frank's men had discovered an anthill outside of the building and near the parking lot. He had suggested to Frank the ants could be used to torment Emerson.

Emerson choked back the bile that had risen in his throat.

"But, once I'm satisfied that you've suffered enough with the ants, we'll kill you. I want you to know that I can be merciful." Frank laughed wantonly. "Jaime, why don't you show our friend the can that you found in the engine repair area?"

Jaime raised the can, which was half filled with gasoline, and thrust it towards Emerson. Emerson heard the gasoline sloshing in the can and could smell the fumes.

"Ants don't like gasoline. So, we'll douse your exposed organs with gasoline to help chase them away." Frank leaned in and toward Emerson. "But, do you know what they like even less? Fire," he said as he flicked a lighter that he had pulled out from his pocket and placed near Emerson's eyes. "Now, isn't that nice of me?" Frank asked sarcastically.

Emerson gasped in horror.

Frank took one gold coin in his hand and approached Emerson. "Pull his head back and put tape over his nose. Then we'll start feeding you some nourishment," Frank said with evil relish and a frenzied look in his eyes.

One of the guards pulled back Emerson's head while the other ripped off a piece of duct tape, and holding it gingerly between his fingers, approached Emerson. As he bent to affix it to Emerson's nose, a bright flash filled the entire room.

"E, hang in there! DEA, drop your weapons," Sam yelled as he stepped around the rear of a large Carver and threw another flash grenade to blind Frank and his men. Other DEA agents appeared with weapons pointed at Frank and his men. Catching Emerson's eye, Sam grinned like a wild man, "E, it's hero time!"

"Kill them!" Frank ordered as he threw his gold coins at Sam and pulled out his knife so that he could plunge it into the bound Emerson. Following his orders, Frank's men opened fire on the DEA agents.

Immediately, the warehouse was filled with gunshots as the force of DEA agents, carrying semi-automatic weapons, exchanged gunfire with Frank's men. The firefight ended within minutes of starting, as Frank's men, who were outnumbered and outgunned, didn't have a chance from the opening shots. The DEA agents were well-hidden after sneaking in the rear doors and catching Frank's men completely off guard. Jaime was killed in the opening salvo, and was followed quickly by two of the others. The remaining two dropped their weapons and surrendered.

When the firefight started, Emerson felt bullets whizzing by his head. He threw his weight to his left and was able to knock his chair to the side and himself to the ground.

Frank pounced on top of Emerson. "Before I go down, I'm taking you out! Just remember what you did to my father and our family. This is payback!" Frank yelled as he raised his knife above his head and prepared to thrust it into Emerson's chest cavity.

Emerson was wide-eyed as he did his best to struggle free.

Frank's arm began its descent, but was suddenly stopped by the vise-like grip of someone's hand. The grip was so intense that it pinched the blood flow and crushed the nerves in his arm. He felt a body move in close to his and the presence of someone's head near his ear.

A deep voice boomed, "Uh, uh. DEA, you're under arrest."

Emerson heard the voice too, and peered around to identify its source. The man's head came into view as he looked around Frank and directly into Emerson's eyes. "That was close. A little too close," he said as he jerked Frank off Emerson and stood.

"Harley! You're DEA?" Emerson asked in astonishment.

"Yep. We've been after this guy for a long time," Harley said as he looked at the table loaded with treasure.

Harley shouldn't have taken his eyes off Frank.

Frank had felt Harley ease the pressure on his arm, and suddenly pulled his arm out of Harley's grip. He twisted free and jabbed his knife into Harley's side. Harley winced with pain and fought like a cornered grizzly. Frank dodged Harley's right arm that swung wildly at Frank's head and began to thrust his blade upward to Harley's unprotected throat.

It never made contact as a nearby gunshot echoed in the cavern-like warehouse. Frank's upward thrust stopped in mid-air and his eyes filled with a look of disbelief. They began to glaze over as blood pumped from a lethal wound to the side of his head. He crumpled to the ground as a voice spoke up, "Good thing I got here when I did!"

Harley and Emerson turned their heads to see a smiling Sam with his left arm in a sling, but a Beretta in his right hand.

Emerson spoke next. "You just had to ruin things for me. I had them where I wanted them," he kidded.

Winking at Harley, Sam teased, "Sure you did."

Changing to a more serious tone, Emerson said, "Where in the world did you come from? I thought Harley killed you."

"That's what everyone was supposed to think. It worked well, didn't it?" Sam asked.

"But, I saw your head recoil from the shot and your head rolled to the side," Emerson said.

Emerson and Harley exchanged knowing glances as Harley freed Emerson from his bindings and helped him to his feet. Emerson rubbed his arms to restore blood circulation and to ease the cramping.

Sam answered, "I knew I had a chance when Harley said he wanted to be the one to put out my lights. I didn't know what he was going to do. As far as my head recoiling, that was easy to do. If you had a gun go off that close to your head, you'd recoil, too. When I realized that he hadn't shot me, I played possum."

"You two have worked more closely together than I originally thought," Emerson said stunned by what was transpiring.

Harley explained, "We've both been involved in law enforcement in one way or another for quite a few years." His dark eyes flashed as he winked knowingly at Sam.

Looking at Frank's dead body, Sam asked, "Who's your friend?"

Emerson responded with a question, "You don't recognize him?"

Sam bent down and looked closer at the fire-scarred face. "Can't say that I do. Don't think I'd forget someone looking like this!"

"It's Francois L'Hoste!"

"No shit!" Sam said stunned. He looked closer and then made the connection. "I thought he was killed when his boat exploded."

"So did I. He told me he was washed ashore on Rattlesnake Island. The guard that we ran into found him and did some home nursing care on him.

"Bad job," Sam commented as he looked at the scarring.

"After things cooled down, the guard arranged his transportation back to the Miami area."

"Yeah, I thought you had written something in your follow-up story about him and his ocean racing boats in Miami," Sam said as he stood.

"How did you find us here?" Emerson asked as the DEA agents helped the wounded.

"I'll answer that one," Harley suggested. Sam nodded his head and Harley explained, "I had slipped a couple of tracking devices in my Sha Sha shoes." He paused and lifted one of his black, flamed shoes and popped out one of the tracking devices from its secret compartment in the sole. "I slipped a couple in the treasure bags in case something happened to me."

"And when he supposedly shot me, he slipped a tracking device in my hand and closed my hand around it," Sam said.

"They pop out easily and no one saw me do it," Harley mentioned.

"Then I saw it and knew that Harley was working a case, but didn't know what was going down until he . . . ," Sam was looking beyond his friends to an approaching man who was wearing a bullet-proof vest, "came over to check on me after you guys drove off behind the Hilton."

Harley and Emerson looked around to see who Sam was talking about and saw another agent standing there. He was tall and slender with graying hair. He spoke first. "Hi guys."

"It's about time that you got here," Harley said. "I was getting ready to blow my cover and try to stop them from pouring the coins down Emerson's throat when you busted in quick-like." Turning to Emerson, Harley introduced the agent. "Meet Sandy Hanson. He's the DEA agent in charge."

Hanson spoke next. "Harley and I have been trying to bust this Frank for the last year, and when Harley told me that Frank was going to be personally involved with this deal, it created quite an opportunity to nail him. We didn't expect that you two would stroll in the middle of this the way you did. We were positioned around Mel Fisher's, but under strict orders not to interfere unless Harley got himself in a jam."

"You sat there and watched the shoot-out between the robbers and the hit men?" Emerson asked.

"We almost interrupted that escapade. Our snipers were watching you, Sam, and Harley closely to protect you. If the bad guys wanted to kill each other off, let them. We were focused on catching Frank."

Emerson was quiet as he listened.

Hanson continued. "When you all left, we helped Sam. Sam's done some work for us over the years, and he showed us the transmitter."

Sam interrupted. "Boy, was I surprised when they showed up! They told me about everything that was going on."

"Of course, we already knew about the transmitter and were waiting to track it. We got Sam medical treatment for his shoulder and caught up with my men who were tracking the treasure, which eventually led us here," Hanson explained.

"Were you here when they took out Al?" Emerson asked.

"We just got here," Hanson said.

"Yes, what happened to Asad?" another man, wearing DEA identification and carrying a semi-automatic, asked as he walked over to them.

"Asad?" Emerson asked.

"Meet Moshe. He's with the Mossad," Hanson said.

"The Mossad?" Emerson asked in surprise.

Sam answered before Moshe. "The guy's real name wasn't Al. It was Asad Malmud. He was a terrorist and they've been tracking this Asad character for years."

Moshe quickly gave Emerson a summary of Asad's terrorist activities.

Emerson listened intently to the explanation and then asked, "And Moshe, how did you end up here tonight?"

Hanson answered before Moshe could reply. "A detective with the Miami police department was running down leads for Moshe. His research indicated that Asad had headed for Key West and Moshe showed up in our offices with photos," Hanson explained. "We had been watching both Asad and Pauley from the time that Harley had tipped us about the heist and Frank's potential involvement. We were after Frank from the beginning and had to let the events unfold to get us to Frank."

"I was actually on the stakeout at Fisher's with the DEA team. I saw everything that happened there and positively identified Asad," Moshe said.

"You too?" Emerson asked in disbelief.

Hanson and Moshe nodded their heads.
"We almost had to restrain Moshe because he wanted to move in and capture Asad. He would have ruined our entire plan," Hanson added seriously.

"Where is Asad?" Moshe asked again.

Emerson quickly explained Asad's gruesome death.

"That's original," Sam thought aloud.

"He deserved that and more in return for the terror he caused others," Moshe commented retrospectively.

Harley spoke next and to Hanson, "I assume you tailed Asad to the power station after I tipped you."

"Actually, we didn't." Hanson said. "We had a stakeout set up there and watched as he planted the explosives. It was raining so hard it not only made it difficult for us to see him, but also difficult for him to see us. We put a tail on him after he left and a good thing that we did!"

"How's that?" Emerson asked.

"Well, first let me tell you what happened at the power station. After he left, two members of the Key West Bomb Removal Squad examined the explosive and seeing that it wasn't booby trapped, moved it away from the power station. We waited until it exploded, then one of the utility workers killed the electrical service to the island, making it seem as if the power station had blown up."

"What about your tail on Asad?" Emerson asked.

"Asad rode over to the hospital and planted a second explosive device there, near the emergency room entrance. We had to rush the bomb squad guys over there as soon as they were done, and they removed it to a safe area where we allowed it to explode harmlessly, too, other than damaging some nearby landscaping."

"Where's the other guy that was with you at Fisher's?" Sam questioned Harley.

"J.B.?" Harley asked.

"Yeah. He was the one with the kids on the houseboat," Sam expounded.

"He took a bullet. Then, our dead friend here decided it would be fun to go fishing. They opened up his wound so that he'd bleed more. Then they threw him overboard as shark bait and went trolling for shark. Didn't take long for them to find some sharks."

Sam winced as he pictured the event. "Hey, I'm thirsty. You guys ready for a little red, white, and brew?"

"As soon as I personally see Asad's body," Moshe said as he produced a photo of Asad for identification purposes. He wanted to be sure that it was the man that they had been hunting for so long.

"I won't be joining you. We've got some clean up to do plus securing the treasure," Hanson said as he joined several of the agents at the table who were repacking the stolen treasure.

The rest of them moved on to the engine repair area to view Asad's body.

As they walked, Sam asked, "E, what are you going to write as far as the stakeout and allowing the bad guys to off each other?"

Emerson didn't answer at first. It would have made for great headlines and controversy, he thought to himself as he watched Moshe turn over Asad's body and smile.

Emerson swung his head around to Sam. "Write about what stakeout? I don't know anything about a stakeout." He smiled at his good friend, Sam.

"Right answer, E!"

The Next Day
Fish Check
Garrison Bight

⌒

Clear sunny skies tempered with a warm breeze created a warm ambiance as the crew of the *Fish Check* readied their gear for an afternoon fishing trip. First mate Gary was arranging the bait in the stern. Captain Steve Luoma was on the flybridge when he saw his afternoon fishermen pull into one of the parking spaces near the craft's stern.

"Hello, Sam," Luoma called as he descended the flybridge ladder to the deck and walked over to assist his afternoon guests on board.

"Sorry we're late," Sam called. "They're still working on clearing debris from the streets and I had to take a detour."

"No problem. It's a beautiful day for fishing in Key West!" Luoma commented as his eyes quickly scanned the brilliant blue sky. "Who do we have here?"

Sam made the introductions, "You remember meeting Emerson?"

"Sure do." Luoma said.

"I told you I'd take you up on that fishing trip offer! Not sure how I'll do," Emerson winced as he turned suddenly. "I've got a couple of bruised ribs that are taped up."

"No problem. Gary can help you out when it's your turn to fish. Right, Gary?"

"Be glad to help," Gary called from where he stood on the bow.

"Not sure if I'll be fishing much, or be on my cell phone, or snoozing. I was up virtually all night writing a story for tomorrow's paper about this escapade down here. Caught a few hours of sleep, finished the story and e-mailed it to Washington a while ago."

Sam continued the introductions. "This is a Harley, a friend of mine."

Luoma nodded his head in greeting.

"Got room on board for a big guy like me?" Harley teased as he took a big step onto the deck. He was wearing his bib overalls again.

"Always," Luoma replied. Looking at Harley's exposed shoulders, he added, "Hope you brought sunscreen. Otherwise you could be in for a nasty burn today."

Harley pulled out a container from his pocket and flashed it at Luoma, who smiled and turned to help the next guests board. He found himself staring into the face of a beautiful, raven-haired, slender woman who was holding a toddler in one arm and struggling to maintain a grip on a fidgety six-year-old. Her eyes looked like she had been crying.

Sam introduced them. "This is Candy and those are her two boys, Mason and Dix."

"Hi boys. Candy, welcome aboard," Luoma said in greeting.

"Thank you. The boys are really looking forward to this," Candy said as she stepped on board with the boys and walked toward the cabin.

"Hey, can I go up there?" Dix asked as he looked at the ladder leading to the flybridge. Without waiting for a response, he scampered up.

Luoma's face broke into a wide smile. "Looks like he's a handful."

Sam spoke softly in reply. "Their father was killed yesterday. Not that I'd say they lost much, but still, he was their father. Harley and I went together to tell her. I thought that bringing them along today would help take their minds off of it."

"How's Candy doing?" Luoma asked.

"She's upset naturally, but she did confide in me that she was preparing to divorce J.B. They lived over in the houseboats."

"Pretty lady," Luoma observed.

"That she is," Sam concurred as he looked appreciatively at her.

Three hours later after Dix had reeled in three fighting wahoo, the boy was seated next to Sam in the cabin. Remorsefully, Dix said as he leaned his head against Sam.

"You know, I'm going to miss my dad. He always called me Hammerhead."

Sam looked down at the boy and his misting eyes. "How about if I call you Hammerhead?"

The boy looked up at Sam and smiled. "That'd be okay."

"Okay then, Hammerhead."

Dix's eyes twinkled.

"How did you like that storm that went through here? We almost got hit by Hurricane Charley," Sam said.

"It was scary. There was a real big wind and we got to sleep in a big shelter with a bunch of people we didn't know. Momma said we were camping out." The words spewed from his lips. "You know what my daddy told me about hurricanes?"

"No. What did he say?" Sam asked.

"He said hurricanes were when rainbows walk."

Sam nodded his head as he put his arm around the boy who leaned comfortably against him and began to fall asleep.

Emerson sat next to Sam and took a peek at the now-dozing boy. "Isn't that cute?" he teased Sam as Candy smiled warmly at Sam.

Sam grimaced as he made a face at Emerson. "So, what are you going to do next?"

"I need a break, and some time for my ribs to heal. I'm going to fly to Pensacola and away from all of this hurricane mess," Emerson said with a look of relief.

"You never know when you'll run into another hurricane here in Florida," Sam warned.

"I thought you only see one, maybe two a year. You've already had Bonnie and Charley," Emerson retorted. "Florida won't see anymore hurricanes this year."

"It's been a funny season this year," Sam mused.

"Well, I'm catching a flight tonight for Pensacola and some long overdue R and R," Emerson replied optimistically. "I'll be sitting on the beach in the warm sun, chilling out!"

The U.S. National Hurricane Center
Miami, Florida
⧼

"I don't like the way this one is building," one of the weather analysts said as he compared his charts to a tropical storm on his computer screen.

"How's that?" his co-worker asked from across the room.

"Looks like this one could be the biggest that we've seen in some time."

"Did you plot its potential track yet?"

"Yes. Looks like it may come ashore in New Orleans or Pensacola."

"Hmmm. Which one is this?"

"Ivan," the analyst said grimly as the plane carrying Emerson took off from Key West International Airport for Pensacola.

Coming in Summer 2006
Promised Land

The next book in the Emerson Moore series!

Promised Land opens in 1805 during the Battle of Trafalgar and onboard *HMS Victory* commanded by Lord Horatio Nelson. When a captured French frigate is boarded, a pressed seaman of British/French descent discovers a wounded priest hiding behind a twelve-pounder on the gundeck. The priest had been sent by the Pope on a secret mission of international intrigue to the United States. The seaman murders the papal envoy, steals a valuable object that the priest was clutching and, after the ship puts into Gibraltar for repairs, flees to France with the hidden secret.

Put-in-Bay-based, *Washington Post* investigative reporter Emerson Moore is lured into a series of murders in Put-in-Bay and the French Quarter of New Orleans. Helping unlock the mysterious deaths are a rogue priest, who was banished from the Vatican to the small Catholic church on Put-in-Bay; Melaudra Drencheau, a flirtatious New Orleans detective; Harry "Elmo" Elms, Drencheau's partner; and Bubbie Drencheau, Melaudra's irascible father who inhabits the swamps along the Pearl River.

From the blue waters surrounding Lake Erie's South Bass Island to the hot, sultry heat of Louisiana's French Quarter, and its dangerous bayous and swamps, *Promised Land* delivers murder, gang fights, dangerous boating incidents, and a colorful cast of characters set within the unique ambiance of each locale.

The trail of the murders leads Emerson Moore to the surprising discovery of a document that may destroy the legitimacy of the United States.